Lie Down in Green Pastures

Other Books by the Author

The Lord Is My Shepherd, Book One in The Psalm 23 Mysteries

I Shall Not Want, Book Two in The Psalm 23 Mysteries

LIE DOWN IN GREEN PASTURES

The Psalm 23 Mysteries

 # 3

Debbie Viguié

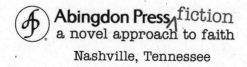

Abingdon Press fiction
a novel approach to faith
Nashville, Tennessee

Lie Down in Green Pastures

Copyright © 2011 by Debbie Viguié

ISBN-13: 978-1-4267-0191-7

Published by Abingdon Press, P.O. Box 801, Nashville, TN 37202

www.abingdonpress.com

The persons and events portrayed in this work of fiction
are the creations of the author, and any resemblance
to persons living or dead is purely coincidental.

All Scripture quotations are from the King James or
Authorized version of the Bible.

Published in association with the literary agency of
Alive Communications, Inc., 7680 Goddard Street, Suite 200,
Colorado Springs, Colorado, 80920

www.alivecommunications.com

Cover design by Anderson Design Group, Nashville, TN

Library of Congress Cataloging-in-Publication Data

Viguié, Debbie.
  Lie down in green pastures / Debbie Viguié.
    p. cm. — (The Psalm 23 mysteries ; bk. 3)
  ISBN 978-1-4267-0191-7 (trade pbk. : alk. paper)
  1. Murder—Investigation—Fiction. I. Title.
  PS3622.I485L54 2011
  813'.6—dc22

                                                    2010053261

Printed in the United States of America

1 2 3 4 5 6 7 8 9 10 / 16 15 14 13 12 11

To Marissa Smeyne
for all your help and support

Acknowledgments

First and foremost I have to thank my father, Richard Reynolds, for his help and his expertise. Thank you to my mom, Barbara Reynolds, for reading and offering honest critiques at every step of the way. As always, thank you to my fantastic editor, Barbara Scott, for her wisdom, insight, and humor. Thank you to Greta Viguié for her enthusiasm and support for this series. Thank you to Nancy Holder, an amazing friend and inspiration, for all of her support. I'd also like to thank Ann Liotta, Juliette Cutts, Calliope Collacott, and Scott Viguié.

1

JEREMIAH SILVERMAN NEVER QUITE KNEW WHAT TO DO WITH HIMSELF ON Thursdays. Thursdays were technically the second day in the week that he had off. Sundays were the first. He hadn't had two consecutive days off since he became rabbi of a synagogue. He had toyed with trying to take off Mondays, but too much seemed to happen on that day. So he took off Thursdays, but usually ended up going in to work at some point anyway. His secretary, Marie, often accused him of being a workaholic. It wasn't true, but there was no telling her that.

At ten in the morning he found himself driving down the street toward the synagogue. He slid into the left-hand lane, preparing to turn into the driveway just past First Shepherd, the church next door.

Seeing no oncoming traffic, he began to make his turn. The hair on the back of his neck raised suddenly, and he twisted his head around just in time to see a car as it slammed into him from behind.

Jeremiah's black Mustang skidded, sliding in a circle as the sickening crunch of metal filled his ears. He saw the face of the man in the other car, eyes frozen wide, head tilted. *That man is already dead*, he realized as his car twisted and then flipped upside down onto the lawn outside the church.

In a moment it was over. Carefully Jeremiah unlatched his seat belt and eased himself onto the ceiling. He kicked the remaining glass out of his side window and maneuvered himself out, cutting his leg on a piece of jagged glass as he did so. He collapsed onto the grass, felt it tickling his cheek, and took several deep breaths. He straightened slowly, checking each bone and muscle as he did. Everything seemed to be okay despite the fact that he had been in a terrible position when struck.

A shadow fell over him. He glanced up, squinting.

Cindy Preston stood there, her long, light brown hair flying around her face, out of breath. Her eyes were wide in surprise. "What are you doing here?"

It seemed like a ridiculous question, as if the answer should be self-evident.

"Recovering from an accident."

"Are you hurt?"

"I don't think so. What are *you* doing here?"

She blinked rapidly and then the corners of her mouth turned up. "I guess I'm here to rescue you."

He wanted so badly to laugh. The thought was ludicrous, especially given all the times he had saved her. Still, there was a dead man in the other car and he thought better of expressing himself. "Thank you," he said instead.

"Ironic, huh?"

"Yes, I guess that is the word," he answered as he struggled to sit up.

She dropped down next to him and put an arm behind his back to help support it.

"The other driver is dead."

"Dead?" she asked, jerking and turning pale. "How do you know?" She glanced anxiously toward the other car and for a moment he thought she was going to leave him to go check.

"I saw his face through the windshield right after he hit me. He was dead before it happened. I'm sure of it."

"A dead man crashed into you?"

"Yes."

"A dead man was driving that car?"

"That's what I said."

She hit a button on the cell phone that she had been clutching in her left hand and raised it to her ear. "Hi, Mark. It's Cindy. There's been an accident in front of the church and I think the one driver was dead before it happened."

She listened for a moment and then continued. "No, I don't know what killed him."

Another pause. "All right, we'll be here."

She hung up.

"You didn't just call Detective Walters, did you?" Jeremiah asked with a groan.

"I did," she said, raising her chin defiantly. "And what's wrong with that?"

"There hasn't been a murder."

"You don't know that."

"The guy probably had a heart attack while driving. It happens."

"And what if it didn't happen today?" she asked, raising an eyebrow. "Do you want to take the chance that this guy was murdered and the killer wouldn't be caught because it seemed like an accident?"

Actually he would rather a killer walk free than expose himself or his synagogue to the scrutiny of the police any more than necessary. He squeezed his eyes closed. There was no way he could explain that to Cindy. No easy way, at least.

No, whether he liked it or not, he was going to have to play the helpless victim this time and hope that it all went away quickly.

"Can you help me stand up?"

"Not until a paramedic looks you over. Mark's calling an ambulance."

"I'm fine."

"Let's leave that decision to the professionals."

He acquiesced and lay slowly back down on the grass, staring up at the blue of the sky. It was March and the weather was starting to get a little warmer. A month before, it would have been too cold to lie on the grass waiting. It got colder in Southern California during the winter than it had in Israel.

He heard the sirens of the ambulance and a moment later he heard Cindy gasp.

"What's wrong?" he asked.

"I know him," she said.

He twisted his head slowly to the side and saw that she was staring through the windshield of the car that had hit his.

"Who is he?"

"It's Dr. Tanner. He used to be a member here."

Of course he did, because that's my luck, Jeremiah thought. As the siren grew louder he began to feel some of the aches and pains caused by the accident. The shock was wearing off and he could already tell he was going to be stiff in the morning.

I'm getting soft, weak, he thought, closing his eyes.

"You're slipping," a male voice said.

Jeremiah opened his eyes and saw Detective Mark Walters staring down at him. "You think so?"

"I do. You're supposed to be the one playing good Samaritan, not her." He nodded toward Cindy.

Actually she's a Gentile, Jeremiah wanted to say, but he was just grateful Mark wasn't calling him Samaritan for once. "I must be getting old," he said instead.

Mark snorted derisively, then got down on one knee. "Seriously, you okay?"

"I'll live," Jeremiah said. "I just won't be happy about it in the morning."

A fleeting smile crossed the detective's face before he stood and turned toward the other car. "Let's see what we've got."

Cindy felt strange. She had been so confident that calling Mark was the right thing to do, but now that he was there she felt a bit foolish. Jeremiah was right; Mel Tanner had probably had a heart attack. The man was in his upper sixties and it would be the most logical explanation for what had happened. How could a murder victim even be driving in the first place?

Maybe he was poisoned, a small voice inside her head whispered. She bit her lip and wished that her deck of cards wasn't in her purse inside the office. She fidgeted with her fingers while she waited for Mark to look over the body.

I'm beginning to see murder victims everywhere. She wondered if she was suffering from some form of post-traumatic stress. The last year she had seen so much death. First there was the Passion Week serial killer. Then there was the string of murders around Thanksgiving. Maybe she thought "murder" because subconsciously she kept expecting to stumble upon another crime scene.

While she waited she watched the paramedics as they checked out Jeremiah. They had ripped open one of his pant legs and were treating a nasty-looking cut. Other than that he looked fine. They insisted on taking him to the hospital for X-rays, and he protested strenuously. To her surprise he lost the argument. With a grimace he climbed into the back of the ambulance and lay down on one of the gurneys.

"Do you want me to come to the hospital?" she asked.

"No. I don't plan on being there more than ten minutes. Besides, with our luck the nurse who thinks we're married will be on duty."

Cindy smirked at the memory of how he had lied to be allowed to see her after she was attacked by a serial killer. The thought of a little payback appealed to her. "That's precisely why I should come. Otherwise she might be concerned that our marriage is in trouble."

"I'm glad one of us can laugh."

The driver closed the door with an apologetic glance at her, then climbed into the front and drove away. Cindy felt oddly reassured that he drove up the street at a reasonable pace without the use of lights or siren. That had to mean Jeremiah was okay.

She turned to find Mark watching her. She gave him a fleeting smile before asking, "Did you find anything?"

He shook his head. "I'll have the coroner examine him, though, nail down actual cause of death. Something like this is usually a heart attack, aneurysm, something like that."

"Thank you. That's what Jeremiah said."

He took out a notepad and pen. "Anything you can tell me about the other driver?"

"His name is Dr. Mel Tanner. He used to go to First Shepherd but now he goes to another church downtown. He's a retired physician. He's still active in the community, though." She flushed and looked away. "I mean, he was."

"Any idea where he might have been headed this morning?" Mark said, ignoring her slip of the tongue.

"No."

"Do you have a current address?"

"No, but he had a lot of friends here. I'm sure I can find someone who has it."

"Thanks. I'll let you know if I need anything else." He glanced at the twisted wreckage of the two cars and then back at her.

"Jeremiah got lucky."

"Yes, he did," she said, trying not to picture him being the one dead behind the wheel. Her breath caught in her throat as the mental image filled her mind anyway.

"And I thought you were the one with nine lives," Mark said.

Cindy shrugged.

"You're not heading to the hospital?"

"No."

He made a tsking sound. "Sounds like divorce court time to me."

She shook her head and rolled her eyes before turning to head back into the church.

As Cindy walked back into the office and took her seat Geanie hopped up out of her chair and walked over. "What happened?" Geanie, the church's graphic designer and webmaster, saved her most creative and flamboyant work for her own wardrobe. True to form she was wearing a fuchsia satin blouse, black leather skirt, pink tights and black boots. Roy, the head pastor, was perpetually dismayed by Geanie's style but church members usually made a point of stopping by the office when they were on site just to see the day's ensemble.

Next to her, as always, Cindy felt extremely conservative even though the sheer sleeves of her cream blouse had seemed so risqué at home.

As Cindy filled her in, she watched in satisfaction as Geanie registered the same shock she herself was feeling.

"That's terrible!"

"I know. At least Jeremiah wasn't hurt, but poor Dr. Tanner."

"Going in a car crash, that's one of my nightmares," Geanie said with a shiver.

"Jeremiah told the officers that he thought Dr. Tanner was already dead," Cindy said, more to herself than Geanie.

"That's just weird."

"I know."

The front door opened and the youth pastor walked in, wearing his almost-perpetual blue jeans, paired today with a green polo shirt. Because of his position he got by with the casual Friday look every day of the week except Sunday. "Wow, did you guys see that accident out front?" Dave asked.

"Cindy did," Geanie answered.

"What a nightmare."

"Dr. Tanner is dead," Cindy said.

Dave turned pale and sat down in one of the chairs reserved for visitors. "Are you kidding?"

"No, why would I kid about something like that?"

He buried his face in his hands and his shoulders heaved. Geanie gave her a puzzled look as the implication hit Cindy. "He drove the bus to camp every year," she realized. "Even after he moved and changed churches."

"Summer camps and winter camps. He was a wonderful man," Dave said. "So good with the kids, so patient. I never knew how he could pay attention to the road with all the noise and chaos around him."

"He was a very nice man," Cindy said, going over and awkwardly patting him on the shoulder.

"I'm going to call Joseph and let him know," Geanie said. "I think the two of them sat on a couple of boards together."

"Why don't you go tell him in person," Cindy suggested. Joseph Coulter was the church's most affluent member. He and Geanie had been dating since Thanksgiving and she was sure he'd rather hear the news from his girlfriend than from someone else.

"Thanks, I'll be back before your lunch meeting," Geanie said, grabbing her purse and heading for the door.

"I'd appreciate it."

Geanie waved as she walked out the door.

After Geanie left, Cindy turned to Dave. "We've almost got a full slate of kids for next weekend. I'd better work on finding you another driver."

"Thanks," Dave said, dragging himself to his feet. "A couple of other churches are having retreats at the same time. I'll call around and see if any of them have room on their buses."

"Do you have Dr. Tanner's address? The police were asking for it."

Dave nodded. "In my office, I'll email it to you."

"Thanks."

He shuffled to the door, then turned. "How are we doing on food for the drive up?"

"Lunch bags will have corned beef sandwiches, courtesy of O'Connell's Pub, and shamrock cookies from Safeway."

"You're a genius."

"Hey, the second day of camp is on St. Patrick's Day. It was a no-brainer."

He smiled slightly. "You've been hanging around the kids too long. You're starting to sound like them."

"There are a lot worse things to sound like."

"Amen."

Detective Mark Walters was not happy. Ever since his dog, Buster, had woken him up that morning he'd had a feeling in his gut that the day was not going to go his way.

Being a homicide cop was challenging on the best of days, nightmarish on the worst. In the past year the worst days he'd had all involved Cindy and Jeremiah. Seeing them together, even though it had been at the scene of an accident, had made his blood run cold.

He called his partner, Paul Dryer, on his cell phone.

"Accident or murder?" Paul asked.

"Accident, so far as I can tell. If it wasn't, though, we'll know soon enough."

"What are the odds, huh?"

Mark snorted. "You ever meet civilians who got mixed up in stuff as much as these two?"

"Once," Paul admitted.

"Really? What happened?"

"It didn't end well," Paul said, voice suddenly devoid of emotion.

There's a story there. Out of respect for his partner, Mark didn't push. "Cindy just called me with the doctor's address and I'm going to have a couple of guys go to his house and reach out to the next of kin. Then I'm heading back to the station."

"Good. We've got actual homicides to investigate."

Mark hung up. Paul was acting touchy. Mark wondered if it had anything to do with the story he wasn't telling.

When he arrived at the police station, he found Paul waiting for him in the lobby, arms crossed.

"What do we have?" Mark asked.

"Randall Kelly, environmental activist. Died ten miles outside of town."

"Let's go."

Once they were in the car Paul explained. "Apparently he was protesting the misuse and destruction of the forestland.

Fire department did a controlled burn in the area early this morning to clear out a lot of the dead trees and dry tinder."

"And they cleared out a little more than they bargained for," Mark said.

"Exactly."

"Sounds like an accident."

"Yeah, but the captain wants us to check it out anyway."

"Why not? I've already been to one accident today," Mark said with a sigh. "So, exactly what homicides were you referencing when I called?"

Paul shrugged. "We've still got a couple older cases to work, like that art dealer from a few months back."

"Or the Iranian student from last year. I know. Trust me, I don't forget a victim," Mark said.

"Hopefully Kelly isn't one of them, just a poor slob who was in the wrong place at the wrong time."

Like Jeremiah this morning.

They reached the burn line and were waved through by firefighters. A minute later they were pulling up a few hundred feet away from the scene of the accident.

Randall Kelly, or rather, what was left of him, was still handcuffed to a charred tree, half of which was little more than embers and ash. The flesh had been burned off the majority of the body with part of the face and arms more intact than the rest.

"Terrible way to die," Paul said.

"You're preaching to the choir," Mark said. "I'd rather be shot any day."

"Can you imagine seeing it coming and not being able to escape?"

"Makes you wonder what he did with the key, why he couldn't free himself."

"Maybe he dropped it? Swallowed it?" Paul said.

19

"Maybe, or maybe someone was supposed to come over today and let him go, friend or family member maybe."

The fire chief was standing at a respectful distance and Mark finally turned away to engage him, catching sight of the coroner arriving on scene out of the corner of his eye.

Mark had met the chief half a dozen times but he introduced himself anyway.

Jim shook his head. "One of these days we'll have to have a barbeque or something, meet under happier circumstances."

"Looks like we've already got something of a barbeque here," Mark said before he could stop himself.

"I trust you know that wasn't funny."

"Sorry," Mark said, wincing. Usually people apologized to him, not the other way around. "Tell me what happened."

"We were doing a controlled burn before the dry season, trying to get rid of a lot of dead leaves, branches, and trees. We're going to be heading into summer with too much dead undergrowth. Better to burn it now than to risk a fire breaking out and burning out of control later."

"I assume you filed all the necessary paperwork, got permits, everything?"

"Of course. We advertised, even posted signs warning people to stay away."

"When did you realize someone ignored those warnings?"

"Helicopter pilot who was keeping an eye on the burn from up above spotted the car about a quarter of a mile off. We doused the fire as fast as we could, but it was too little, too late. It took us an hour to find him. We were hoping someone had just left the car, but then, well, I smelled burned hair and a minute later I found him. That's when we made the call to you boys."

"How did you know who he was?"

"The registration in his car. It made sense, too. He raised such a stink a couple years back when we were going to do the burn. He even managed to get a temporary restraining order, called for environmental impact studies, blah, blah."

"What happened?"

"While everyone was busy messing around some idiot set off a fire with a cigarette butt. Fire wiped out more than a dozen houses."

"I remember that," Mark said.

"Yeah, well, we hadn't heard much from Mr. Kelly since then. Figured he'd learned his lesson, just sorry others had to pay his tuition."

"More often than not that's what happens," Mark said. "So, I guess he forgot it and headed out here to try and do the same thing all over again."

The fire chief stroked his chin and stared toward the body. "I'm not entirely convinced that's true."

"What makes you think that?" Mark asked sharply.

"You ever seen a rat caught in a trap?"

"Can't say as I have."

"They get desperate enough they'll gnaw their own leg off to get free."

"Randall Kelly wasn't a rat," Mark noted.

"No, but he was in a trap same enough. What would you do to save your life?"

Mark turned and looked at the skeleton. "You mean would I gnaw my own hand off?"

"No need. All you'd have to do is dislocate or break one of your thumbs."

"Spend much time running from the police when you were a kid?" Mark joked even as he stared at the body. Jim was right. All Randall would have needed to do to escape was free one hand. If he had struggled hard enough he could have broken his thumb even if he didn't mean to.

"Why weren't you struggling, Randall?" he whispered.

True to her word Geanie returned just before lunch, freeing Cindy up to head to her meeting at O'Connell's Pub. She arrived a couple of minutes early and settled into a booth. The pub was authentic Irish, at least as far as one could get in California. She had always liked the food and every once in a while she would come in and watch people talking and playing darts. She didn't participate even though she was a pretty good dart thrower. Cindy was always too shy to get up in front of people and perform like that.

"One day," she promised herself under her breath as she stared longingly at the dart board. Of course, it looked much different than the one she had on the back of her bedroom door at home. This one didn't have a picture of her brother on it. *I wonder if I can even hit a board without using his face as a target?* she thought, smiling to herself.

"I hope I didn't keep you waiting," Gary O'Connell said as he slid into the booth and took up position across from her. The real estate agent was in his late thirties with light brown hair, hazel eyes, and the world's cheesiest smile. She always wondered who had the wider, whiter smiles—movie stars or real estate agents.

They shook hands. They had met once before, at the office of the lawyer who had handled the estate of Marge Johnson, a church member who had died the year before and left her possessions to various church staff and members. To Cindy she had left a house.

While Cindy appreciated the gesture enormously, the house was too large for her needs and she was afraid of what the upkeep costs were going to be. Gary O'Connell had been the Realtor recommended to her.

"How are you doing today, Cindy?"

"Not bad, you?"

"I'm still in business so I can't complain. At least not too loudly," he joked.

She smiled. "I've been meaning to ask you. Any relation to the pub here?"

He nodded. "My brother Chris owns this place."

"Well, tell your brother I'm a fan of his corned beef sandwiches."

"Let me guess. You have them once a year."

"More like once a month," she said with a smile. "I told you, I'm a fan."

"I will be sure to pass that along."

"Thanks."

He gave her that cheesy smile again, then pulled a folder out of his leather satchel. "So, Cindy, let's get started. I've brought some paperwork for you to sign and we'll talk about the process and what you can expect from it and from me."

"Thanks, I really appreciate it," she said, taking the papers. "I've never sold a house before. I've never even owned a house before."

"I'll do everything I can to make the whole thing as painless as possible."

"What do you think the chances of even selling it right now are?"

"I'll be honest with you, not great. Still, we'll do all that we can."

"It must be a difficult time to be a real estate agent," she said as she started skimming the papers.

"What can I say? It's a killer market. Last agent standing and all that."

"Well, good luck," she said, glancing up.

"To both of us," he smiled.

The waiter came over and Cindy ordered a corned beef sandwich.

"The usual," Gary said, relinquishing his menu.

"That must be nice," she said as the waiter walked away.

"What?"

"To go somewhere often enough they know you and know what you want to eat."

"But on the other hand, it really throws people off if you're in the mood to mix it up a little and order something else."

They spent the next forty-five minutes talking and eating. Cindy listened as Gary outlined his plan for selling the house.

"How long have you been in real estate?" she asked when he took a breather.

"Fifteen years. I've mostly done commercial, but the last year and a half I've been forced to branch out and now I do residential as well."

"One-stop shopping."

"That's me. Hurry, hurry, hurry, step right up and satisfy all your real estate needs," he said, mimicking a midway barker.

She couldn't help but laugh. When they were finally finished she made her way back to the church feeling optimistic about her chances of selling the house.

Geanie was clearly relieved to see her and Cindy soon discovered that word of the accident had spread and she spent the rest of the afternoon fielding calls. Several times she wondered how much worse it was next door where Jeremiah's secretary, Marie, was probably having to explain to every member of the synagogue just what had happened to their rabbi. She felt sorry for them both.

By the time Cindy left work she was exhausted. When she got home, she walked into the kitchen, grabbed a marker from a drawer, and put a big red X over the day on the calendar. She then flipped ahead to May. Eleven weeks remained on her countdown to her Hawaii trip that she had planned for Memorial Day weekend. Eleven weeks to paradise. Eleven weeks to vacation. Eleven weeks to lose those last few pounds so she could wear a bikini.

She sighed. The bikini was probably a pipe dream. Still, she forced herself to make a salad for dinner instead of eating her leftover pizza from the night before. Once finished, she found herself fidgeting, not really sure what to do with the rest of her evening. She was too tired to work on a project and too amped up to watch television.

She finally opted to call Jeremiah and check in on him.

"Hello?" he answered, sounding a little groggy.

"Did they miss me at the hospital?" she teased.

"They did, but I covered for you."

"Glad to hear it. Are you okay?"

"Nothing some aspirin and a few days won't fix."

"Good. I was worried about you," she admitted.

"Did you hear anything more about the other driver?"

"No."

Her phone beeped in her ear. "Can you hold on a sec while I see who's trying to call?"

"Sure."

She pulled her phone away from her ear and looked at the caller ID.

Mark Walters.

A chill danced up her spine. Why would he be calling except to tell her that she was right and there was another killer on the loose?

25

2

"Jeremiah, it's Mark on the other line. Can I call you back?" Cindy asked, forcing herself to take a deep breath.

"Sure," Jeremiah said as she switched over.

"Hi, Mark."

"Hi, Cindy. How's the rabbi?"

"Fine," she said, flushing slightly. She didn't know why the question made her uncomfortable.

"Figured as much. Listen, we need to ask you some follow-up questions. You at home?"

"Yes."

"Great. See you in five minutes."

Cindy hung up and briefly debated calling Jeremiah back. Before she could, though, there was a knock on the door. She opened it to find Mark and Paul standing there, faces grim.

"That was a quick five minutes," she said as she gestured them inside.

"We were parked out front," Paul explained.

"Let's sit down," Mark said.

They took seats around the kitchen table and they both pulled notepads out of their pockets. Cindy wrinkled up her nose. Both men smelled of smoke.

"It wasn't just a heart attack that killed Dr. Tanner, was it?" she asked, her mouth dry.

"We don't know much at the moment but we're trying to rule out possibilities," Mark said. "We are, however, fairly certain that he was dead or unconscious when the accident happened."

"Of course he was dead. Jeremiah said so," she replied.

"That may be, but I'm not sure how much Jeremiah actually saw rather than imagined. That was a nasty accident," Paul commented.

Cindy felt anger rising in her and it caught her off guard. Why should she feel suddenly so defensive over them doubting Jeremiah's account of the accident? Was it because she had relied on his conclusion when making the decision to call the police in the first place?

She took a ragged breath and asked, "How do you know the driver was dead or unconscious, then?"

"The accident investigator," Mark said.

"He found something?" she asked.

"More like he didn't find something. Skid marks. Dr. Tanner never once hit the brakes during the entire thing."

"And had he been awake he would have been pushing the brake pedal as hard as he could," she said.

"That's the logical assumption," Paul said. "So, we want to go over the accident with you again and ask you some more questions about Dr. Tanner."

"Anything I can do to help," Cindy said.

She felt like all she did was repeat herself for the next half hour until she'd told the story from her point of view a dozen times. Finally they shifted topics.

"Do you know of anyone who would want to hurt Dr. Tanner?" Paul asked.

Cindy shrugged. "He was a kind man, well thought of, but I don't know enough about him to be able to answer that. I'm guessing that's a question for his family."

"Anyone at the church know him better?" Mark asked.

"Joseph Coulter sits on a board with him."

"And just which board would that be?"

"The GPNC Board. The board was created to oversee use and care of the Green Pastures Nature Camp. The camp is about an hour-and-a-half drive from here and was created by several churches and non-profits in the area years ago for use as a camp and a retreat. Kids go there to summer camp from all over the area. Adults go to religious retreats."

"I'm familiar with it," Paul said. "They were both on the board?"

"Yes."

"Anyone else at the church have close ties with him?" Mark asked.

"Dave Wyman, the youth pastor, relied on him to drive the bus to camp whenever it was needed. He took the news really hard this morning."

"Ah yes, Wildman. Heck of a nickname for a youth pastor."

"Anyone else?" Paul asked.

"Not that I know of. If you want, I could set up an appointment with Pastor Roy—"

"No, thank you," Mark interrupted, visibly wincing.

Cindy remembered the first and last time Mark had tried interviewing the head pastor and the look of utter frustration on his face when he left Roy's office.

"Okay, I think we're done here," Paul said, snapping his notebook shut and putting it away.

He stood and Mark followed suit. Cindy rose reluctantly to her feet.

"I've got a question for the two of you. I know you're not smokers, so why do your clothes smell like smoke?" she asked.

Mark grimaced. "I'm sure you'll read about it in the papers tomorrow. We were investigating an accident. An environmentalist got caught in a planned burn to clear out undergrowth before the dry season."

"That's terrible! How does that involve you, though? You're homicide detectives."

"Anytime somebody finds a body like that we get called. Strictly routine," he said.

She noticed that he didn't look her in the eye when he said it. "You've always had a terrible poker face," she accused.

He shrugged.

After the detectives left she called Jeremiah back, but it just went to voicemail. She hoped that meant he was getting some rest. She flopped down on the sofa and turned on the television.

"And next up on the Escape! Channel is Kyle Preston's newest show *Dare Me*. See the first part of Kyle's journey as he attempts to go over a waterfall in a barrel."

She clicked the TV off in disgust and headed for her bedroom. Once there she began throwing darts at his face on her dartboard. The picture was actually a better one of him. He looked serious and intense, like he actually was contemplating what an idiot he was for always putting himself in such danger.

Jeremiah ached all over when he woke up. He stood gingerly and walked into the bathroom where he inspected himself in the mirror. There was bruising on his left cheekbone. He pulled off his shirt and saw the welts and bright purple bruises left by his seatbelt. The cut on his leg was hurting and starting to itch. All in all, he had gotten off lightly. Except for the bruise on his face no one would realize anything had happened to him.

He debated briefly going into work. He knew he should, but all he really wanted to do was go back to bed and catch up on some reading. He took a shower, which did little to make him feel better. Having made up his mind he put on a pair of sweats and a T-shirt and picked up the phone.

His secretary answered on the third ring.

"Hi, Marie, sorry for calling you at home. I just wanted to let you know that I'm not going to be in today. I'm still recovering from yesterday."

"Recovering? From what?"

"The car accident. Didn't you hear?" he asked, surprised. He always assumed that Marie heard anything that happened at or near the synagogue within five minutes.

"You were in a car accident?" she asked, voice rising an octave.

"In front of First Shepherd. A guy had a heart attack and rear-ended me."

"And you didn't think to tell me?"

He winced. "Actually, I thought you'd have figured it out when you saw my car. Cindy came running out of the church right after it happened and insisted I go to the hospital."

"In the future, you call me when something like that happens," she fumed.

"Sorry. I wasn't thinking straight. The car flipped and I was pretty out of it." He felt only slightly guilty playing it up. The last thing he wanted from Marie was a guilt trip.

"Oh! Are you hurt?"

"A little, but it's not bad. I decided I'd take it easy today so that I can do my best in the morning."

"I can call someone to handle the service tomorrow if you need me to."

"No, but thank you."

"Are you going to be able to do the Schuster funeral on Sunday?"

"Yes."

"You need me to bring anything by?"

"I can manage. I've got plenty of food in the refrigerator and I'm planning on sleeping most of the day."

"Okay, but you call me if there's anything I can do."

"I will," he promised, relieved when he hung up. He checked his voicemail and realized he had missed a call from Cindy the night before. He decided to call later and see what, if anything, she had found out from the detective.

At the church things were relatively quiet. A few members showed up around ten to pray together for Mel's family. Among them was Joseph. When they were finished he walked into the office.

"Looking for Geanie?" Cindy guessed.

"I was going to take her to lunch."

"She's at the print shop. She'll be back soon."

"Mind if I sit here and wait?"

"Be my guest," Cindy said. "I'm so sorry about Dr. Tanner."

"Thanks. It's going to be strange holding a meeting this week without him," Joseph admitted. "He's been the iron fist keeping the rest of us in check for years."

Cindy smiled at that. "And just how far amok could the rest of you actually run without it?"

"Farther than you'd think," he said seriously.

"I'll take your word for it."

"How are things going with you?"

31

She shrugged. "Nothing to complain about."

"Anything ever happen with that computer programmer you were going to go out with a few months ago?"

"We went on exactly three dates and decided we should just be friends."

"Hey, that beats our record. We only went on half a date."

"I guess I'm just too picky. Either that or I fear change."

"Speaking of change, I noticed a For Sale sign up in front of the house Marge left you. Who are you using for an agent?"

"Gary O'Connell."

"Seriously?"

"Yes, why? Have you heard something bad about him?"

"No, no. It's just that he usually does commercial transactions."

"Apparently times are tough for Realtors," Cindy said with a shrug.

"Well, I'm sure he'll do a great job for you. I've been dealing with him on and off for the last couple of weeks. He is persistent."

"You're not moving, are you?" she asked in alarm.

"No, no. He's representing a land developer, Max Diamond, Diamond Industries. He's made a bid to buy the church camp."

"I didn't think it was for sale."

"It wasn't, but he made an offer anyway. Stirred up a bit of a hornet's nest, too."

"Why would that be?"

"Until Max Diamond came sniffing around the biggest point of controversy this year was whether or not to rename Green Pastures to something that sounded a little more exciting," Joseph said.

"How could the board even consider selling?" Cindy asked. "They're set up to protect and govern the use of that land for all the churches, scout troops, and clubs in the area. What would happen to it if Diamond Industries purchased it?

"That's where it gets a little tricky. There's a lot of improvements that should be made to the actual campsite itself. The buildings are twenty years old, most of them erected as temporary ones until more permanent structures could be built and the infrastructure is practically non-existent. The truth is that renovations have been sorely needed for years but there's just no money anywhere to accomplish that. The camp itself only occupies one small section of a huge parcel of land. Max Diamond has come in and offered to buy the entire parcel, give us a fifty-year lease on the camp and the surrounding acreage, and pump enough money into it to really bring it into the twenty-first century. Some people think it's the answer to prayer and others of us think we're being offered a devil's deal."

"The one time I went to a retreat there you couldn't turn on the hot water in the sinks without turning the shower water to freezing," Cindy said.

"Exactly. And at least once a week the entire plumbing system backs up. So, you can see where this is shaping up to be a fight."

She nodded. "But if the board accepts the offer suddenly the land is leased and not owned."

"Exactly. And of those who believe that somehow the camp will still maintain its character, its tranquility and its isolation, half believe that fifty years are long enough. After all, they'll be dead before the lease is up."

"And others of you are trying to plan for future generations."

"And that's the fight in a nutshell. Mel was the chairman of the board and he was one of the strongest opponents of the proposed purchase. But then, he's always been a visionary."

The door opened and Dave entered, a sheet of paper in his hand. His face lit up when he saw Joseph. "Any chance you're here to sponsor a couple more kids for camp? I've got two who would love to go if someone would pay for them. Imagine the fun they'll have, the things they'll learn, the excitement on their faces."

"Not what I was here for, but how can I say no after that?"

"Awesome." Dave dropped the paper on Cindy's desk and she could see it was a list of the kids signed up for camp. "Cindy, add Brenda and Zac to the list. Joseph, can you give Cindy a check today? I'm going to go leave messages for the kids."

With a triumphant grin, Dave left.

"I don't have my checkbook. Can I pay in cash?" Joseph asked her.

"That would be fine. I'm sorry that he ambushed you that way."

Joseph fished his wallet out of his pocket. "It could be a lot worse. He could have asked me to go as a chaperone. I'd much rather pay. A weekend with Wildman and dozens of hyper, screaming teenagers is not my idea of fun."

"I hear you. Still, thank you so much for doing this. I don't know Zac, but I know Brenda will really appreciate it."

The door opened and Geanie announced herself with a squeal of excitement. She ran to Joseph and gave him a quick kiss.

"Lunch?" he asked.

"Yes, please. Cindy, do you mind?"

"Go for it. I'll take my lunch break when you get back."

Geanie and Joseph left hand in hand and Cindy smiled at the sight. The two of them were good together and she was beginning to wonder if it might not be the real thing.

Not that she would know the real thing if it bit her. After the failed attempt at dating after Thanksgiving she was beginning to wonder if she just had too much of a problem opening up and trusting. She could never be herself on a date without worrying about how she could get hurt.

Because there was always a way you could get hurt.

Her cell rang and she fished it out of her purse in the drawer just before it went to voicemail.

"Hello?"

"Hi, it's Jeremiah."

"How are you feeling today?" she asked.

"Glad to be alive and in one piece. A little sore and stiff, but otherwise fine. I am taking the day off."

"I'm glad to hear it. Do you need me to bring anything over?"

He laughed.

"What is it?"

"Nothing. I'm fine, really. What did the detective have to say last night?"

"They're pretty sure Dr. Tanner was dead when he hit you; there were no skid marks on the road."

"I could have told them that. Come to think of it, I believe I did."

"Apparently yours wasn't the only accident they were investigating yesterday."

"Oh, what was the other?"

"An environmentalist burned to death after handcuffing himself to a tree in a planned burn zone."

"Strange."

"I thought so, too." She paused, hoping he would say something more on the topic.

She was disappointed when he finally said, "I need to go and get some sleep."

"Oh, okay."

"Have a good day."

"You, too," she said, hanging up. She felt disappointed and she asked herself why. Was it because she wanted to talk to him more about the accidents or because she just wanted to talk to him more? She blushed at the thought.

Leave it to me to find yet another way I could get hurt.

3

Cindy was tired when she got home. No sooner had she thrown her purse and keys on the table than the phone rang. She briefly debated letting it go to voicemail, then finally picked it up.

"Hello?"

"Hi, Cindy, it's Gerald Wilson. I made it into town and I wanted to confirm our interview for tomorrow afternoon."

"Yes, absolutely."

"Does two still work?"

"Yes."

"Wonderful. I'm staying at the Courtyard."

"I'll meet you in the lobby at two."

"Excellent. I'm looking forward to it."

She hung up and felt a flutter of nerves and excitement. She'd almost forgotten that tomorrow was the day she was being interviewed for a book about her role in stopping the Passion Week Killer the previous Easter. Gerald Wilson was writing a book about crime, myths, and legends in the area. He had contacted her a couple of months before to set up the interview.

Feeling a bit better she grabbed some orange juice and contemplated her options for the evening while drinking it. Before she could make a decision the phone rang again. It was her mom.

"Hi, Mom."

"Hi, honey. How are you?"

"Good, I'm being interviewed by that writer tomorrow for the crime book."

"How nice. Remind me to send you the latest stack of articles on your brother. There was a fabulous one in *Travel and Leisure* and another one in *National Geographic*."

"Great," Cindy said, beginning to feel the frustration settle in. Would it kill her mom to acknowledge her accomplishments? "So, why did you call?" she asked.

"I just wanted to make sure you were going to be watching your brother's television special tonight. He's bungee jumping off the Golden Gate Bridge live."

Cindy cringed and felt a cold knot settle in the pit of her stomach. "Why, why would he do something like that?" she whispered to herself.

"It's all a promotion for that new show of his."

"Isn't that illegal?"

"Honey, he's a *star*. Besides, his network takes care of all that kind of thing."

"But he's jumping . . . over water . . ."

"Yes, isn't it exciting?"

Cindy closed her eyes. Her mother was crazy. That was the only explanation for why she could condone Kyle's reckless behavior.

Her mother continued talking but Cindy stopped listening. She walked into the bedroom with the phone still pressed to her ear and pulled the darts out of Kyle's face. She took careful aim and then realized that throwing the dart at his picture wasn't going to make the terrible feeling inside her go away.

"Mom, I have to go," she interrupted.

"Oh, okay, dear. Just make sure you watch."

"Uh-huh."

As soon as she had hung up she grabbed her purse and keys and left. Twenty minutes later she was sitting in the pub ordering a corned beef sandwich and eyeing the dartboard.

Two large guys were playing a game of darts and she watched while waiting for her opportunity. The older guy was winning, nailing the center of the bull's-eye almost every time.

The pub was more crowded than it ever was at lunch when she usually went. On the walls and on the tables were little shamrock signs reminding patrons that St. Patrick's Day was coming. The corned beef and green beer would both be ever present on that day. Cindy knew from experience, though, that they dyed 7-Up green as well for those who weren't imbibing.

"I'll do everything I can," she heard a familiar voice say from the booth behind her.

She turned and saw Gary sitting with a man about ten years his senior with salt and pepper hair and a strong jaw.

"Frank Butler has been sniffing around that property. He'd love to beat me out of it, but I won't let that happen. I won't let anything get in my way. I will have that property."

"I understand, Mr. Diamond," Gary said.

"I'm not sure you do, Gary, but that's okay. I just need you to keep talking to that board, remind them how good my offer is. I'll take care of the rest."

It sounded ominous to her and she couldn't help but stare at the land developer in fascination.

He drained his drink, stood up and buttoned his jacket, and then exited the bar. Cindy turned back around, feeling guilty for spying. After what Joseph had told her, though, she was curious.

A minute later the dart players wrapped up their game. Now would be the time to take her chance to play. She started to stand up and a hand descended on her shoulder.

"Needed another corned beef sandwich, huh?"

She looked up to see Gary. He was smiling, but his face and eyes looked strained.

"What can I say? They're just that good."

"Chris! Come here, you've got to meet one of your biggest fans," Gary said, gesturing to the taller of the dart players.

Chris walked over and extended his hand. Cindy shook it as Gary did the introductions. "Chris, this is one of my clients, Cindy Preston. She's a fan of your corned beef sandwiches. Cindy, this is my brother, Chris, who owns the pub."

"It's nice to meet you," Cindy said, feeling a bit embarrassed.

"An' it be a pleasure to meet anyone who loves me corned beef, particularly a pretty lass," Chris said in a thick Irish brogue. He winked and leaned in close. "The customers appreciate it if ye have a bit o' the Irish about ya."

"Oh, I see," she said, not sure what else to say.

Both men laughed and Cindy had the uneasy feeling that the joke was on her. "Can I interest ya in a friendly game o' darts?"

"No, thank you," she said. It was bad enough to make a spectacle out of herself in front of strangers, but with Gary there and now having met his brother she wasn't sure she wanted to embarrass herself that way.

"Not much for darts?"

She shrugged, not really wanting to explain herself.

Both men laughed again. "I'll check on your sandwich," Chris said.

Gary sat across from her. "I can't believe you two haven't met. Most nights he's out here talking with all the customers, playing darts."

"I've never come for dinner before, only lunch," she explained.

"That makes sense then."

"Anything new about the house?" she asked after a minute of silence stretched between them.

"Since yesterday? No."

Chris returned with her sandwich and set it down with a wink and a flourish.

"He's quite a character," Cindy said after he had gone.

"Always has been. Even when we were kids he was larger than life. And I was the baby brother he took care of. I wouldn't have made it as far as I have without him," Gary admitted.

"It's nice to have someone you can rely on," Cindy said, wishing that she felt that way about someone.

What about Jeremiah? a voice whispered in her head.

"It's more than nice. But then I guess we do anything for family, you know?"

Cindy didn't say anything. Instead she just picked up her sandwich and bit into it. *I would have done anything for my sister,* she thought before she could stop herself.

"So, you planning on getting your Irish on next week?"

"Absolutely," she said, still chewing.

"One day a year the whole world is Irish. It's fun for most, but it's important for those of us who are Irish to remember our roots, our culture."

"Your family?"

"Exactly," he said with a broad grin.

Cindy was a quarter Irish on her father's side, but she had no desire to share that with Gary. She wished he would get the hint and go away. She wanted to be alone.

You don't want a family? the insidious voice pressed.

She sighed and wondered if she ignored the voice and Gary long enough whether they would both go away.

Mark hated breaking bad news to relatives. Randall Kelly's sister, Maureen, was sitting in a chair in her living room, her luggage forgotten by the front door. She had just arrived home from a business trip and he and Paul had finally been able to get hold of her to tell her about her brother's death.

"I don't understand how this could have happened," she said once her sobbing had eased.

"Did you know that your brother was going to protest the planned burn yesterday?" Paul asked.

She shook her head violently. "No, he would never have done that. Not after what happened a few years ago. He managed to keep the fire department from doing the burn on time and a real fire started and several people lost their houses and everything they owned. A lot of people blamed Randall for that, but not any more than he blamed himself. He locked himself in his house for three weeks. He wouldn't even see me. There's no way he would have done that."

"Are you sure?" Mark asked.

"Positive. He wasn't even supposed to be here Thursday morning. He was supposed to be going up to that church camp that the land developer is trying to buy. He wanted to see it for himself before trying to rally the community in opposition to the proposed purchase."

Mark and Paul exchanged quick glances. "You wouldn't happen to know the name of the camp, would you?" Mark asked.

She squeezed her eyes closed. "It sounded like that old TV show *Green Acres* . . . Green . . . Green Pastures."

"Green Pastures?" Paul repeated.

"Yes. He was planning on protesting the sale."

Two victims and both of them having something to do with the church camp. Mark didn't like it.

"Is there any reason you can think of that he would have done that down in the burn area?"

"No."

Mark flipped through his notes, not really looking for anything, but just thinking about the implications of what she had said. "Do you know if your brother had approached anyone involved with the sale yet?"

"I'm not sure. I left Wednesday morning. I don't think he had talked to anyone at that point."

"So you think he chained himself to a tree to protest the purchase?" Paul asked.

She half laughed. "I know it's cliché. He liked the image. He thought it was powerful."

"Could you describe for us the method your brother used when he tied himself to a tree?"

"He always used cable ties."

The detectives shared another quick look.

"Always?" Paul questioned.

"Yes."

"Why cable ties?" he pressed.

"Because even if he fell asleep or someone tried to pull him away the plastic couldn't hurt the tree like metal from a chain or something else could."

"So he wouldn't handcuff himself to a tree?"

"Never. That would risk damaging the tree if the metal rubbed against it."

"Did your brother have any enemies?" Paul asked.

"You don't become a crusader for any cause without making enemies. That's what he used to tell me."

"Any that would want to see him dead?" Mark asked.

"I—I don't know. I mean, there hasn't even been anything really happening for at least a year. He's been spending most of his time trying to write a book."

"Anything in there that could make people angry?"

She shrugged. "I don't know. He wouldn't let anyone read it until he was finished."

"We're going to need to get a copy of the manuscript," Paul said.

"It should be on his computer at home."

They stayed with her until her friend was able to come over and be with her and then they left. Once they were in the car Mark looked at the clock and groaned. His wife, Traci, was not going to be thrilled that he was home so late on a Friday. There was no help for it, though.

"Are you thinking what I'm thinking?" Mark asked.

"That Traci's going to kill you? Yes."

"Wonderful."

"Are you thinking what I'm thinking?" Paul parroted.

"That this was no accident," Mark said grimly. "It was murder."

"Green Pastures again. Think Kelly's death has anything to do with Dr. Tanner's?"

"Let's not go there until we get something more on cause of death for the doctor. I'm hoping we can leave him in the accident column and chalk it all up to coincidence."

"Yes, because we see so many coincidences every day," Paul said sarcastically.

"You're always so comforting."

"I'll send someone over to Kelly's house to get a copy of the manuscript and I'll start reading through it. You should go home."

"I hate to agree with you, but it sounds like a plan to me. We should also call up to Green Pastures and see if anyone up there saw or talked to Kelly."

"If he even made it up there."

"Exactly," Mark said.

Mark closed his eyes. He knew that seeing the secretary and the rabbi again had been a bad omen.

Jeremiah awoke early Saturday morning. He had slept through most of Friday. He had clearly been more exhausted than he realized. *You're getting soft*, he told himself as he sat up gingerly.

Captain, a large German shepherd, was on the bed staring at him with soulful eyes.

"I'm okay, boy," Jeremiah said as he stood up.

He took the dog for a quick walk and then returned to the house where the two shared a sandwich.

He usually used Fridays to finish preparing for Saturday services but fortunately he had taken care of everything earlier in the week. He debated briefly about calling a taxi or having someone pick him up but finally opted to walk. It would help keep all his muscles from stiffening up completely.

When he made it to the synagogue, he found Marie waiting for him. Whenever she was in the office before services it wasn't a good sign.

"What's wrong, Marie?"

"We need another counselor for the high school weekend retreat at Green Pastures."

"I thought we had only fourteen kids attending."

"We do. Nine boys and five girls. Larson is the boys' counselor, but Eileen's sister had her baby this morning and she flew back East to be with her."

"Okay, I'll make an announcement," he said. "Hopefully someone will step up."

Shabbat services usually lasted three hours. The bar mitzvah of the youngest Levine boy caused the services to run slightly longer. The boy took his time, carefully and seriously reading from the Torah, embracing his entrance into manhood.

Jeremiah couldn't help but envy him a little. *What must it be like to grow up in safety in America instead of in jeopardy in Israel?* he wondered.

When the services were over, he made an appearance at the celebration afterward. It was expected and the festive environment was refreshing.

"Rabbi, can I speak with you?"

He turned. It was Noah, the oldest of the Levine boys. He had his hands shoved in his pockets and his shoulders hunched.

"Yes, of course."

He followed Noah to a corner of the room where they sat on folding chairs. Once they had settled Jeremiah asked, "What's on your mind?"

"I'm going to be graduating from high school in two and a half months. I want to enlist in the army, but my parents want me to go to college first. Actually, I think they're hoping that if I go to college I'll grow out of wanting to join the army."

"They want you to be safe and to get a good education, provide for your future," Jeremiah said.

"I know. They've explained all their reasons, and they are good ones, but it's not what I want to do."

"Have you explained your reasons to them?" he asked.

"I've tried. I'm just not sure they understand." The boy sighed and rubbed his forehead with his hand. "I'm not sure I understand," he admitted.

"Talk to me about enlisting in the military. What does it mean to you? Why do you feel you want to do it?"

"That's just it. I'm not sure I want to so much as I feel compelled to."

Jeremiah smiled. "In Israel we are compelled to. Here in America you have a choice. It's either something you want, something you don't want, or something you think you should want."

"I hate school," Noah admitted. "The thought of going straight to college just makes me sick inside. It makes me feel trapped."

"You could get a job, work for a few years first."

"I want to be able to do more than work at a fast food joint and I'm not really interested in most of the skilled trades like mechanic and carpenter."

"So, what makes you feel that going into the military will be better than going to college or getting a job?"

"I feel like I'd actually be doing something, helping out, you know? And I could learn a lot in the process, maybe figure out what I want to do with the rest of my life. My little brother, he's smart, loves to read and study. He wants to be a doctor someday and I think he'll make it. He hated Boy Scouts. He quit after six months. Me, I hate studying, but I loved Boy Scouts. I made Eagle Scout when I was fourteen."

Though he had no experience himself with Boy Scouts Jeremiah still knew that was young to achieve the distinction. "What did you like about it?" he asked.

"Everything. It made sense to me. I knew where I stood, what I was doing, what I had to do to excel and achieve the next thing. I loved the outdoors aspects. And I felt like I was accomplishing something real."

Jeremiah cleared his throat, aware that what he said next would likely have a huge impact on Noah with consequences that were as yet unforeseen to them both. "Some people do very well in the military. They like the structure; they like serving; they can both follow and lead. There's nothing wrong with choosing that for a career or even for a short-term experience.

However, there are costs, even beyond the obvious physical dangers. It can isolate you from friends and family, even change you. It can become hard to relate to people who aren't in the military. And then, if you do see combat, you'll have to live with the knowledge that you've killed people. Some can and some can't."

"I had thought about the danger, and that I might have to fight, but I didn't think that it could change me," Noah admitted soberly.

"It will change the way you think, respond, react. The military is very good at creating fighting machines. Unfortunately, there is no off switch for what you will become. It will be part of you for the rest of your life."

"Thank you, sir, you've given me a lot to think about." Noah glanced across the room. "I think my mom wants me for pictures."

Jeremiah stood. "Go be with your family. Days like this are precious."

"I'll think about what you said."

"I hope so," Jeremiah whispered to the boy's retreating back.

4

CINDY WAS TEN MINUTES EARLY FOR HER MEETING WITH GERALD WILSON. She sat down in a chair in the lobby of the Courtyard and waited nervously. A couple of minutes later a tall, thin man with thick glasses and steel gray hair entered the lobby, saw her, and walked straight over.

"Miss Preston, it is wonderful to finally meet you," he said, extending his hand.

She stood and shook it. "How did you know it was me?"

"My dear, before I retired I worked thirty years in forensics. You are the right age to match the voice I spoke with on the phone. You have a tense air of uncertainty that says that not only are you nervous but also you don't know who it is you're meeting and what they look like. You're here in the lobby early and that very habit of arriving early at places was what caused you to stumble upon the body in the sanctuary when no one else was around except a stranger next door with the same proclivity toward being early."

She was impressed. "Wow, you must have been very good at your job."

"I was," he said with a bright smile. "But, in this case, I cheated."

She tilted her head to the side.

He pulled a newspaper clipping out of his pocket. It was an article about her and it had her picture.

"Oh!" she said, laughing.

"A word of caution, my dear. Now that you are so famous, please do not assume that everyone who can call you by name when they see you, knows you and is someone you have just forgotten. Rather it may be a complete stranger, possibly one who seeks to do you harm."

She flushed. How many times had she forgotten someone's name after they had been introduced? Enough times that she always assumed she was the one in the wrong when someone she didn't know seemed to know her.

"How do I know you're really Dr. Wilson?" she challenged.

He laughed. "Very good."

He pulled out his wallet and showed her his driver's license. Cindy stared at it, but realized she wouldn't know a fake driver's license if she saw one. She nodded finally and he put it away.

"Since this is a Courtyard, should we adjourn to the courtyard?" he asked.

She nodded and followed him. The hotel was built as four blocks of rooms forming a square with a glass roof over the top and an elaborate courtyard in the center boasting walkways, plants, two restaurants, and dozens of benches and secluded tables. It offered a feeling of tranquility to business travelers and Cindy couldn't help but relax slightly as she sat down at a white table surrounded by greenery with the sound of a fountain nearby.

"This is lovely," she said.

"Yes, it is. When I travel I try to choose places like this. The people I interview are reliving horrific experiences and I've found it's helpful for them to be in a tranquil, soothing environment when they do."

"That's very thoughtful of you."

He shrugged. "Some would call it mercenary. The longer I can keep people talking, the more of their story I get." He smiled at her in a way that took some of the edge out of his words. "Now, as you know, I'm writing a book about crime and the myths and legends surrounding it in this part of the country. It's the fourth book of the kind that I'll be writing. I brought copies of my other three for you if you want them."

"Thank you, I'd appreciate that."

"Not at all. I want you to be able to trust that I'll handle your story with sensitivity and not try to turn it into some tabloid article."

She laughed at the thought. "I've got the brain of the killer alive in a jar?"

He shrugged. "Something like that. Some people can be so tactless and will do anything to sensationalize a story. I prefer to let the facts speak for themselves. After all, if there's anything I've learned, it's that fact really is stranger than fiction."

He pulled a digital recorder out of his pocket and set it on the table. "Now, do you mind if I record our conversation?"

"No, I guess not."

"Good, then let's get started."

As Cindy began talking to him and answering his questions about the Passion Week Killer she was surprised at what a good interviewer he was. He allowed her to tell the story in her way and then he asked her questions that she had never stopped to think about before. He slowly dissected every crime scene, every horrific moment and instead of finding it traumatic she actually felt somewhat freed. It was the first time she'd been able to tell someone who hadn't been there in the moment how she felt and what she thought about everything that transpired.

After about an hour he switched the recorder off. "You're doing just fine," he told her. "Most people aren't used to being interviewed and it can be quite comical at times, but you're doing very well."

"Thank you," she said, smiling tentatively.

"Let's take a break for a minute and have something to drink. What can I get you?"

"A Coke would be great."

He left for a minute and returned with two glasses of Coke. Cindy accepted hers, savoring the feeling of the cold glass in her hand, and took a long swig. It was amazing how much better it felt to be doing something other than talking about herself.

"So, what else are you investigating? You said your book was dealing with events local to Southern California."

"Yes. Pine Springs has provided me with an excellent opportunity in that regard. You see, in addition to the story you're already familiar with, Pine Springs is also somewhat infamous for playing host to a rather bizarre cult almost a quarter of a century ago."

"Really? I hadn't heard."

"Oh, yes, it's a fascinating story, actually. A religious leader, a crazed zealot named Matthew, lived in the mountains. He would come into town every two weeks for supplies and to attract new followers. Converts gave him all their worldly possessions, you know, pretty typical fare. People complained, but the police couldn't find anything to pin on him. Everyone who went with him went voluntarily.

"Then a couple of children from wealthy families were kidnapped. Ransoms were paid but the children were never found. Everyone suspected Matthew, but there was simply no proof. Finally, after three years, the entire cult just vanished.

Poof! No one knows what happened to them. There are endless theories, some more plausible than others."

"Like what?" Cindy asked.

"Vigilante justice is a popular one, but it seems far more likely that the cult actually migrated, south perhaps."

"I've lived here for a few years and I've never heard that story."

Gerald shrugged. "Most people don't like to talk about it, but the rumors are there. Every couple of years a treasure hunter goes looking since it's rumored that much of the group's wealth was converted to gold and jewels and kept with them."

"Fascinating. I can see the allure," she said.

He smiled. "So can I. Who wouldn't want to stumble upon that kind of find?"

He finished his soda and put the glass down on the table. "Okay, returning from the distant past to the recent past. Are you ready to continue?"

"Just about. Who else are you interviewing?"

"I'm planning on speaking with the detectives on this case when they have a minute to squeeze me into their very busy schedules. I don't blame them. I would put bringing killers to justice above discussing solved cases with a writer any day."

"You miss it?"

"Does it show? Actually, I miss the thrill of solving a riddle, of figuring out who did it. I don't miss the trauma of seeing what people are capable of doing to each other and the pressure to find killers before they escape."

"Hence, you write the books you do. Solved any riddles?"

"I think I've got the Lizzie Borden case solved, but I'm keeping that one to myself," he said with a wink.

Cindy laughed and shook her head.

"So, hopefully I can speak with the detectives who worked your case soon."

"You should also talk to Jeremiah."

"I would love to. Unfortunately when I approached you I also approached him and was told in no uncertain terms that he would give no interview. I was also strongly urged not to use his name or the name of the synagogue. He was very adamant about it."

"Why?"

"Many people value their privacy. I can't blame them for that. Being in the public eye changes things. Plus, people cope in different ways. Some people find it helps to talk things out. Others feel a deep need to repress stressful events."

She didn't see Jeremiah as the repressing type. Besides, he had spoken of the events with her since they had happened. She had noticed, though, that he wasn't necessarily fond of being in the spotlight.

"Okay, so what do you want to know now?" she asked.

He asked her more questions that she interspersed with a few of her own. It turned out that Gerald Wilson was a fascinating man with amazing stories from his time as a forensics investigator. After the interview was finally concluded it was dinnertime and he treated her to a meal at the nicer of the two restaurants at the hotel.

He regaled her with stories of his cases and also of the things he had discovered traveling around the country to research his books. When she finally left the hotel and made it home it was just past ten.

Cindy got ready for bed, but found that she was still too wound up to sleep. She hopped on the internet and tried looking up the cult Gerald had mentioned. Unfortunately there wasn't much information, even less as it turned out, than he had already given her.

She sighed. *I guess that's one mystery I won't be solving.* She sat back in her chair.

Then, of course, there was still the mystery of what had happened to Dr. Tanner. She thought about the conversation she had overheard in the pub the night before. She did a search on Max Diamond. Well over a million hits came back.

She tried again, searching for "Max Diamond controversy." A quarter of a million hits. "Well, Mr. Diamond, you must be one interesting character."

She tried again, replacing the word *controversy* with the word *scandal*, and was gratified when ten thousand hits came back. She skimmed the first three pages. Everything seemed to be linked to one of his accountants embezzling money. Hardly what she was looking for.

She tried again. "Max Diamond murder." Her heart skipped when a dozen hits came back but quickly sank when she realized they were all environmental websites accusing the land developer of murdering trees.

It was pointless, and she glanced at the clock to see that it was past one in the morning. She had to go to bed. She shut down her browser and headed for the bathroom. After brushing her teeth she sat down on the edge of her bed and yawned.

It was hard to believe that Dr. Tanner's funeral was the next day. Could it really have been just an accident, a cruel twist of fate that had killed him and involved her and Jeremiah?

It can't have just been an accident.

Accident.

She jumped to her feet and returned to her computer where a moment later she was typing "Max Diamond accident" into the search window.

Several thousand hits came back and she scanned them closely. There were a lot of articles about a handful of accidents on construction sites for property owned by Max Diamond. There were several reports of a minor car accident he was involved in a few years before. She kept going through the pages, something telling her that she was close to what she was looking for.

On the sixth page she found it. There was a two-year-old article from a Nebraska newspaper about the closing of a land deal between Max Diamond and an area rancher. The rancher had tragically lost his wife the month before to an accidental overdose of prescription medication.

Cindy printed the article and then searched for more information. She found a couple of other articles about the death including the obituary. None of them gave more information than accidental overdose. The obituary came with a photo of a smiling woman in her late forties.

Max Diamond's words came back to Cindy. *I won't let anything get in my way.*

She stared hard at the picture of the woman. "Did you get in his way?" she whispered.

Cindy was miserable in the morning. Worse, she had no one she could talk to about it. As she prepared to go to the funeral service for Dr. Tanner she dressed slowly. She was exhausted, having finally forced herself to go to bed around three. It was more than just the exhaustion that was bothering her, though.

Cindy hated funerals. The first funeral she had ever attended was for her sister and since then she had done her best to avoid them, only attending two that she couldn't get out of. Both times she had nearly collapsed, the memories from the first one overwhelming her.

She didn't want to go to Dr. Tanner's funeral. Indeed, there was no reason for her to go. They hadn't been friends or known each other. They had been acquaintances who shared nothing more than a casual nod when passing each other. There were no people there who would need her shoulder. Most people there probably wouldn't know or notice her.

But something deep inside her wouldn't let her stay home. She couldn't forget what she had overheard Max Diamond say in the pub. In her gut she didn't think that Dr. Tanner's death had been an accident.

Even if that's true, what do I possibly expect to find? she wondered.

She was wearing a black skirt and a plain white blouse. The only all-black thing she owned was a little black dress she was saving for just the right occasion. *Such a fairy tale. Like I'll ever have a reason to wear it or anyone to wear it for.*

She was tired. She hadn't slept well the last couple of nights and she knew her mind had been fretting over the death, unable to let it go. She had begun to wonder if she needed it to be a murder to help make sense of it. Otherwise, someone having a heart attack while driving and crashing into another car was just one more horror of the world that she couldn't protect herself from.

No one is safe ever, not anywhere.

She didn't like feeling that way. Ironically since her two brushes with killers in the last year the thought had slowly started to control her less. Murder was understandable even if abominable. Senseless accidents, random incidents, and fate weren't.

She went to her jewelry box and selected a simple gold cross necklace. *God understands those things even if I don't,* she thought, trying to comfort herself. At last she was finished getting ready.

Moment of truth. Are you going or not?

She grabbed her purse and headed out the front door, trying to ignore the shaking of her hands as she locked it behind her. It was a short drive to the cemetery. By the looks of things a couple of funerals were scheduled for the day. She followed the small signs to the parking area for the Tanner funeral.

They were having a graveside service and she followed several others across the grass to where chairs had been arranged near a casket. She hung back, not wanting to take a chair as they were already filling up fast. That way she could leave quickly and quietly if she needed.

Just looking at the mourners was enough to make her chest tighten and she found a nearby tree she could brace herself against for support. *You're okay*, she told herself over and over again. She took several deep breaths, trying to remind herself why she was there.

She tried to see the faces of the people as they passed by, but not their expressions. Grief, sorrow, confusion, anger, she didn't need to see the emotions to know that they were there.

Joseph and Geanie walked past and Geanie gave her a little wave, which Cindy returned. Dave and his wife showed up close after them.

As the funeral began Cindy looked around. Most were sitting or clustered around those who were. There were a few, like herself, who chose to be scattered farther away.

Finally her gaze fell on Paul and a chill raced up her spine. Something told her that the detective wouldn't be there if they still believed Dr. Tanner's death was an accident.

She began to ease her way slowly over to him, the heels of her black pumps sinking into the earth with each step. She noticed that, like she had been, he was surveying everyone and everything around them. With a grimace Paul dipped his head toward her to acknowledge that he saw her.

When she reached his side she stood quietly, waiting for the service to conclude. Once it did, though, she intended to find out what exactly was going on. It was a relief to stand there with him because it let her focus on her purpose and not on the sounds of crying that reached her ears or the words of the pastor memorializing the deceased.

When the service was finally over she turned to Paul. "It was murder, wasn't it?" she asked, careful to keep her voice low.

"We don't know anything of the sort," Paul said, his voice frosty. "I'm here to pay my respects. And, if you must know, I'm here to talk with Joseph about a different matter."

"A related matter?" she guessed.

"No," he said, but the flicker of his eyes gave him away.

"So, something is going on," she said triumphantly.

"Miss Preston, leave well enough alone, for your own safety and my sanity."

"But I can help," she protested.

"No, you can't. Look, if you're really that bored and need something to occupy your time, might I suggest a hobby. Or a boyfriend."

"I'm not bored," she said, allowing her anger to show. "I helped out a lot the last two times something like this happened."

"What you did was nearly get yourself killed. What you're doing now is interfering with a police investigation."

She took a step back. Before she could think of any way to respond, Joseph and Geanie walked up.

"Hey," Geanie said, giving her a quick hug.

"Hi, Cindy. Detective, everything okay?" Joseph asked.

"I have a few questions I'd like to ask you."

"Sure."

"Can we step over here a ways?"

Paul and Joseph moved away from the gravesite and the exiting mourners and Cindy and Geanie followed. When they stopped walking Paul glared at Cindy. Joseph, following his gaze, said, "We can speak freely in front of them."

"You're on the board for Green Pastures, correct?"

"Yes."

"And land developer Max Diamond is trying to buy the camp, correct?"

"Yes."

"Have you had any contact with a man named Randall Kelly?"

Cindy felt her pulse begin to quicken. She had read in the papers that Randall Kelly was the environmentalist who had been killed.

"No, but his name sounds familiar."

Paul pulled a picture out of his shirt. "You haven't seen or talked to this man for the last few weeks?"

"No."

"Has anyone mentioned an environmental activist to you in connection with Green Pastures?"

"No, sorry," Joseph said. "Why?"

"We believe that he was murdered last week. We're trying to figure out why and by whom. Is it possible that Dr. Tanner could have had any contact with him?"

"I don't think—" Joseph broke off in mid-stream, a thoughtful look crossing his face.

"What is it?" Paul pushed.

"Wednesday night Mel mentioned that he was going to be meeting with somebody who might be able to throw some more light on the whole situation."

"Did he say who?"

"No."

"Did he say what time or where he was going to meet this person? Was the meeting for that night or the next morning?"

Joseph shook his head. "I don't know. I wish I could be more help."

"That's okay. Please call me if you remember anything else," Paul urged.

"I will."

Paul turned and headed for the parking lot, leaving the three of them alone.

"What's going on?" Joseph asked.

"I'm not sure," Cindy said, "but I'd bet it has something to do with Green Pastures and Max Diamond. I overheard him Friday night talking about the sale and I believe he means for it to happen, regardless of who has to get hurt."

"Or killed?" Geanie asked.

Cindy nodded.

"That's ridiculous," Joseph said. "Max Diamond is a very wealthy man. If he loses this battle, he'll just move on to the next one without breaking a sweat."

"I'm not so sure about that," Cindy said.

"I am," Joseph countered.

"I'm sure the police will figure it out," Geanie said quickly.

"I hope so. I did want to ask your opinion on something else, Cindy," Joseph said.

"What?"

"Tomorrow night we're having another board meeting. Among other things we need to find a replacement board member. I was thinking of throwing Jeremiah's name out for consideration. Do you think he'd do it?"

"Why are you asking me?

"The two of you seem pretty close, so I wanted to try and gauge his reaction by talking to you first."

"We're not exactly close," she said. "I really don't know, but you can try. He'd make a wonderful addition to the board, I'm sure."

"That's what I think. Well, I'll see what can be done. Are you going over to Dr. Tanner's house?"

"No, I was just here for the funeral."

"Okay. Take care, Cindy, and don't worry. The police have everything under control." Joseph and Geanie turned to go.

How he of all people could say that was beyond her. If it weren't for her, he himself could have been killed or falsely imprisoned based on everything that had happened with his purebred dogs, the murderer, and the homeless charity back in November.

She stayed until the last mourner had left. Frustration was building within her. It felt like every two seconds someone was either telling her that she was crazy or that she was in the way.

She glanced back toward the casket and pain nearly overwhelmed her. It was about more than just her sister this time, though. Dr. Tanner had been a good and decent man and someone had killed him. She was sure of it.

"No one believes me now, but I'll prove it," she vowed.

Funerals are hard on everyone, Jeremiah reflected as he stared upon the faces of the mourners. They were there to grieve the loss of a young woman who had passed away after a long illness.

He read some words from one of the Psalms and then gave a brief eulogy for the woman. Then the older family members passed around a small knife, which they used to cut their clothes on the right side, representing the hole the deceased had left in their lives. It was an outward sign of mourning. Some of the younger family members chose to wear a black ribbon instead of rending their clothes. "Dayan Ha'emet, Blessed is the Judge of Truth," Jeremiah said as they performed the ritual.

At the conclusion of his words the coffin was lowered into the ground and many came forward to take their turn shoveling some dirt upon it. This act was the ultimate act of love and kindness, for the deceased could not do it herself, nor ask others to do it, nor thank them for their labor on her behalf. It also offered closure to those grieving.

When that was finished the mourners then recited the Kaddish prayer. "Praised be the name of G-d. He created the world according to his will. Life has a plan and a purpose. We hope for the coming of G-d's kingdom on earth, when things as they are, will be changed to things as they ought to be."

Those in attendance who were not immediate family then formed two lines facing each other, which the mourners passed through on their way to the cars.

"May you be comforted among all the mourners of Zion and Jerusalem," Jeremiah said as they passed by. Others also offered condolences.

When it was over, the crowd dispersed. Some would be going to her home to sit quietly with her family and discuss her life and to provide a simple meal, probably hard-boiled eggs and bagels. He had been to a couple of non-Jewish funerals and had been surprised at the amount of food and people that showed up at the house of the bereaved after the funeral. It had seemed too festive to him.

He was the last to leave and as he headed toward the front of the cemetery he tried not to let the images of other funerals, ones where he had been a mourner, fill his mind.

He pulled his cell phone out of his pocket, preparing to call a taxi to take him back home when a familiar car rolled up beside him.

"Need a ride?" Cindy asked.

"Yes," he said, pocketing his phone and moving around to the passenger side.

"What are you doing here?" she asked once they had begun moving.

"I was presiding over a funeral. And you?"

"Attending one. Dr. Tanner's."

"Were you close?"

"No, but I wanted to go. I still don't think it was an accident. I think he was killed."

"And what makes you think so?" he asked.

"My gut tells me."

"And your gut's never been wrong?"

"I—I don't know," she stammered slightly.

"Look, Cindy, leave those sorts of determinations to the police. That's what their job is."

He could tell that he had irritated her. They drove in silence the rest of the way to his house.

"Thanks for the ride," he said, forcing a smile as he exited the car.

She stared at him stonily. "You're welcome."

He sighed as she drove away.

Monday morning Mark was sitting at his desk going through and cleaning up his notes about the Kelly case and waiting for Paul to get off the phone. His partner had been on the phone since Mark had gotten in and his curiosity was beginning to get the better of him.

Finally Paul walked over, his face grim. He pulled up a chair and sat down.

"I'm not going to like this, am I?" Mark asked.

"No, because I hate it."

"What did you find out?"

"We got hold of the manuscript Kelly was working on. I've got a couple guys reading through it. I skimmed it. It's inflammatory, but he doesn't name names or point fingers as much as I expected. I don't see anything in there that could have gotten him killed."

"Okay."

"I called up to the administration office at Green Pastures."

"And?"

"Randall Kelly did go up there on Wednesday to look around and talk to some of the staff."

"Did you get names?"

"Better than that. He spent most of his time talking to a gentleman who fancies himself a park ranger. I got that guy on the phone and he was more than happy to tell me all about Kelly and their conversation. Apparently all that land up there is not only a camp but also one of the only breeding grounds for a rare type of bird."

"And that could have sent Kelly on a crusade easy," Mark said. "Did our would-be ranger have any idea why he might have been in the burn zone?"

"No, because when Kelly left apparently he was in quite a rage and said he was heading to talk to Max Diamond and get the whole project stopped."

Mark whistled low. "I guess we're going to be paying a visit to Mr. Diamond this morning."

Paul nodded.

Mark stood up but his partner didn't join him. Mark looked at him questioningly.

"There's more," Paul said.

Mark sat back down. "What is it?"

"Autopsy report came back on Dr. Tanner. He had a heart attack all right. It was induced by poison."

5

Mark blinked at his partner. "Dr. Tanner was murdered?"

"Yes."

"Two deaths and they were both connected in some way to Green Pastures."

"We were right; I don't think it's a coincidence," Paul said.

"Then we definitely need to go see Max Diamond this morning."

"He's staying at a local hotel while he's working on this deal."

"Let's go, then."

"Ready when you are."

They got up and headed outside to Paul's car. When they arrived at the hotel they were relieved to find the land developer was still in his room. They headed on up and were admitted by the man himself.

Max Diamond would be imposing under any circumstances. He was well over six feet tall with the build of a linebacker and an iron handshake. Mark looked him dead in the eyes and didn't give an inch as the developer tried to use those facts to his advantage. Mark didn't care who Max was or how big he was; he wasn't going to be intimidated by anyone.

"Detectives, come in and sit down," Max said after they had introduced themselves.

The living room area of the suite was tastefully furnished despite the fact that it was larger than most apartments. As soon as they had taken their seats Paul pushed a picture of Randall Kelly across the coffee table toward Max.

"Have you ever seen this man before?"

"Of course," Max said without hesitating.

"Do you know who he is?" Mark asked.

"A pain in the butt, but like all such pains he's not worth much attention. He's one of those environmental activists. Why, has something happened to him?"

"What makes you ask that?" Paul said.

Max Diamond laughed. "Gentlemen, I'm not stupid. Detectives come around with pictures asking if you know somebody there are very few reasons why. Either he committed some sort of crime, accused me of some sort of crime, is missing, or is dead."

"Very good, Max," Mark said. "In this case, dead."

"I can't say I'm sorry. He was an annoying little pest. He confronted me late Wednesday, all bluster about how he was going to make sure the deal for that camp didn't go through. Something about birds. I've dealt with his kind before so I wasn't overly concerned. They usually go away in their own time."

"If you pay them off?" Paul asked.

Max shrugged. "I've never had to. I'm an expert on getting the community on my side, despite whatever concerns people like him have."

"And just how do you do that?" Mark queried.

Max smiled. "That, gentlemen, is a trade secret, so to speak. Are we done or do you have more questions?"

"Oh, we have more questions," Mark said, irritated and refusing to be dismissed so easily. "Were there any witnesses to your little conversation?"

"Sure, he got me while I was having a drink downstairs at the bar. He wasn't exactly quiet. His type never are. There were probably a dozen witnesses. You could start with the bartender, I'm sure."

"And what time did this all take place?" Paul asked.

"Between six and six-thirty. I had dinner reservations at six-thirty. I invited him to join me and continue our philosophical discussions. I think that upset him and he left."

"And how did you spend the rest of your evening?" Paul asked.

"Dinner here at the hotel. Around ten I retired to my room where I stayed until eight in the morning when I came down for a late breakfast."

"How are your negotiations going with the Green Pastures board?" Mark asked, changing topics.

"Well. I'm sure they'll come around to my point of view. Although I have to hand it to the chairman, he's a tough one. Smart, shrewd, and principled."

"You sound like you almost admire him."

"I do in a way. He's not like that weasel," Max said, pointing to the picture of Kelly. "He knows how to create something, how to be a success, not just stand in other people's way. Still, he's a reasonable man, and in the end I think we'll make a deal."

"Not with him you won't," Paul said.

"Oh, and why is that?" Max asked, looking bemused.

"He's dead."

And for the first time since they had been there the look of smug superiority vanished from the developer's face. Surprise mingled with a touch of sorrow twisted his features. "Dr. Tanner is dead?"

"Yes, he is."

"I'm very sorry to hear that. What happened?"

"He was killed."

Max looked uncertain for just a moment, like he didn't know how to respond, and then the mask descended again. "That's unfortunate, but hopefully his replacement on the board will be easier to work with. I wish you luck in catching his killer."

As they left the hotel, Mark couldn't help but marvel at what a piece of work the developer was. Once in the car he turned to Paul. "Do you have to work hard to become that much of a jerk or is it a gift?"

Paul smiled briefly. "You know what they say. Some are born with it; the rest aspire to it."

"You think he killed Kelly?"

"Personally, no, but I wouldn't be at all surprised if he hired somebody to do it."

"If we can prove that, it's good enough for me," Mark said. "How about the doctor?"

"He actually seemed surprised by that one."

"I agree. So, two different killers?"

"Maybe, I don't like it, though. It's too much of a coincidence," Paul said.

"The murders have to be connected. We just have to figure out how."

Marie popped her head into Jeremiah's office. "You have a visitor," she said. "It's one of the Gentiles from next door."

"You mean Cindy?" he asked.

"No, this one's a guy. Said his name was Joseph."

What could Joseph possibly be doing here? Jeremiah wondered.

"Go ahead and send him in."

He rose and shook the other man's hand when he entered and then they both took their seats.

"Joseph, it's been a while," Jeremiah acknowledged.

"Yes, it has."

"What can I do for you?"

"I'm here to invite you to serve on the Green Pastures board."

"Excuse me?" Jeremiah said, blinking in surprise.

"With the death of Dr. Tanner I've been elected the acting chairman and I want you to fill the vacant position."

"I'm sorry, I'm just not interested."

"Hear me out. I'm not so much asking you as begging you. As rabbi you're a community leader with a vested interest in the future of Green Pastures. I need someone like you right now while the decision is being made whether to continue the camp as it is or to sell it to Max Diamond in exchange for a lease on the land and more than enough cash to fix the infrastructure of the immediate camp area."

"I'm not a businessman, Joseph."

"Exactly. We've got too many businessmen on the board, myself included. What we need is a religious leader to help us examine the pros and cons and decide the future of Green Pastures."

"I still don't—"

Joseph held up a hand to interrupt him. "Please don't give me an answer right now. Just think about it. If you could serve for three months until we get this matter settled then I'd happily accept your resignation and we could both move on. But right now I have to replace Dr. Tanner and I would much prefer someone like you sitting at that table with me. Your community needs you."

"I'll think about it."

"That's all I need for the moment. Thank you," Joseph said, rising and extending his hand once more.

"You ever planning to go into politics?"

Joseph laughed. "No, why?"

"No reason," Jeremiah said, shaking his hand.

As soon as Joseph had left, Jeremiah sank back down in his chair. Of course he had to refuse the offer. Serving on a board like that was far too public and politically charged. He didn't need the scrutiny. He couldn't help but wonder why Joseph had come to him instead of one of the pastors of his own church, though.

There was definitely a certain irony to the whole situation. *Dr. Tanner, why did you have to hit my car?* He sighed and turned back to his work.

Cindy could barely keep her eyes open Monday afternoon as she stared at her computer monitor at work. She had been up half the night doing some research online, trying to figure out if there was a poison that could cause someone to have a heart attack. As it turned out there were several, although most of them would have killed Dr. Tanner before he even got in his car.

She had discovered that a few, like cyanide, could have caused the delayed heart attack. Most of them, though, would be nearly impossible to obtain.

Unless you were wealthy and connected.

"Earth to Cindy!"

Cindy jumped and turned to look at Geanie.

"Helloooo, are you with us?" Geanie asked.

"Sorry. What?" Cindy asked.

"Camp. Wildman. Questions."

Cindy just stared back at her, allowing her confusion to show on her face.

"Wow, you really were spacing out," Geanie said.

"Sorry. What's going on?"

"Marie just confirmed that we're holding space for sixteen people on our bus up to Green Pastures. I was wanting to know if you had a final head count from Pastor Dave and a driver for the bus? I'm also supposed to remind you that depending on how many he needs seats for we might need to send up the van as well."

"Okay, I'll get on it," Cindy said.

She reached for the phone, yawned, and thought better of it. Instead she got up and left the office, heading for the youth room and Wildman's office. The youth pastor beamed when he saw her.

"Any chance you got a bus driver?" he asked hopefully.

"I've got calls out. I'll do some follow-up this afternoon."

"Oh," he said, clearly disappointed. "So, what brings you here?"

"Do you have a final head count for students and counselors attending? The synagogue is sending sixteen people up and I want to make sure we have seats for everyone."

"I just finalized the list," he said, standing to grab a piece of paper from his printer and hand it to her.

"Thanks," she said, scanning the list quickly. "Oh, good, Brenda is going to be able to go," she said. Cindy had gotten to know a little bit about the girl during the Thanksgiving food drive. Brenda's family was very poor and she attended church by herself.

"Yes, she was thrilled when I told her we'd found a scholarship for her."

"She deserves a little happiness," Cindy said.

"Well, hopefully this will be the best camp experience ever!"

"I'm sure it will be," Cindy said. *Especially since I think this will be her only camp experience.*

She left the youth room and headed back to the main office. When she stepped inside, though, every thought of nailing down a bus driver vanished as Mark stood up from where he had been sitting next to her desk.

She rushed over to him, dropping the camp list next to her phone. "What is it?" she asked.

"It turns out you were right to call us last week," he said. "Dr. Tanner was murdered."

"I knew it!" she said, far more exuberantly than she should have, given what it was that she knew. "Sorry," she said, wincing.

It didn't seem to faze him. "I just wanted to ask you some more questions."

"Are you sure Paul is going to be okay with that?" she asked before she could stop herself.

Mark rolled his eyes. "Paul has issues with civilians being in the line of fire. And rightly so. Unfortunately, I have to be a little more flexible sometimes."

"Geanie, can you cover for me?" Cindy asked.

The other girl nodded, a bemused expression on her face.

A minute later Cindy led Mark into one of the Sunday school rooms, the very one they had had a similar meeting in nearly a year before.

Mark took one look at the miniature chairs and groaned. "Seriously? There aren't any rooms with adult-sized furniture in this place?"

"None that aren't in use or about to be in the next half hour. There's always some kind of meeting going on around here."

"Fine," he said, sinking down onto a tiny plastic orange chair. "You should know I'm going to talk to the rabbi next."

"Of course," she said, secretly thrilled that he had come to speak with her first. She leaned forward eagerly on her own tiny plastic chair.

"Like I said in the office," Mark began. "Dr. Tanner was definitely murdered."

"Was he poisoned? Was it a poison-induced heart attack?" Cindy asked, somewhat breathlessly.

"You know, with imagination like that you should become a policeman or a mystery writer. Personally, I'd recommend writer. It's usually safer."

"Usually?" she asked, staring intently at him.

He cracked a smile and she found herself laughing.

"You're in a really good mood considering we're here to discuss murder," he observed.

"It's just such a relief," she admitted. "Everyone was treating me like I was crazy."

"Crazy like a fox." He took a deep breath. "Yes, it was poison and it induced the heart attack."

She resisted the urge to throw her arms up in the air and make the touchdown gesture. She mentally shook herself. *Get a grip, we're talking about the brutal murder of someone you knew, a good, decent man. This isn't a game. You don't get points for outguessing the police or being clever. A man is dead and that is a great tragedy, not a reason to party like you just won the Super Bowl.*

"How was he poisoned? By whom?" she asked after she had forced herself to take several deep breaths to clear her head.

"We don't know yet. The coroner thinks, though, that he was poisoned within an hour of dying."

"Would he have known he was poisoned?" she asked. "I mean, would there have been any symptoms?"

"Probably not."

She could tell from his facial expression that Mark was saying that to make her feel better. The truth was he really didn't know, but he didn't want to say that and risk making her feel worse.

"And you don't know if the poison was swallowed or injected?" she asked.

Mark shook his head. "In case you missed it, I'm the one here to ask you questions, not vice versa. But, for your information, it looks like he swallowed it."

"Which would mean that all you'd have to do is figure out where he had breakfast that morning," she said.

"The accident happened at ten in the morning. Yes, it could have been breakfast, or brunch, or it could have been a cup of coffee he grabbed somewhere."

"True."

"Almost all murders committed are done so by friends or family. So, tell me what you know about his family. Any of them up for something like this? Did anyone here at the church hate him for any reason in particular?"

"Like what?" she asked, startled by the question.

"Like anything. Grudges? Any hints of adultery?"

"No, nothing like that."

"And yet he changed churches after years of attending this one. Usually people don't do that without a good reason."

"I think I told you last week that he moved and started attending a church closer to him."

"Paul's checking with the minister there," Mark said. "If he was going to church regularly elsewhere then why was he in front of First Shepherd when he had his heart attack?"

"I don't know."

"You say there's meetings going on here all the time. Any on Thursday he would have likely been trying to attend?"

"I—I don't think so," she said, startled at the thought. She had assumed his driving in front of the church had been random, unrelated. Maybe it wasn't.

"What meetings were happening here Thursday morning?" Mark asked.

"There was a women's luncheon that started at eleven," she recalled. "There was also a prayer meeting scheduled." She closed her eyes and visualized the calendar, hoping to remember so she wouldn't have to go get it.

"Anything else?"

Her eyes flew open as she remembered. "There was a scout leaders' meeting."

"Who was there?"

"Representatives from the area for all the different scouting groups. Boy Scouts, Girl Scouts, Cub Scouts, Campfire Girls, Brownies, Sea Scouts, too, I believe."

Mark leaned in close, his eyes blazing at her. "Would any of those people have had any reason to know Dr. Tanner?"

"Larson Beck. He's a Cub Scout leader for the area. He and Dr. Tanner were both on the board—"

"For Green Pastures," Mark finished with her.

"Oh! Do you think Dr. Tanner was coming to see Larson?" Cindy asked.

"I'd be willing to bet on it," Mark said. "And I'm not a betting man."

With that terrible poker face, you shouldn't be, she thought.

"Joseph told Paul yesterday that Dr. Tanner was supposed to meet with someone Wednesday night or Thursday morning to help shed light on the sale of the camp."

"It's possible he was talking about Larson."

"But Larson would have been able to voice his opinions directly in the board meeting."

"Unless he was afraid of something or someone," Mark said.

Cindy shook her head. "Larson Beck isn't afraid of anything."

"Everyone's afraid of something," Mark said.

And some of us are afraid of everything, like me.

Cindy felt like she was grasping at a thought that kept just barely eluding her. It was important; she could feel it. "What if . . ."

She stopped, feeling the pieces slowly falling into place.

"What?" Mark pushed.

"What if whoever he met with killed him?"

Mark was nodding. "Maybe. I'm guessing that whatever that meeting was about certainly was connected to his murder."

A flash of understanding crossed Mark's face.

"What is it? You figured it out, didn't you? Tell me," Cindy pleaded.

"It's just speculation at this point," he said, talking more to himself than to her.

"I don't care. This whole thing has been speculation. Let me know what you're thinking. I can help. I know I can."

"What if Dr. Tanner and the person he met with were both killed?" Mark asked.

"I don't understand—" she started to say and then stopped. "You mean the environmentalist?"

"Exactly. He was planning on causing a huge uproar over the proposed land sale. Turns out some rare birds use that area as their nesting ground. What if—"

"What if he was the person Dr. Tanner was meeting with when he told Joseph there was someone who could shed light on the whole situation?" Cindy finished.

"Yes."

"And somebody else linked the two of them together and killed them both?"

"That's about the size of it," Mark said.

"But who would do that?"

"Someone who wanted to make sure Max Diamond bought Green Pastures, no matter the cost."

"No matter the cost," she echoed, her blood turning to ice in her veins. She thought of what she had read on the internet about the rancher's wife. She thought about telling Mark, but so far it was an isolated incident. Another thought occurred to her, though. "There are other board members who are against the sale," she whispered. She stood abruptly to her feet.

"Where are you going?"

"I have to warn Joseph."

6

Settle down," Mark told Cindy, pushing her back down into the chair. "If the murders are linked and the killer is going after people opposing the sale, we don't want to tip our hand too early."

"But Joseph—"

"Is both a potential victim and a potential suspect at this point," Mark said.

Cindy blinked. "Suspect? How could he possibly be a suspect?"

"At this point anyone connected with Green Pastures is a suspect as far as I'm concerned," Mark said. "I don't think Joseph had anything to do with these murders, but I don't want to accidentally tip off whoever did by telling Joseph too much."

She bit her lip and fidgeted in the hard, plastic chair, feeling very much like a kindergartner who had just been told she had to sit quiet the whole day. Kindergartners weren't putting their friends' lives in jeopardy, though.

"He's a friend, and so is Geanie. I can't risk them getting hurt."

"Don't worry. We'll do everything we can to protect them now that we have at least a theory about what is going on here."

Cindy remembered police protection that had not gone so well in the past, but decided it was not the time to bring it up. She didn't need to antagonize Mark.

"Do you have a list of people who sit on that board?" he asked.

"No, but Joseph can give you that." She blanched as she remembered her conversation with him the day before.

"What is it?" Mark asked.

"I know he's thinking of asking Jeremiah to replace Dr. Tanner."

"Of course he is," Mark said with a sigh. "Because, you know, any way that you or the rabbi can get more drawn into this mess. Sometimes I think the two of you are conspiring to give me a heart attack or gray hair at the very least."

"I was at the pub the other night," she said, deciding she needed to tell Mark her suspicions regardless of whether it contributed to his premature graying. "I overheard Max Diamond say that he wouldn't let anything stop him from buying the camp."

"That doesn't mean anything unfortunately," Mark said. "You could convict and execute me a dozen times over based on the things I say during the day. People exaggerate or are misinterpreted all the time."

"Well, I looked him up on the internet and a couple of years ago he bought a ranch in Nebraska a month after the owner's wife accidentally overdosed on prescription drugs."

Mark sighed. "That could be a complete coincidence. Do you even know if the wife opposed the sale? That would at least be something."

"I don't know," she admitted.

"Max Diamond is a suspect just like everyone else, but I've met the man and I'm not sure he's behind these killings. He's not a nice man and of course you want to blame him because of it."

"It's not that," Cindy said.

"All right, thank you for your help," Mark said as he stood up. "Call me if you think of anything else."

"What do you want me to do in the meantime?" she asked.

He looked at her like she had grown a second head. "What do you mean?" he asked.

"What can I do to help?"

"Nothing. Cindy, you're not a cop. This isn't your job. What you need to do right now is leave well enough alone and let us professionals handle it. Meanwhile, I'm sorry for pulling you away from your actual job."

He left the room and she stared after him. "But I can help," she whispered.

Jeremiah was less than thrilled when Marie showed Mark into his office. Mark closed the door and took a seat across from Jeremiah. "Hello, Rabbi."

"Detective."

"I just came from next door. Heads up, the secretary has got her teeth in this and I doubt she'll be letting it go any time soon."

Jeremiah leaned back in his chair and did his best not to react. "What exactly is it she's got her teeth into?"

"The man who hit you didn't just have a heart attack. He was murdered."

Jeremiah had been afraid that might be the case. He hadn't wanted to believe it, but Cindy had seemed so sure and it would make life too simple if it had just been an accident. Simple was something life hadn't been in way too long.

"I'm sorry to hear that."

"That he was murdered or that she's determined to get herself involved?"

"Both. But frankly I am curious as to why you're here."

"If she's getting herself involved I know it will drag you in, whether you want it to or not. There's a connection between you two."

"I don't know what you're talking about."

"Fine. Play that game. I also want to pick your brain more about the accident."

"I've already told you everything I could remember," Jeremiah said.

"I know, but I'm going to need to go over everything with you one more time."

Jeremiah answered Mark's questions as quickly and with as much detail as possible. Just having the detective in his office made him uncomfortable.

What's wrong with me? he began to wonder. The car accident was the least suspicious thing he had been involved in that the detective had questioned him about since they had met. Still, he felt the urge to just walk out of the interview, hit the street, and keep walking.

Three years he had been rabbi at the synagogue. Three years he had lived in the same house, gone to work at the same place, bought his groceries at the same store, seen the same people.

I'm restless, he realized. It was the longest he had been anywhere since he was a kid and something inside of him was telling him it was time to move on. The realization frustrated him and he balled his hands into fists.

He stared at the detective and wondered how many seconds of silence and peace it would buy him if he reached across his desk and snapped the man's neck. *Calm down*, he warned himself.

"Rabbi, are you okay?" Mark asked.

Jeremiah just stared at him.

"Rabbi? You don't look so good."

Jeremiah shook himself hard. "Reliving the accident is stressful," he lied.

"Gotcha. Well, I think we're done, so I'll go and let you de-stress," Mark said, standing up.

You don't even want to know how I de-stress, Jeremiah thought as he forced himself to smile at the other man. It felt more like he was baring his teeth, but he forced himself to meet the other man's eyes.

Mark took a step backward. It was involuntary, Jeremiah could tell. There was no quickening thought in Mark's eyes, just a slight dilation that betrayed fear so subtle that he wasn't even aware of the emotion.

"See you later," Mark said, heading out the door a touch faster than he might otherwise have.

Jeremiah gripped the edge of his desk. He was losing control and that wasn't a good thing. He needed to clear his head before he did or said something he couldn't take back. He strained his ears and could hear Marie on the telephone in the outer office. Perfect. He wasn't in the mood to explain himself. He scribbled a simple note on a piece of paper. *Going to appointments, out for the rest of the day.*

He grabbed his coat on his way out of his office. He dropped the note on Marie's desk, waved, and left before she could hang up the phone. He made it to the parking lot without running into anyone and drove quickly home.

Once there he changed clothes and then clipped a leash on Captain's collar. "Feel like a run in the park, boy?"

The dog barked joyously. He had learned what the word *park* meant and he looked forward to the exercise as much as Jeremiah did. Ten minutes later they were in the park and Jeremiah felt the rush of release as he uncoiled his muscles and raced along the path. Captain ran beside him.

He had spent most of his life alone, but over the last four months he had found himself getting used to the dog's presence. He had never had a pet before but he understood why people valued them so highly. Still, Captain was more than a pet. He was a comrade.

"Whatever happens, boy, it's you and me," he told the dog.

Captain barked and butted Jeremiah's hand with his nose even as they ran. The dog had come to him upon the death of his previous master. A man Jeremiah had recognized from his past, a man who had been murdered before Jeremiah could talk to him. And the murder was still unsolved.

Maybe that's what's wrong with me, has me so unsettled, Jeremiah thought. It was a simple explanation, too simple, he feared.

He was also getting enmeshed in the community, too much so for his taste. The invitation from Joseph to be on the board was a sign of that.

But isn't that what you've been trying to accomplish? Isn't that the whole point of a new life, one free from too much scrutiny?

He began to run faster, but the headache that was forming couldn't be outrun. Neither could his problems. He was going to have to make some decisions about the course of his life soon before they were made for him.

It was close to quitting time when the office door opened and Brenda walked in. Cindy looked at the girl in surprise and then gave her a big smile. "Hi, Brenda, remember me?"

Brenda smiled shyly. "Of course, Miss Preston."

Cindy cringed at the title and how old it made her feel, but kept her smile firmly in place. "Is there something I can do for you?"

The girl held an envelope in her hands, gripping it with white knuckles. "Is Pastor David here?"

"I think he's left for the day. Can I help?"

Brenda walked forward and handed the envelope to Cindy. "I wrote a thank you letter for my camp sponsor."

"Oh, wonderful. I know who it is so I'll make sure he gets it."

"Thank you," Brenda said, coloring.

Brenda's family was very poor and Cindy could guess what it meant to the girl to go to camp. The girl hovered anxiously and Cindy sensed there was something more.

"What else do you need?"

"I was going to ask Pastor David to write me a letter of recommendation. I'm going to try to get an after-school job."

"Oh, I'm sure he'd be happy to write you a letter. I'll ask him in the morning."

"Thank you," Brenda said, biting her lip.

"You're welcome. Do me a favor and have fun at camp, okay?"

"Okay," Brenda said with a smile.

"Do you want me to give the letter to Joseph?" Geanie asked after the girl had left.

"I'd really appreciate it," Cindy said.

Geanie got up and took the letter from her, looking at it contemplatively. "He's a really good man."

"Was there a question?" Cindy asked, puzzled.

"I'm just . . . I'm scared. You know?"

Cindy blinked at her, startled. "Of what?"

"I'm in love with him," Geanie admitted. She shuddered after she had said it. "That's the first time I've admitted it."

"So, I take it he doesn't know?"

Geanie shook her head.

"Do you know how he feels?"

"I know he likes me, but beyond that . . . no. I think that's what scares me so much," Geanie said.

"You could tell him how you feel."

Geanie laughed as if that was the funniest thing she had ever heard. "The guy should say it first. It doesn't work well the other way around."

"Oh," Cindy said. Staring at Geanie she could see the other girl's emotions, her love, her fear. She felt a pang of jealousy. She had never been in love, not even close. She had never let herself go there.

That would require opening myself up, being vulnerable.

But staring at her friend Cindy wished that she could know, if even just once, what it felt like to care about a man that much. Tears suddenly stung her eyes and she turned away so that Geanie wouldn't see them and get the wrong idea.

When she locked up the office as they left a while later Cindy contemplated the rest of her evening. She didn't want to go home and try to amuse herself with television. She had nowhere to be, though, nowhere to go.

Or I could go see Larson Beck and find out what he knows, if anything, about all of this.

She turned around at the church gate and headed back to the office. Larson's phone number was in her files connected with the scout meeting. She called the number from the office phone and on the third ring he answered.

"Hi, Larson, this is Cindy Preston. I'm the secretary at First Shepherd."

"Hi, Cindy. What can I do for you?"

She felt suddenly awkward, but she took a deep breath and continued, "I'd like to talk to you about Dr. Tanner's accident. I think it might be connected to the purchase offer for Green Pastures."

There was silence for a moment and then Larson asked, "What makes you think that?"

"I have my reasons, and I can explain it all to you. I just wanted to know if we could meet and talk?"

"Sure, okay. Coffee at Joe's downtown in half an hour?"

"I'll be there," Cindy said.

She relocked the office and the church gate and drove to Joe's in a state of excitement. Gerald Wilson was right; the thrill of solving riddles was addictive.

But not safe, a part of her mind whispered, reminding her of the cost.

She flipped open her cell and called Jeremiah, wanting to catch him up to speed and invite him to the meeting. It seemed odd that they hadn't spent much time talking about the crime.

She got his voicemail. "Hi, it's Cindy. I talked to Mark and I know he was on his way to talk to you about the fact that Dr. Tanner was murdered. I'm going to see Larson Beck. We think Dr. Tanner was on his way to see him when he died. Give me a call."

She had to park two blocks away. When she finally made it into Joe's coffee shop, Larson was already at a table sipping his coffee. He waved to her and she ordered herself a raspberry hot chocolate. A minute later she was sitting across from him.

"Thanks for meeting me."

"You said murder. I'm all ears."

He listened while she brought him up to speed, displaying shock and sorrow alternately as she described the scenario she and Mark worked out.

"And you think he was coming to see me when he was killed?"

"Yes. Had he called you, made plans to meet with you?"

"No, nothing. I wish he had. I've been against the sale of Green Pastures from the beginning. I think it's a mistake to give it up and have to take someone else's terms to be able to use it. That camp is too valuable to the community. I'm up there with groups half a dozen times a year. I'm going up this weekend as counselor for the synagogue.

"I just can't believe someone's willing to kill over this, though," he continued. "I wouldn't think Max Diamond would need the land that badly and none of the board members stand to gain anything personally whether the sale happens or not."

"I just want you to be careful," Cindy said. She was disappointed that he didn't seem to have any light to shed on the situation, but she hoped that she could at least keep something from happening to him as well.

"I will be," he said. "Thanks for the warning."

They left the coffee house and Larson walked her toward her car. It was dark and a light rain had begun to fall. There was no one else on the street and Cindy glanced around nervously. She trusted Larson, but something didn't feel right.

A man stepped out from a doorway directly into their path and Cindy saw the glint of metal in his hand. "Your wallet and your purse," a deep voice rasped.

Cindy screamed as Larson lunged toward the mugger. The gun went off and Larson fell against her. Together they crashed to the ground.

7

Mark was heading home when Paul called him. "What is it?" he asked, hearing the tension in his partner's voice.

"Get over to the hospital now."

There was a click as Paul hung up. Mark turned on his siren and hung a U-turn in the middle of the street. He slammed his foot to the floor and screamed around startled drivers who hadn't had time to register his coming and pull over.

He spun to a screeching halt in the emergency room parking lot and sprinted inside. Paul met him just inside the door. Sitting on the ground rocking back and forth, head on her knees, was Cindy. There was blood on her clothes but she appeared uninjured.

"Is it the rabbi?" Mark asked.

"No. Larson Beck. He was shot by a mugger a few minutes ago. Doctors are in with him now."

"It wasn't a mugger!" Cindy wailed. "They just wanted you to think it was one!"

Mark dropped down beside her. "Cindy, it's Mark. Who wanted us to think that?"

She looked up at him. Her eyes were red and swollen, the pupils dilated unnaturally. She was shaking from head to toe and he could see that she had gone into shock. She was holding her right arm at an unnatural angle and he realized the shoulder was dislocated. He swore and didn't bother to hide it. A dozen nurses and doctors flying around her and not one of them had realized she was also in need of medical attention.

"Nurse!" he shouted.

"What is it, Detective?" a woman bustled up.

"This woman has gone into shock and her arm's dislocated. Admit her now."

"Yes, sir," the woman said. "Gurney!" she shouted.

Mark helped Cindy to stand and then to sit down on the gurney.

"I don't want to lie down," she told him.

"Do it for me," he urged.

She did and grunted in pain.

"Cindy, who wanted us to think this was a mugging?" Mark asked again.

"The same people who wanted you to think all the other murders were accidents," Cindy said.

A nurse wheeled her off then and Mark stood and stared after her, belatedly realizing that he, too, was shaking.

"I've said it before and I'll say it again, civilians shouldn't get involved," Paul said.

Mark turned on him, anger settling in the pit of his stomach. "For all we know she's the only reason that our victim is alive."

Paul grunted but didn't say anything.

"I need a drink," Mark said.

"Coffee in the hospital cafeteria is all I can offer you."

"We should leave our number so they can call the moment there's anything to report."

"I already have," Paul said. "Let's go get that coffee and talk."

As they walked to the cafeteria Mark called his wife and told her not to wait dinner for him.

"It's nice that she's so understanding," Paul said.

"Yeah, but I wish it wasn't necessary," Mark answered.

After they had their coffee in hand they selected a table at the far end of the cafeteria. The one nice thing about the facility was it was designed so that people could obtain a measure of privacy if they wanted it.

"I heard on the scanner that there had been a shooting involving a man and a woman. I had a bad feeling and I was two blocks away so I got there right as the ambulance did. I saw who it was," Paul said.

He took another swig of coffee and continued, "Larson was down. There was a lot of blood. I'm not sure if he was hit in the chest or the shoulder. A witness who had been parking her car said she had seen a man in a ski mask running away from the scene. She was the one who called 911. Cindy went with Larson in the ambulance, but no one looked at her to realize what kind of shape she was in until you did. Including me. I'm sorry."

"We should have interviewed Larson tonight," Mark said.

"Looks like Cindy tried to do that for us."

"I wish I knew what she found out."

"Hopefully we'll know shortly."

"We have to put an end to this, Paul."

"I think you need a vacation," his partner observed.

"And you don't? What are you, a machine?"

His partner didn't dignify that with an answer.

They sat in silence, each lost in his own thoughts. Finally Paul's phone rang and he snatched it up and listened intently for a moment before ending the call.

"We can see Cindy."

Mark was on his feet and had tossed his coffee cup in a moment. "Any word on Larson?" he asked as they hurried back through the hospital's halls.

"Still in with the doctors."

Cindy was dazed but still conscious when they entered her room.

"You know, you really do need to stop ending up in here," Mark said, trying his best to crack a smile.

"Not my fault," she muttered.

"Can you tell us what happened?"

"We had coffee. He didn't . . . know anything."

"What about the shooting?" Paul pressed.

"Walking to my car and guy came out of doorway. He had a gun . . . wanted wallet, purse. Larson tried to knock away gun . . . it went off . . . Larson fell on me, knocked over . . . hit ground. Ambulance."

She was getting more incoherent and her eyes were glazing over as the exhaustion and medication took over. Within moments she was asleep.

"I don't think she's waking up anytime soon," Paul said.

"Agreed. But as much as we need to talk to her she needs the sleep more."

"If nothing else we know where she'll be for the next several hours. Hopefully this scare will put an end to her trying to get involved."

Somehow Mark doubted that. He remembered how terrified she had been when the Passion Week Killer had been on the loose. If that hadn't stopped her from wanting to get involved then he didn't know what would.

One of the nurses Mark had seen earlier came into the room and checked on Cindy. When she was finished she turned to them. "The doctor is coming here in a minute to speak with you."

Sure enough the doctor appeared shortly looking as tired as Mark felt. He checked Cindy's chart and then turned to them. "She's going to be okay. The shoulder will be stiff for a few days and I'm going to prescribe some physical therapy to help strengthen and heal everything."

"That's good news," Mark said.

"What about the guy who was shot?" Paul asked.

"He's going to be okay, too. Bullet went into his shoulder and we were able to get it out. We're going to keep him for a few days. He lost a lot of blood and we want to guard against infection, but otherwise he should be just fine."

"When will he be able to talk?" Mark asked.

"Not until tomorrow morning at the earliest. He's heavily sedated and won't be waking up anytime tonight, I can assure you. Even if he did, I think he'd tell you he was attacked by pink rabbits or some such nonsense with the amount of medication he's got in him."

"So, there's nothing more we can really do here tonight," Mark clarified.

"That's correct, gentlemen. Hopefully you'll have better luck in the morning."

Tuesday morning Jeremiah could tell there was trouble the moment he stepped inside the main office at the synagogue.

"We need a male counselor for the retreat," Marie said.

"I thought we needed a female counselor? That was the announcement I made Saturday."

"We did, but someone stepped forward."

"Good, so what's the problem?"

"Larson Beck."

"The boys' counselor . . ." Jeremiah said, waiting for Marie to jump in.

"Not anymore. He's in the hospital."

"What's wrong with him?"

"I don't know."

A warning bell went off in the back of Jeremiah's mind. Hadn't Cindy said something about Larson in the voicemail he had deleted the night before?

"Well, there's still time to find someone," he said.

"They leave Thursday night. That's two days."

"That's cutting it close. I'm sure you'll come up with someone, though," he said, moving toward his office.

"I have."

Something in the way she said it made him stop, turn, and look at her. "Who?" he asked, a terrible suspicion filling him.

"You."

"No, I can't. It's out of the question."

"We're already having a special guest cantor for services on Saturday. You could be gone."

"It's not just that." He blinked, unhappy that she had clearly been thinking it through. "I've never been a camp counselor."

"It's just like being a rabbi. Just outdoors part of the time."

"I'm allergic to trees," he lied.

"Which is why you always go jogging in the park downtown?" she said, not budging an inch and scolding him for the lie with a lift of her eyebrows.

"I'm not good with kids."

"Sure you are. I've seen how you are around them. They love you."

And there, burning just below the surface, his temper began to slip. He was the one in charge, not her. "I'm not doing it," he snapped at her.

She flinched and took a step backward. She opened her mouth to say something, then closed it and her shoulders slumped in defeat. She went and sat down at her desk. "Then

I'll just have to call the parents and tell them the trip is canceled," she said quietly.

"Good, do that."

There was no way he was going to spend three days in the wilderness with a bunch of teenage boys. He was having a hard enough time controlling himself lately, hiding, and being put in that environment was the last thing he needed.

He sat down and stared blindly at his computer screen. "I need a vacation," he whispered. He hadn't taken a real one in a long time.

Deep down, though, he knew that wasn't the answer.

Cindy woke up in a hospital bed with only the vaguest idea of how she had gotten there. Her shoulder hurt and she felt like she was in a fog.

"Good morning," a cheerful voice said.

She turned her head slowly and was surprised to see Gerald Wilson sitting in a chair nearby smiling at her.

"What are you doing here?" she asked the writer.

"I called the police station this morning hoping to track down those detectives for at least a quick interview and heard about what happened to you. I figured I'd come down and check on you."

"Thank you," she said.

"Can I get you anything?"

"I'm thirsty."

"Say no more."

There were a pitcher and cup on the table near the bed and he quickly poured her some and handed it to her. She started to reach for it with her right hand, then thought better of it as it sent a twinge to her shoulder. She took the cup and managed to sip a little of the water before handing it back.

"Thank you."

"So, it seems you've gotten yourself caught up in another crime," he said.

"Unfortunately."

"Maybe I should save room in my book for one more chapter?" he suggested.

She shook her head slowly, wincing at the headache she seemed to have. "I don't think this one has the legendary qualities you're looking for."

"You never know," he said. "Sometimes the most innocuous-seeming things can set us upon quests we could never have imagined the scope of."

"Quest . . . funny word," she said, feeling her eyelids beginning to droop.

A nurse came in and checked on her and Cindy submitted to the brief exam and questions. Seemingly satisfied the nurse scribbled on her chart and informed her that a doctor would be in later to talk to her.

No sooner had she left than two familiar forms darkened her door. "Detectives," she said as Mark and Paul walked in.

"Cindy," Mark said, ducking his head slightly.

"Miss Preston," Paul acknowledged her.

Both men turned and looked at Gerald.

"Gerald Wilson," he said, introducing himself.

"The writer?" Mark asked.

"The same. Are you sirs the detectives who worked on the Passion Week Killer case?"

"We are," Mark confirmed.

"I'm anxious to interview you both. Perhaps when we're done here?"

"Perhaps," Mark said.

He turned to her. "How are you feeling?"

"Not great," she admitted.

"I'm not surprised."

Mark eyed Gerald and then looked at Paul.

"Why don't we step outside for a few minutes?" Paul suggested to the writer. "You can tell me about this book you're writing and maybe I can answer some of your questions about the case."

"That would be excellent." Gerald beamed as he accompanied Paul outside.

Mark sat down on the edge of the hospital bed and looked at her. "Tell me what happened," he said.

She told him every detail she could remember up to the ambulance arriving to take them to the hospital. "What's wrong?" she asked.

"I'm sorry you got hurt, especially when it didn't get us any new information."

She shook her head. "But it did. The killer went after Larson, which means it is all related."

"That's true. Good work," he told her.

"You don't happen to know when they're going to let me out of here, do you?"

"I'm guessing they'll let you go today. You dislocated your shoulder but appeared to have no other injuries."

"That's good."

She was feeling drowsy again.

When she awoke again her visitors were all gone and a doctor was standing at the foot of her bed reading her chart.

"Can I go home?" she asked.

"I don't see why not," he said. "Everything looks good. You've got someone who can pick you up and stay with you tonight?"

She nodded.

"Good. Make your call while I get the paperwork in order."

He left the room and she turned and stared at the phone, debating whom to call. She finally called the church office and got hold of Geanie. When she heard what was going on the other woman agreed to pick her up at noon.

Around eleven Cindy was finally feeling clearheaded. She got dressed and a nurse helped her put her arm in a sling to keep her shoulder still. Then Cindy managed to make her way to Larson's room. He was awake when she walked in and gave her a watery smile.

"How are you?" she asked.

"Looks like we both got winged," he said, eyeing her sling.

"Dislocated shoulder. Hardly matches up to being shot," she said.

"Maybe I should think twice next time before lunging at the guy with the gun."

"I don't think that would have stopped him from shooting," she said.

"Me either."

She stared at him for a moment in surprise.

He looked at her and grimaced. "What you said in the coffee shop made a lot of sense. Still, I didn't want to believe it. Then that guy jumped us and I knew it was true."

"How?"

"The timing for one thing. And for another, he demanded you hand over your purse and you weren't carrying one."

"You're right. I hadn't even thought about that," Cindy said. "I left it in the trunk of my car and I just had my keys and some cash for the coffee in my pocket."

"Exactly."

"But he could have assumed."

"I don't think so. I think a thief would have been hyper observant of the thing he was trying to steal or its absence. No, I think it was a ruse. I think he was there to kill us."

"Us?" Cindy asked, sinking down into a chair.

"Us. If the killer wasn't aware that you were on to him before, he certainly is now."

Larson was right and she felt the same fear constricting her throat that she'd felt the last time a killer was aware of her presence. Just like then, she was in the wrong place at the wrong time and it was bound to get her noticed.

And killed, if I'm not careful.

"Have the police been in to see you yet this morning?" she asked, changing the subject slightly.

"They left about twenty minutes ago. I told them the same thing. I think it upset them even more than it's upset you."

She flushed. "They've had to spend a lot of time worrying about my safety."

She knew it was their job, but they had had to do excessive worrying in her case. What did you get someone for something like that? Sending a fruit basket with a note thanking them for saving her life repeatedly seemed a little silly. But sitting there she realized that she should do something for Paul and Mark, job or not. They had more than earned it.

"Is there anything that I can do for you?" she asked.

"Yeah, catch this guy. You're good at catching killers. Least, that's the word on the street."

She looked at him bemused. "Oh, really."

"Really."

"I'll put it at the top of my to do list."

"Fantastic. Also, if you could let the folks at the synagogue know what happened I'd appreciate it. I left a rather cryptic message there this morning when I was making calls to let them know I wouldn't be able to be a camp counselor this weekend."

She felt sorry for him and the kids. "You're going to ruin your iron man reputation," she teased.

"Tell me about it. The doc said 'no', though. So did my son."

"Oh my gosh, I completely forgot. Is he okay?"

"Yeah. His grandmother was babysitting last night. After I had coffee with you I had a couple of late meetings to get to. One of the officers swung by the house last night and let her know what happened."

"That's a relief."

"For you maybe. I already get lectured on how I take too many needless risks. Somehow camping seems to pale in comparison to this. Who knows, maybe she'll stop complaining when we go on camping trips. After all, out in the forest you just have to worry about animals, not assassins."

"True. Good luck with that," Cindy said.

"Thanks. At any rate she should be happy for a while. The police said they were going to put a protective detail at my house once I go home."

"I'm surprised they don't have one here."

"I heard them discussing it as they left."

"I'm sorry I dragged you into all this."

He shook his head. "You didn't do anything, Cindy. Way I see it, you saved my life. Thank you."

"You're welcome," she said, feeling embarrassed and not knowing what else to say. "Well, I've got to get back to my room."

"They sending you home?"

"Yeah."

"Lucky. See if you can smuggle me in some cheesecake."

"I'll see what I can do."

Cindy made it back to her room and only had to wait a few more minutes for Geanie to appear. "Ready to get out of here?" she asked, popping into the room with a wheelchair.

"More than. Did you clear it with the nurse?" Cindy asked as she sat down in the chair.

"Maybe I did, and maybe I didn't," Geanie said mischievously as she wheeled her out of the room.

Cindy twisted around so she could stare at her. "You're in a good mood."

"Yup."

Geanie waved at the nurse at the nurses' station who responded by waving a packet of papers in the air. Geanie grabbed them and handed them to Cindy. Topmost was a prescription for pain medication.

"Thanks," Cindy said.

Geanie wheeled her out to her waiting car and once they pulled away from the hospital Cindy gave the other woman her full attention. Geanie's cheeks were glowing and her eyes were sparkling. A perpetual grin was turning up the corners of her mouth.

"Joseph said it, didn't he?"

"Yes!" Geanie burst out as if she had been about to explode with the news. "He said it last night when he dropped me off at home and kissed me good night."

"And then you said it back?"

"Of course."

"Congratulations," Cindy said, leaning her head back against the headrest and closing her eyes. "The two of you are in love."

"I'm thinking we're not the only ones," Geanie said coyly.

"What?"

"Those came for you this morning," Geanie said, gesturing to the backseat.

Cindy turned around and stared. There on the floor was a vase with a dozen red roses.

8

"Who are they from?" Cindy asked.

"There's a card, but I didn't open it. I'm guessing if someone sent you red roses you have a pretty good idea who it is," Geanie said.

"Not a clue," Cindy admitted. "I suppose it's possible someone heard I was in the hospital?"

"I doubt it. We hadn't heard a word until you called in a couple hours ago. That kind of news usually travels fast."

Cindy turned back forward. The motion of the car and the medication in her system were not making for a good combination. She would find out soon enough who the mystery sender was.

"Who'd you leave in charge of the office?"

"No one. I put a sign on it that said we'd be open again at one."

"You're going to have a fun afternoon. You know how people get when the office isn't open when they expect."

"I know, but what was I going to do, leave Wildman in charge of the phones?"

Cindy giggled despite herself at the image. "It would be entertaining at least. And no one could complain that the office was closed."

"Yeah, but somehow I think the other complaints would more than make up for it."

"Good decision."

"Could we swing by Joe's coffee shop so I can get my purse out of my trunk?" Cindy asked after a minute.

"Absolutely."

A few minutes later they pulled up and Cindy stared at her car. "You think I can drive?" she asked.

"I think I forbid it. The nurse told me, and I'm sure the doctor told you, that they wanted you to keep the arm still for a couple of days until you start therapy."

"Fine."

Cindy handed Geanie her keys and the other woman retrieved her purse. Then they continued on their way. Once they reached Cindy's house Geanie insisted on helping her inside.

"There's nothing wrong with my legs," Cindy complained.

"Yeah, well as the designated transporter from the hospital it's on me if you get hurt before you're safe and sound in your own house. If you fall on your head inside your house it's on you, not me."

"You're so kind," Cindy said sarcastically.

"I know; it's one of my many strengths."

As soon as Cindy was seated at the kitchen table Geanie went back out to the car for the flowers and set them on the table in front of her. She plucked the card from amidst them and thrust it toward Cindy.

"Open it!"

"Help, I can only use one hand."

"Oh, sorry!"

Geanie slid the card out of the envelope and then handed it to Cindy. She sat down and stared at her expectantly.

She's in love and now she wants everyone else to be, Cindy realized.

Cindy looked at the writing on the card.

> We've got our first request for a showing!
> Meet me at the house Tuesday night at 6 and
> bring the flowers. Gary.

Cindy couldn't help but feel disappointed. "It's from my real estate agent."

"Oh. That's . . . different."

"He's going to show the house tonight and he wants me to bring these. I remember him talking about 'staging' the house for showings. I'm guessing these are part of the plan."

"Some plan. Tell him next time to bring the flowers himself and not to get a girl excited."

Cindy nodded. "I guess it's possible he has an ulterior motive. I mean maybe he could be flirting with me."

"Is it so hard to imagine?" Geanie asked. "You're a wonderful woman. Any man would be crazy not to see that."

"Thanks. Now would you mind sending that out in a memo?"

Geanie pretended to stagger back in shock. "Wait, are you open to dating? Actually open? Because, you know, I'm not a bad matchmaker if I do say so myself."

Cindy could just imagine what sorts of guys Geanie would try to match her up with. She wasn't sure she was quite desperate enough to risk it. "Hold that thought, Yente."

She almost laughed at Geanie's deflated expression.

"Thanks for getting me here. I officially release you from your transporter duties," she said instead.

Geanie glanced at her watch. "I've got another fifteen minutes to get you comfortable before your sitter arrives."

"My sitter? What on earth are you talking about?"

"Well, Joseph and I discussed it and you really do get into quite a lot of trouble when left to your own devices. So, he's coming over here when I leave to watch you and get you anything you need while you rest."

"I don't need a sitter."

"Do you want me to call that nice police detective and get his opinion on the topic?"

"No!"

"Then I suggest you behave," Geanie said with a smirk. "Now, can I help you get into some pajamas?"

"I think I can manage."

"You ever had your arm immobilized before?"

"No."

"Then you can't. Let's go."

Fifteen minutes later Cindy was in her pajamas and on the couch with a blanket and pillow. The doorbell rang and Geanie flew to open the door. She gave Joseph a huge kiss, which he laughingly returned. Then he came in and observed Cindy.

"I brought provisions," he said, holding up a grocery bag in one hand and several DVDs in the other.

"At least we won't starve or need to resort to watching reruns of game shows," Cindy joked.

"Joseph thinks of everything," Geanie said, blushing as she said his name. "Okay, I've got to run, but I'll be back later tonight. Call if you need anything. Either of you."

"We will," Cindy and Joseph chorused together.

Joseph closed and locked the door after Geanie when she left and turned to Cindy with a grin. "Isn't she amazing?"

"She is. I'm just glad that you're paying attention."

"Trust me. I am," he said, sobering quickly.

Cindy was taken aback by the transformation. Joseph carried the groceries into the kitchen. "Can I get you something to eat or drink or some crackers to settle your stomach?"

"No, thank you."

"When is it time for your next dose of Tylenol?"

"Not for another three hours."

He brought her a glass of ice water.

"I said I wasn't thirsty," she protested.

"That's what you said, but trust me, I know how dehydrated a person can get without even realizing it when they're under stress."

He was right. She'd only had a couple of sips of water early that morning. She took the glass and began to drink it slowly, resting between sips.

Joseph settled into a chair and looked her over. "How are you?"

"I'm okay, really. Everyone's making a fuss for nothing."

"Uh-huh. Tell that to someone who believes it."

"My shoulder hurts, but no permanent damage done."

"How's Larson?"

"He's going to be okay, too."

"That's a relief. I keep going over the last few days in my mind and there's one thing I can't decide."

"What's that?" she asked.

"Which one of us is the psycho magnet?"

"I don't think I understand."

"Until last year you and I both lived rather quiet, straight-forward lives. Now, three separate killers have wreaked havoc in our lives. I realize you were much more on the front lines the first time around than I was, but the Passion Week Killer invaded my property, hurt people there. I just started thinking that I'm cursed. It makes me worry about Geanie, about what might happen to her now that she and I are close."

Cindy's heart ached for Joseph. "I'm so sorry, Joseph. It's me. I'm the psycho magnet."

He shook his head. "The second killer was targeting my friends and colleagues and using me to get to them. I'm one of the board members standing in the way of the current killer and people are dying because of it. Both the second and the third killers you just happened to be in the wrong place at the wrong time. At least once because of me."

"Joseph, please, you're scaring me," Cindy whispered.

"Not half as much as I'm scaring myself," he admitted.

"It's not you. It can't be," she said. "And it's not me either. These things, they would be happening despite us. If you weren't on the board there would still be those who oppose the sale."

"True."

"Come on, you're always the optimistic, laid-back one," she begged. "What's wrong?"

He dropped his head into his hands for a moment and then slowly looked up at her. "I guess I'm just worried because I'm really happy right now and I don't want anything to ruin that. I'm also contemplating . . . a life change. And when a man does that he begins to think of all sorts of things, like the safety and well-being of others."

"What sort of life change, Joseph?"

He bit his lip and then looked at her. "You know, it's funny. I know a lot of people. I'm friends with a lot of people. And yet, none of them are what I'd consider good, close friends. In fact, you're probably the best friend I have."

She stared at him stunned, unsure what to say. "I'm honored, Joseph. I consider you one of my closest friends, too."

What he had said rattled her. Aside from him and Geanie, she didn't have many people she actually would consider close either. *Even having friends means risking something*, she realized.

"So, I guess if I'm going to talk about this with anyone, by rights it should be you," Joseph said.

"You can tell me anything."

"I'm thinking of asking Geanie to marry me."

Cindy stared at him for a moment and then squealed in delight. "That's wonderful!"

He smiled and it lit up his eyes. "It is, isn't it? I mean, I finally found the perfect woman for me. And to think, she was right under my nose for so long. I even have you to thank for bringing us together really."

"Glad to do it," Cindy said, unable to fight back the tears.

"So now, I'm thinking. I love her more than anything. I want to be with her. But am I cursed? Is she going to get killed?"

"Joseph. You say I'm your best friend."

"Yes."

"Look at how much danger I've been in in the past year, the number of times I could have been killed."

"Yeah."

"I'm still here. Look at your dog, Clarice, who I know means the world to you. Look how much danger she was in and she's fine, too."

"That's true."

"You can't protect those you care about from danger. You can just be with them when they go through it. And people don't die while God's not looking. It's terrible and tragic, but if it was Geanie's time to go, she could just as easily be killed in a car crash in Pennsylvania as she could by a killer invading your life. Easier, actually."

Joseph shuddered and a weight seemed to lift off his shoulders. "I guess you're right. I've been giving the evil in this world too much power and God too little. Thank you."

"You're welcome."

"And you know what else?"

She shook her head.

"You've done the same."

She stared at him, stunned.

"Best friends are honest with each other, yes?"

She nodded, not trusting herself to speak.

"You've worked so hard to build a safe little life for yourself where nothing and no one could hurt you. But you of all people should know that you can't control everything. You can't stop accidents from happening or fate from intervening. I think we've connected in this last year because for the first time, you've started living life instead of running from it."

And now she was crying in earnest, great shuddering sobs that wracked her body and wrenched her heart.

Joseph knelt down and put an arm around her. "It's okay. I'm here."

Jeremiah picked up his phone in the office. "Hello?"

"Hi, it's Cindy."

She sounded shaky, like she had been crying. He took a deep breath, not sure he was ready to deal with whatever she had to say.

"What's wrong?"

"Larson wanted me to call and let the synagogue know what happened to him. Apparently he left a very vague message earlier this morning."

"Marie said something about him not being able to be a counselor because he was in the hospital."

"That's true. So, maybe not as vague as he thought."

"What's wrong with him?" Jeremiah asked. He really should go out and make a visit if it was anything serious. It was expected.

"He was shot last night."

"What?" Jeremiah roared, rising to his feet.

"He's going to be okay. The killer got him in the shoulder. He's going to be in the hospital for a few days, though. His son is staying with his grandmother for the duration, but I'm sure they could use some support."

"What happened?" Jeremiah asked.

"I warned him last night that he could be in danger since he was one of the board members opposed to the sale of Green Pastures. When we were leaving the coffee shop we were attacked."

"Were you shot?" Jeremiah asked.

"No, just a dislocated shoulder. I was lucky."

Lucky. She has the strangest concept of luck. She was nearly killed.

And I wasn't there to protect her.

"Are you still in the hospital?"

"No, I got home about an hour ago. Geanie came to get me and Joseph's staying with me."

It should have been me staying with her.

"Is there anything you need?"

"No."

"You take care of yourself, get some rest, you hear?"

"I'm going to take a nap and then later on check in with Mark."

"Why do you need to check in with Mark?"

"I have a meeting tonight with my Realtor who is also Max Diamond's Realtor and I'm wondering if I should feel him out."

Something inside him snapped.

"Cindy, what are you thinking? You're not a police officer. It's not your job to hunt down criminals."

"But if I can help—"

"You're a church secretary. That's what you are. That's all you are. You need to stop thinking of yourself as Nancy Drew."

There was silence on the other end of the line. He knew he had hurt her; he could feel it. But he couldn't stop himself. She had to stop putting herself in the line of fire.

"All you're going to do is get yourself killed and leave the rest of us to deal with the mess."

When she spoke again her voice was strangled sounding. "Thank you for expressing how you really feel. It seems to be a day for that. I'm sorry that I've been an inconvenience and a burden. I won't trouble you with my concerns any more. Please pass on to Marie the information about Larson. He deserves to have *his* church and *his* rabbi supporting him at a time like this. You don't need to concern yourself with me. I've got people from my church who care. That is enough for me. Good day, Rabbi Silverman."

She hung up the phone and he slammed his receiver down into the cradle and glared at it.

She's going to get herself killed. What is she thinking? Does she think she can take these risks because I'll be there to look after her, to shoot the bad guy for her? I won't anymore. I can't. This is not how my life is supposed to go. I'm a rabbi and that's all I am; that's all I can be. Rabbis don't go around solving crimes. The biggest mysteries they have to solve are matters of scriptural interpretation and whose Passover dinner invitations to accept.

He rose to his feet and stormed out of his office. Marie looked up at him timidly.

"I'm going to the hospital to see Larson. He was shot. The grandmother's taking care of his child. Call whoever you call and get some food arranged for them."

"Okay," Marie said, voice barely a whisper.

He broke the speed limit driving to the hospital, but he was past caring. He tried to cool down. He was a rabbi and rabbis didn't march into hospital rooms of injured parishioners and scream at the top of their lungs.

What's wrong with me? Why can't I pull it together? I never had problems controlling myself in the past.

Then again, he'd never had to exert so much control for so long before. Everything was a lie. Every word, every action was carefully studied and measured for effect. He couldn't just be himself and the mask that he had so carefully constructed was cracking, revealing the real him piece by piece. It was intolerable and he didn't know how to handle it. Everyone thought that starting over was easy, but it wasn't. Some habits, some desires never died. They just went underground and built up pressure.

Like a volcano.

He parked at the hospital and made himself take several deep, calming breaths before going inside. He was no good to Larson in the condition he was in. No good to himself.

Finally he got out of the car, still focusing on taking the long, deep breaths. He crossed the parking lot, forcing himself to observe the tactile sensations. He thought about the feel of the breeze on his face, the smell of the cars, the feel of the asphalt beneath his shoes and the rubbing of his socks against his toes. He willed himself to be in the moment, experiencing only that which was tangible and real. And when he walked into the hospital he was able to smile at the nurse on duty and ask for Larson Beck's room number.

When he got upstairs he found an officer stationed outside Larson's room, fortunately no one he knew.

"Rabbi Silverman," he said.

The officer nodded. "You're on the approved list."

Jeremiah walked in.

Larson was asleep, his face contorted in pain. His shoulder was bandaged with enough gauze that he looked a bit like a mummy. There was a half-eaten Jell-O cup on the tray in front of him.

Jeremiah sat down in the chair and forced himself to look at the man.

He was almost killed leaving a meeting with Cindy. A meeting Cindy called and invited me to. A call I ignored.

He should have known better. Every time he tried to ignore a call from Cindy something terrible happened.

Why would someone want to hurt Larson? He's a kind man, a generous man.

There were only two possible solutions. Either it was a random attack or an act of desperate people. Given the other acts of desperate people that had resulted in two deaths in the last several days he couldn't convince himself that the attack was random.

And, somehow, random didn't happen to Cindy. Chaos and terror and violence happened to Cindy, but it was never random. Why was that? Why did she always seem to be the center of a cyclone? Cyclone Cindy.

It frightened him. Every time he interacted with her she helped chip away more of his mask. Being around her wasn't safe for either of them. But staring at Larson he realized that being apart wasn't necessarily a good idea either.

She's a meddling amateur, in over her head. But she never asked for the things that have happened to her to happen. It's not her fault people kill each other. Adonai, what is the plan for her? For me?

Larson groaned and his eyes fluttered open. He forced a smile. "Hello, Rabbi."

"Larson. How are you feeling?"

"Like I was kicked by a mule."

"I'm not surprised. It *looks* like you were kicked by a mule."

"Well, then at least there is balance."

Balance. That was exactly what was missing from Jeremiah's life. Still, he forced himself to smile and talk to Larson about what happened, his recovery, his family. He stayed for half an hour and when he left he knew that he had provided Larson comfort, though he had found none for himself.

Driving away from the hospital, he decided to go home. It was past four and he couldn't bring himself to look at Marie again and remember what he had said to her.

Like it or not, Green Pastures seemed to be at the center of every drama that was present in his life. People were being killed for it. Kids were being disappointed because their counselor couldn't go.

For three years Jeremiah had avoided going to Green Pastures despite many opportunities. It seemed that anytime someone wanted a retreat they wanted to have it there and they insisted on inviting him. He had turned down dozens of invitations from members of the synagogue as well as from leaders of other synagogues who were having leadership and rabbinical retreats at the campground. Numerous scout troops had asked for blessings as they traveled to the campsite up in the mountain. Donations were constantly being made for the camp and there wasn't a month went by that he didn't hear about some event happening there.

Still, he had managed to avoid actually stepping foot onto the site itself. He had encouraged the charitable giving, helped find scholarships for kids to go, and pushed people into volunteering their time all while remaining safely in Pine Springs and not venturing into the woods outside.

He hadn't been in the wilderness since before he had come to America to change his life. He had planned on keeping it that way. He had no desire to be in the great outdoors with a bunch of other people, smelling the smells of the forest, hearing the sounds of the night, reliving memories better left buried.

He sighed. But people were dying over the place now. Things had to change.

It was time he saw Green Pastures for himself.

9

At five-fifteen Geanie returned, relieving Joseph of Cindy-sitting duty. As he left, Joseph flashed Cindy a smile and a wink. The two of them shared a fantastic secret and she would never dream of revealing to Geanie that she knew Joseph was thinking of proposing.

"Did you two have fun?" Geanie asked.

"We did," Cindy said. She had been grateful that she hadn't been alone when she hung up the phone from talking with Jeremiah. Joseph had apologized for giving her the same lecture a couple of days prior and helped her not to dwell on how unpleasant the entire thing had been.

"Are you sure you're up to meeting your Realtor tonight?" Geanie asked. "I'm sure he could show the home just as well without you."

"I want to go," Cindy said. "I want that house sold. I also want to talk with him about some other things. You're just in time to help me change."

When Cindy was appropriately attired Geanie grabbed the vase of roses and put it once again on the floor of her backseat as Cindy climbed into the passenger seat.

"Thanks for driving me."

"You're welcome."

The house wasn't that far away and they were soon pulling up out front.

"I can't believe you're selling this place," Geanie said.

"It's far too big for me."

"It's really cute."

They got out of the car and walked to the front door, which was opened for them by Gary. They said a quick round of hellos on the porch.

"This is a really nice house," Geanie said as they walked inside.

"I guess so. I hadn't thought very much about it," Cindy said, trying to look around and see it with fresh eyes.

"It's got three bedrooms, two bathrooms, and an in-ground hot tub," Gary chimed in as he took the roses from Geanie.

"Hot tub?" Geanie asked, eyes widening. "And you're thinking of selling this place?"

"Not *thinking* of, I *am* selling this place," Cindy said.

"You're crazy."

"Thanks for the diagnosis."

"This is clearly far more house than Cindy needs and when she does buy a house, she's going to want to do so with a significant other," Gary hastened to say.

Cindy smiled. *Relax, Gary. I'm selling and you'll get your commission*, she thought, but didn't say it out loud.

"Here, let me show you the rest of the house," she said to Geanie.

As they went from room to room Geanie became more enthralled with the place. "How much are you asking for it?" she finally asked.

Cindy told her and Geanie nodded her head thoughtfully. "You know, I've got some money saved up to buy a house some day."

Cindy felt a momentary panic. Geanie couldn't buy this house, not when Joseph was going to be proposing in the near future. "Geanie, could you go around and make sure all the lights are on, and everything looks good?"

"Isn't that Gary's job?"

"Yes, but I wanted to ask him a couple of questions."

"Sure."

"Thanks."

Cindy moved back to the living room where Gary was meticulously arranging the roses in their vase. "Thanks for those," Cindy said.

"You're welcome. It's just my little good luck charm. Superstition most would call it. But I think red roses send the right message to home buyers. Here is a place of romance, renewal, beauty. You want to live here."

"I'm all for anything that works."

"What happened to your shoulder?" Gary asked, finishing with the vase and turning to look at her.

"I was with Larson Beck from the Green Pastures board last night when someone tried to kill him."

"What?" Gary asked, blinking at her like he couldn't have heard her right.

"Somebody tried to kill him. He's going to be okay, but he'll be in the hospital for a while. He was shot and I ended up with a dislocated shoulder."

"Are you joking?"

"No. I was released from the hospital a few hours ago. Geanie tried to convince me to stay home, said you could handle showing the house without me."

"Absolutely. Go, get some rest."

"But I had to come."

"What on earth for?"

"I wanted to talk to you about one of your other clients."

"Who?" Gary asked, still looking bewildered and not entirely convinced of what she'd been saying.

"Max Diamond."

The doorbell rang.

"Max, uh, what do you—"

The doorbell rang again and Cindy sighed. "You better get that. We'll finish talking after they go."

Within moments Cindy found herself being introduced to a nice, older couple who were being escorted by a brash brunette woman who never stopped talking even during introductions.

Cindy scurried to get out of their way as they tramped through the house.

"How's it going?" Geanie whispered as she came up beside her.

"Look at their expressions. He's got this death stare going and she's complaining of blisters and looking like she's going to cry. I think I heard their Realtor make a reference to 'the first house this morning.' I'm guessing at this point they're not even seeing what they're looking at."

"Doesn't bode well for your chances of a sale with them."

"I'm guessing not."

Seven minutes later the trio trooped out without a backward glance and Gary closed the door behind them.

"That's it?" Cindy asked, feeling a bit dismayed.

"That's it," Gary said, sounding cheerful but looking tired.

"Wow. Somehow I thought there'd be . . . more to it . . . I guess."

"That's how most of them are. Seven minutes were long. Some people only spend two minutes on the first look through."

"Again, wow."

"I'll go turn off lights and close windows I just opened," Geanie said.

Once she had left the room Gary turned to Cindy. "Were you really serious before?"

"Yes."

"I am so sorry. I just can't fathom who would want to hurt either of you. You don't have any jealous ex-boyfriends, do you?"

"No, nothing like that!"

"We live in a terrible world."

"I wanted to talk with you about Max Diamond."

"Sorry, you did say so. Unfortunately, I don't think he's in the market for a small single-family home."

"That's not what I wanted to know."

"Sorry, you talk. I'll listen," Gary said apologetically.

"I overheard him the other night in the pub say that he wouldn't let anything stand in his way of buying Green Pastures. I wanted to know, what sort of man do you think he is?"

"He's a very successful businessman. He's blunt, he's ambitious, aggressive, a visionary, all the things that help a person succeed in his line of work I guess. Why?"

"I mean, do you think he's capable of hurting people to get what he wants?"

"I, I'm not sure I get your meaning," Gary said. "I mean he's a keen negotiator and I hear he can be quite ruthless when dealing with his rivals, so I guess so. People generally come out on the losing end financially when dealing with someone like that. That's one of the reasons I think the offer he's made to buy Green Pastures is so extraordinary and generous. Everyone would win."

"Would he be willing to kill someone to create that win?" she asked, realizing that she was getting nowhere by being subtle.

"Kill someone? I seriously doubt Mr. Diamond is capable of anything so brutal," Gary said, looking shocked at the suggestion. "And who would he even kill?"

"Maybe a board member who doesn't want the deal to go through."

"Larson? You think he attacked Larson?"

"More likely hired someone to do it," Cindy said. "I'm guessing he's got more than enough money to do that."

"But the idea is ludicrous. There are so many other ways he can persuade people. I know he wants the land really badly and would do nearly anything to keep his competitor from it, but I just can't see him taking it that far."

"Good people often have a hard time ascribing evil to the actions or motivations of others," Cindy said quietly.

Gary bit his lip. "That could be," he said at last. "I don't want to believe it, so maybe that's why I don't. I'm sorry. I wish I could be more help."

"All sealed up. I think we're done here," Geanie said, returning.

"I think so," Cindy agreed. "Thanks for at least talking it out with me, Gary."

"Anytime. If I do . . . hear or see anything . . . I'll let you know."

"I would appreciate it."

Back in the car, Geanie looked at her. "You don't seem happy."

"Disappointing conversation."

"Home?"

"Please. I think I need to go to bed."

"That's the first sensible thing you've said tonight."

"Marie, I need to talk to you," Jeremiah said Wednesday morning as he sank down into the chair across her desk from her.

"What is it?" she asked warily, folding her arms over her chest.

For almost three years he had been the rabbi. Marie had mothered him, smothered him, protected and bullied him. Never had she feared him, though. He had let the mask slip just a little and she hadn't liked what she'd seen beneath. It was up to him to make it okay for her if he expected to stay there any longer.

Part of him wanted to move on, but he had worked so hard to build a life, a reputation, a new identity there. It would be hard to start over.

He dropped his eyes to his hands, a less threatening posture than locking eyes with her.

"I'm so sorry for what happened earlier. I guess I didn't realize how badly I need a vacation. I thought I was fine, but I'm really tired. Then the accident, it just really threw me. You mentioned me being a camp counselor and I could just picture trying to drive the kids to camp and being hit again, but with all them there. I just couldn't deal with it. I look okay, but I'm still hurt, physically and emotionally. The thought of taking on more responsibility just overwhelmed me and I snapped. I'm sorry you had to see that."

She reached out and grabbed his hands with hers. "It's perfectly understandable. You should have taken more time off."

"You're right." *She'll love hearing that.*

"Of course I am," she said, voice warming to him. "Look, don't be so hard on yourself. We all have our breaking point. You just need to tell me when you're feeling overwhelmed. I'm here to help you."

"I know. It's just . . . hard . . . sometimes."

He risked looking up at her. Her face had melted with concern and he could tell she was already forgetting her fear of what she had seen beneath his façade. "Forgive me?" he asked.

"There's nothing to forgive," she said.

And she meant it.

"Did you find anyone else to take the kids up?"

She shook her head. "We were set to have space on First Shepherd's bus. They're having a retreat the same weekend. But without a male counselor for the cabin we can't send our kids."

"I'll do it."

"No, that's too much stress," she said, shaking her head.

"I couldn't stand the thought of disappointing the kids. Some of them never get a chance to do anything like this except through us. I promise I'll take some time off once I get back."

"Are you sure?"

"Yes." He stood up. "Could you call the parents and tell them it's back on?"

She smirked. "I never called to tell them it was off."

"What would I ever do without you, Marie?"

"Let's not find out," she said.

"Agreed. I'll be in my office if you need me."

He just wished it would be that easy to make amends with Cindy. Part of him, though, warned that they were both better off with her hating him and keeping her distance.

It was late morning before Cindy woke up. After she had made it to the kitchen she called Geanie.

"I'm awake," she announced.

"Good. I was beginning to worry. I was going to come over on my lunch hour. I still can."

"No, I'm good, but thanks anyway. Anything going on I should know about?"

"We're all squared away for camp. We've got the bus and the bus driver I found arriving tomorrow afternoon. We have permission slips and payment from everybody."

"Did you coordinate with Marie at the synagogue?"

"Yup. They were having trouble finding a replacement counselor, but Jeremiah agreed to go."

Jeremiah. She thought of the angry words he had said to her and she thought about him trying to wrestle a group of high school boys up at the camp. She felt like she was going to be sick, but she wasn't sure which thought was causing the reaction.

"You still there?"

"Yeah, sorry," Cindy said. "It sounds like you've got everything under control."

"Yup. You just concentrate on healing up."

Cindy promised and then hung up. She grabbed a banana and scarfed it down as she headed for her computer. She dragged the mouse over to the left-hand side and after a few minutes was able to retrain herself with that hand.

"Okay, Max Diamond, no one else might think you're capable of murder, but I do. And I'm going to prove it."

Six hours later with her left hand cramped from working the mouse and doing all the typing she shut down her browser in defeat. The only thing that she could find even remotely linking Max Diamond to murder was the rancher's wife. Maybe she had been the first, or maybe she was just the only one that had been mentioned in the same article as his name.

Or maybe it's a coincidence and he didn't kill her, she thought. She was out of options and there was only one way to find out the truth. Her shoulder was a little stiff but it was her hand and the pounding in her head that forced her to take some Tylenol, shovel a few forkfuls of leftovers in her mouth, and hit the couch, calling it an evening.

She slid her arm out of the sling and moved it slowly. So far, so good. She had heard the doctor say when he put it back in that it wasn't the dislocation that was so much the problem as how long it had spent that way with the tissues swelling around it.

I should have paid attention to what he did so I could put it back myself if it ever happens again, she thought as she drifted off to sleep.

Jeremiah packed his backpack slowly, cautiously. He felt like he was retraining himself. So many of the things that he wanted to pack by instinct were no longer necessary nor were they even remotely appropriate.

They're going to feed you, he reminded himself as he shunned the box of protein bars. Finally, just to help himself let it go, he slipped three of them in the bag anyway. *Midnight snacks*, he reasoned, though he did not indulge in such things at home. *Or really lousy camp food*, though he knew there was nothing they could serve that would be worse than things he had eaten before.

They're going to house you, inside, and give you bedding, he thought as he discarded a blanket and a tarp he could sleep on.

And there will be heat in the cabins, he told himself as he discarded a few heating packs.

He picked up the camp packing list that Marie had provided him with, the same one they sent home with all the kids to help them prepare for camp. *Don't add to the list*, he chanted to himself as he reread it.

Nowhere on the list did it say to bring a survival knife, compass, fishing hook and line, waterproof matches, or rope. Which meant all of that had to stay behind.

He ran down the list one final time.

Clothes. Check.

Underwear. Who could forget that?

Socks. Dangerous to forget that.

Jacket or sweatshirt. Jacket, Norwegian, thin but very warm. The Norwegians know cold.

Swimsuit. Packed, and it will stay that way if I can help it.

Towel. Ditto.

Hat. Check.

Sunscreen. Got it.

Mosquito repellant. Absolutely.

Pajamas. Check, but would rather sleep in my clothes.

Notebook. Got it.

Pen. With the notebook.

Toothbrush, toothpaste, hairbrush, deodorant. Travel sized for convenience.

$5 (optional). Why do they have this on every list for every trip the kids ever do? What could they possibly be buying and do parents actually send the money? Nine kids and me. Better make it $50.

His bag was packed, but he couldn't bring himself to zip it closed.

"It's just a trip to sleepaway camp. It's like a motel but with bunk beds. You don't need anything else," he said out loud.

Captain whined and Jeremiah scratched the German shepherd behind the ears. Marie had agreed to stop by to feed and walk him while he was gone.

"Wish you were going with me," he told the dog. "I think I'd feel safer."

10

CINDY HAD HER FIRST PHYSICAL THERAPY SESSION ON THURSDAY MORNING, and it went well. Afterward she had Joseph drop her off at her car, which was still parked by the coffee shop.

He followed her home. After they parked, he asked, "How does the shoulder feel?"

"Good as new," she lied. "The therapist said there was no reason I couldn't drive, but I should take it easy."

"Do you need anything before I go?"

"No, I'm all set. Thank you for taking me."

"You're welcome."

After Joseph left, Cindy came to a decision. She needed to talk her theories through with someone, someone who was on the outside who might be able to give her a fresh perspective.

She headed for her car and minutes later found herself in the lobby of the Courtyard.

"I'd like to call up to Gerald Wilson's room," Cindy said.

The agent at the front desk picked up a phone and called. "Sir, there's a woman named—"

"Cindy Preston."

"—Cindy Preston here to see you. Okay, I'll send her up."

The agent hung up. "He's in Room 514."

"514," Cindy repeated.

The agent nodded toward the elevators and Cindy shortly found herself knocking on the door to Room 514.

Gerald opened the door and welcomed her in.

"You're leaving?" she asked, noting the suitcases packed and next to the door.

"Actually, you just caught me."

"But have you finished gathering all the information for your book about Pine Springs?"

"All that I intend to gather here, yes."

"Were you going to leave without saying anything?"

"Yes, my dear, I'm afraid so. Terribly rude of me, I know, and I do apologize."

"Why?" she asked, sensing that something more was going on beneath the surface.

He sat down on the edge of the bed and folded his hands over his knee. "I had planned to stay for another week or two, but something happened last night that changed my mind."

"What?"

"A man broke into my room in the middle of the night, held a gun to my head, and told me that my time here was finished. I believed him, so I'm going now."

Cindy was stunned. "Someone broke in here and ordered you to get out of town?"

"Very Old West theatrics, but that's the size of it."

"And you're going?"

"Did I mention the gun?"

"But don't you want to find out who did this to you?"

"Not as badly as I want to keep on living," he said.

"But that's one mystery you can't walk away from!" she said, sinking into the chair near him.

He reached out and grabbed her hand. "My dear Cindy. I'm not you. When someone threatens to kill me I have less of a desire to find out 'who' and more of a desire to avoid discovering 'how' the hard way. I did all my work in a laboratory, not the field. I'm not used to being threatened and frankly my life is too precious to me to risk it on trying to find out who was behind it. It's enough for me to know that it's not safe to stay. So, I'm going."

She was deeply disappointed. For some reason she had expected more from him. Maybe it was because when he had said he enjoyed solving riddles she had felt like she could finally explain her own fascination with the mysteries that had come into her life. She cleared her throat and fought the urge to cry. "Do you even have a clue why?"

He shrugged. "I guess I asked questions of someone who didn't want to be asked."

"About me?"

He smiled. "I'm nearly done with your chapter, but I suppose it could be linked to you."

"It's either me or the cult."

"Like I said before. Some people find the past too painful to talk about. Apparently someone here finds it very, very painful."

"But I was hoping to get your perspective on the recent happenings, see if you thought I was totally crazy."

"You might be a lot of things, but crazy is not one of them," he said. He glanced at his watch. "I was going to call a taxi to take me to the airport. If you're willing to drive me, I'd be happy to hear your theories and give you my opinions."

"Deal."

"Then let's get going. I don't want to stay a moment longer than I have to," he admitted.

Mark was frustrated. It had been two full days and they were no closer to finding whoever had attacked Larson and Cindy. Nor had they had any success in figuring out exactly where Dr. Tanner had been the morning he was killed. The only places they had successfully eliminated were his house, Randall's house, and the donut shop across the street from the police station.

"We finally got something," Paul said, hanging up the phone.

"What?"

"A neighbor of Dr. Tanner's remembers seeing him driving downtown two hours before he crashed into the rabbi's car."

"Downtown is not on the direct route between the doctor's house and the church."

"And since the poison was lethal in an hour and most businesses downtown are closed that time of morning odds are good he was stopping somewhere to get some breakfast or some coffee."

"Let's start canvassing the local eateries, see if anyone remembers him. It's a long shot, but it's at least a reasonable area to search," Mark said. "And let's start with Joe's since that's where Cindy and Larson were attacked."

"It would be nice and neat and clean if it turned out to be where the doctor was poisoned," Paul noted.

"Yeah, probably too neat and clean the way our luck's been running on this case."

"We can always hope."

Maybe it's time we started doing a little more than hope, Mark thought grimly. *Maybe it's time we started praying.*

Driving Gerald to the airport was probably not what Cindy's physical therapist had in mind when she said to take it easy. Still, at least it was the local airport and she didn't have to drive him all the way to Los Angeles. Her arm really was feeling a lot better, too, and she began to think that everyone was being overly cautious.

He listened intently while she explained what had been happening and what she thought it all meant.

"What do you think?" she asked at last.

"While I agree that clearly it is all connected and that Max Diamond would seem to be some sort of instigator with his proposed purchase of Green Pastures all the evidence you have against him is completely circumstantial. I truly don't believe that in the end he's your killer."

"That's not what I wanted to hear."

"I know. And it's possible I'm completely wrong. It wouldn't be the first time."

"What am I going to do?" Cindy asked.

Gerald laughed. "I don't know, but I can't wait to find out."

"Thanks."

"I can tell you one thing. Whatever you do, it won't be what I would do in your shoes."

They had pulled up to the terminal and Cindy turned to look at him. "Promise to call and tell me how it all turns out," he said.

"I will," she said.

"And I will let you see your story before it's in print. That's something I don't do."

"I appreciate it."

Jeremiah thought the workday would never come to an end. His backpack sat ready in the corner of his office and he had brought jeans and a polo shirt to change into before the bus left for camp. Fortunately the girls' counselor was no stranger to Green Pastures or weekend camps. She assured him that she knew where everything they would need for the weekend, including candles for Sabbath ceremonies, were located in the administration building.

He could tell when the kids had started to arrive by the noise from the direction of the parking lot. After a few minutes he took a deep breath and went to change his clothes. When he was finished he grabbed his backpack and presented himself to Marie, who looked him over.

"You sure you got everything?"

"I packed everything on the list you gave me," he said. "I was surprised at how detailed it was. Seriously, who forgets to pack underwear?"

"You'd be surprised at what people forget to bring," Marie said. "Most people read the list and don't think beyond it, boys and girls. That's why underwear and deodorant and pajamas are all on the list."

"Sounds like the kids are here."

"And already hyper. It's going to be a fun bus ride," she said, almost to herself. "Here, I'll walk you outside."

The bus was in the First Shepherd parking lot, right near the break in the hedge that separated the two parking lots from each other. The girls' counselor was already present and already lining people up and checking them off.

On the other side of the hedge Pastor Dave Wyman was doing the same with their kids. Finally the bus doors opened and kids streamed inside. Jeremiah followed slowly, until he, Dave, and Marie were the last ones standing outside.

"Guess I'm going to get to see firsthand why all the kids call you Wildman," he told Dave.

"Lucky you," the youth pastor said with a grin.

"Are you sure you're going to be okay?" Marie asked as he got ready to board the bus.

"I'll be fine," he assured her.

"You got everything you're going to need?"

"I believe so. Got my clothes, my toothbrush, some lesson plans. I should be just fine."

"These camps can be brutal, you know, screaming kids driving you crazy all the time. Someone will get homesick; someone will just get sick."

"If you'd prefer I didn't go," he said, making as though to step away from the bus.

"No, no, I'm sure everything will be just fine. I mean, it's just sleepaway camp. What could go wrong?"

"Absolutely. Listen, could you do me a favor?"

"What is it?" she asked.

"If you see Cindy could you tell her that I'm sorry. I kind of snapped at her the other day."

"I'm sure she deserved it," Marie said icily as she folded her arms across her chest.

Just like you deserved it when I snapped at you? he thought. He didn't say it out loud, though.

"I was pretty harsh with her."

"Fine, if I see her, I'll tell her," Marie said. He could tell from the look on her face that she was planning on going out of her way to avoid seeing Cindy. He sighed. There was nothing he could do about it at the moment.

Dave clapped Jeremiah on the shoulder. "Glad to have you with us!"

"Glad to be here," Jeremiah said, faking his smile.

"All your kids loaded up?"

"Yup and Mrs. Goldstein as well."

"Awesome. That just leaves you and me."

Reluctantly Jeremiah climbed onto the bus ahead of the youth pastor. He found an empty seat toward the back behind a couple of his kids and claimed it.

Dave took up position at the front of the bus facing everyone. "Anyone forget anything? Speak up now."

There were no takers so the youth pastor continued. "Welcome campers! And for those of you who are here with First Shepherd I want you to welcome aboard our neighbors from the synagogue."

"Hello!" dozens of kids shouted.

Jeremiah's kids waved and smiled. It was an adventure for all of them.

"All right remember stay in your seats, no bugging the driver. If you need something raise your hand. Now who's ready to go crazy!"

All of the kids including his screamed and Jeremiah winced at how deafening the sound was. He stared in disbelief at Wildman.

How does he handle this week in and week out?

"Okay, let's get this party started!"

More excited screams as the bus lurched forward.

"Let's start singing. We'll begin with 'Father Abraham.'"

Jeremiah blinked in disbelief at the title.

"Ready? Go!"

And then kids and counselors alike began to sing. "Father Abraham had many sons, many sons had Father Abraham. I am one of them and so are you. So let's all sing along. Right arm. Left arm. Right leg. Left leg. Right hand. Left hand. Right foot. Left foot. Let's all praise the Lord!"

Two of his students who were sitting in the seat in front of him turned and looked at Jeremiah in bewilderment. He understood their confusion. It was going to be a long bus ride, though. Best to make the most of it.

"When in Rome," he said with a smile. Then he began to sing along.

There's no turning back now, Jeremiah thought as the bus headed onto the freeway.

11

"There's no turning back now," Cindy told her reflection in the mirror. She had come home after dropping Gerald at the airport and wrestled with herself while she came to a decision about what she was going to do.

Fear rippled through her, but mingled with it was another sensation, one she had almost forgotten she could feel. Excitement strummed her nerve endings making them vibrate and sing. So many momentous things had happened in the past year and yet she had only felt the fear.

Maybe it's because that's all I let myself feel; that's all I know. It made sense. She had worked so hard to be safe, built a nice little life for herself, so simple, so confined in a little bubble of her own design.

What would Lisa have thought if she could have seen it? Her sister wouldn't have approved. Cindy knew she would have made it her mission to push her out of her comfort zone. *Just like she always used to. She was too busy pushing me to worry about herself.*

Maybe that had been Lisa's secret all along. In Cindy's memory her sister loomed large as a reckless, fearless character.

Had she really been those things or were her memories tainted by that final, chilling one that still haunted her dreams?

What if she wasn't reckless?

The thought gave her chills. If Lisa wasn't reckless then it was true that safety was merely an illusion. Cindy almost stopped breathing.

What if she wasn't fearless?

Then she did the things she did because she could overcome her fear. She had made it her servant instead of her master.

And so can I.

Cindy began to breathe again. And then, very slowly, she began to smile at her reflection.

Mark threw his half-eaten hamburger in the trash. The feeling in his gut that had started the morning of the car accident had continued to grow with the passing of the days. Even though he was sitting in a cool, temperature-controlled building he was sweating like a guilty man under the interrogator's lights. Something was wrong.

No matter how many ways he went over it everything pointed to Max Diamond. Still, he'd bet his paycheck that the man wasn't behind the murders. "What are we missing?"

Paul only grunted at him. The stress was clearly getting to him as well. He was becoming far less communicative.

Cindy found Max Diamond in his hotel's lounge, texting and looking at his watch. It appeared as if he was waiting for someone.

"Mr. Diamond?"

He glanced up at her. "Yeah, sweetheart?"

"I'd like to talk to you."

"I don't need another drink at the moment."

"I'm not a waitress," she said, taken slightly aback. That gave him pause and he really looked at her for a moment.

"You know, St. Patrick's Day isn't until tomorrow," he said, eyeing the green blouse she was wearing.

"I'm aware." Just being near the man made her angry.

"Let me guess. You're here because you have some sort of beef with me, am I right?"

She nodded.

He waved to the empty chair at his table. "My guest is late, so come, entertain me."

She sat down, slamming the folder she was carrying onto the table hard enough to make the ice in his drink rattle.

"So, why are you here, honey?"

"I'm here because you've been killing everyone who opposes you buying Green Pastures."

He blinked rapidly, then said, "Sorry, what?"

"Don't play innocent with me," she said. "Dr. Tanner, the chairman of the board, was against the sale. You had him poisoned last Thursday. Randall Kelly, the environmentalist, was planning on rallying the community against the sale and you had him killed and his body burned also last Thursday. Monday night you sent someone after Larson Beck, another board member opposed to the sale, with orders to shoot and kill him. Larson was shot and I was injured in the attack, but we both survived."

"Another board member was almost killed?"

"Three days ago, at your behest."

Max Diamond put his hands on the table. "I knew the police were looking into Tanner's and Kelly's deaths, but no one said anything to me about Beck. Now, I don't know where you're getting your crazy ideas, but when those people were hurt I had a lot of witnesses who saw me."

"I'm not saying you did the dirty work yourself. I'm saying you hired someone to do it for you," Cindy hissed.

"That would be the smart thing to do if I had anything to do with this, which I didn't. I want that land, lady, but I'm not willing to kill for it. I'm not that kind of man. Frank Butler, he might kill for a land deal, but not me."

"Really, because you've done it before," Cindy said, pulling the picture of the rancher's wife out of the file and putting it on the table. "I know it wasn't an accidental overdose. You killed her. What was the problem? She didn't approve of her husband selling that ranch to you?"

Max turned completely white when he saw the picture. He reached to touch it with a shaking hand. Then, he lifted his eyes to her and she saw pure rage in them. "Get out. Now," he said, raising his finger and pointing to the door. "Your five minutes are up."

She reached for the picture but he slammed his fist down on top of it. "If I ever see your face again, I'm calling the cops and I'll have you in court so quick your head will spin. Do you hear me?"

Cindy didn't know what to do. She had honestly believed that he would say or do something to give himself away. For just a moment she wondered if she could have made a mistake, but looking at him she knew that if there hadn't been a dozen people nearby he would have choked the life out of her with his bare hands.

Cindy turned and fled the hotel.

The bus was on its final leg of the journey as it climbed farther up the mountain. It eased over a bridge crossing a stream and twisted along the road for another fifteen minutes, making several of the kids around Jeremiah turn slightly green.

"If you're going to be sick, warn somebody," Jeremiah cautioned one youngster.

Another of his charges, Bobby, leaned over and tapped him on the shoulder. "Rabbi, I'm going to be—" and the boy vomited on the floor at Jeremiah's feet.

"I meant before—" Jeremiah ground out as all around him kids flew to open windows.

Shrieks and choruses of "eewwws" announced up and down the length of the bus exactly what had happened.

"Hold tight, we're almost there!" Dave shouted from the front of the bus.

Jeremiah lifted his legs, keeping his hiking shoes out of the mess as the bus made a hard turn. The bus came to a stop with an anguished screeching of brakes and the kids pushed and shoved each other in their hurry to disembark.

Bobby was the last to exit, still looking green and more than a little embarrassed. He muttered something that Jeremiah guessed was supposed to pass for an apology.

Dave came back with paper towels and set to work cleaning up. "Worst part of camp. Seems like every year someone has to throw up," he sighed.

Jeremiah reluctantly exited the bus and found his nine charges clustered together, waiting as the bus driver offloaded luggage. As the bags started coming off Jeremiah eyed them dubiously. Most were duffel bags, some seemingly longer and heavier than their owners.

What on earth did these kids pack for a three-night stay? he wondered. For himself, everything he needed was in the backpack that he had taken on the bus with him. While he waited he pulled out of it a crude camp diagram that Wildman had given him, which showed the location of their cabin. A schedule was also attached and Jeremiah was pleasantly surprised to see that so far they were right on target.

In forty-five minutes they were all supposed to meet up with the other groups at camp for an informational meeting and welcome. Then it was off to dinner.

He took a deep breath. This was doable. Noah was the last of his kids to get his bag, one that was considerably more manageable than the others, and once he had it on his shoulder, Jeremiah signaled his troops to move out.

The kids fell into a straggly line behind him, groaning under the weight of their ponderous bags. He wondered if it would serve as an object lesson and would teach them to pack lighter in the future. Somehow he doubted it.

A ten-minute walk brought them to their cabin, which bore the proud sign Sequoia on it despite the fact that none of the trees near it were sequoias. Jeremiah shook his head and swung open the door and stepped inside.

The kids parted around him like a river and flowed into the cabin, jostling each other for the prized bunks. The cabin had five sets of bunk beds and most of the kids were trying to claim top bunks. Jeremiah let his backpack slide off his shoulder into his hand and lobbed it across the room to the top bunk on the far wall. It landed in the middle of the bed just as three kids came to a screeching halt in front of it.

They turned and looked at him wide-eyed.

"Mine," he said.

Noah he noticed was the only one not fighting for a top bunk and the boy quietly put his bag on the bunk under Jeremiah's. When he saw Jeremiah staring at him he shrugged. "Some of these kids have never been to camp. I've been in the top bunk loads of times."

Jeremiah tried not to smile. Noah saw it as the others did, as a fun place to be, an honored place. He saw it as strategic defense. From that bunk in that spot he would be able to see everyone's faces as they slept without getting up. He would have a clear line of sight to the front door and the bathroom door and be beside the one window.

He looked at his watch. "All right, settle in. Use the restroom. We're moving out again in twenty minutes."

There were laughter and chatter as the boys did as instructed. He hopped up on his bunk and observed the proceedings with amusement. Jeremiah flipped open his cell. No service. At least he wouldn't have to contend with Marie calling every hour to check up.

Three minutes before it was time to head to the meeting hall he lined them up on the porch and checked them off mentally: Noah, Bobby, Stuart, Tray, Jared, Samuel, Ben, and the twins Micah and Malachi.

Then he faced them squarely. "Listen up, men, I expect this to be a weekend of learning, growth, exploration, and fun. The way to accomplish these things is to listen, to participate, and to follow orders. I expect you to do what I tell you to when I tell you, the first time with no talk back. Are we understood?"

"Understood," they all said.

He shook his head. "Are we understood?" He raised his voice, punching each word.

"Understood!" they shouted in unison.

"That's better. Now fall in after me."

He turned and marched them off toward the meeting hall. The meeting hall, as it turned out, was one large room with an octagonal stage area at the bottom and stairs deep enough for three rows of chairs, each rising toward the back of the building. There were no chairs present, though, and he guessed those were reserved for adult retreats.

The kids instead sprawled on the floor. His own group threw themselves down, some on their stomachs, others sitting on the edge of the stair. Jeremiah crouched down to a perch on the edge of the stair next to Noah and watched as the other groups raced in and took up similar positions around the room.

He caught a couple of teenage girls giggling and waving at his guys and he felt his stomach clench. He hadn't thought about dealing with that aspect of camp.

After what felt like a long time every group seemed to be present. Someone wearing a T-shirt bearing the camp logo got up at the front with a microphone.

"Howdy, campers!"

"Howdy!"

"I'm Chuck and I'm going to be your master of ceremonies this weekend. So, welcome, and I just wanted to go over a few camp rules. First off. Lights out at 10 p.m. No exceptions."

There were groans all around though Jeremiah suspected that was later than some of the freshmen were allowed to stay up at home.

"Second. No girls in guys' cabins and vice versa."

More groans, mostly from the older kids.

"Third. Listen and follow the instructions of your counselors and camp coordinators. We are here for your safety."

"And the final rule, and it's a biggy. The Golden Rule. Which is what?"

Around him kids began to chant, "Do unto others as you would have them do unto you."

"Absolutely. Now, who's ready to have fun!"

A deafening roar went up from hundreds of voices and Jeremiah wondered if he'd survive the trip with his hearing intact.

"So, for those of you who are new to Green Pastures, let me just give you a brief history. Twenty years ago the local churches and scouting organizations decided they needed a place in the wilderness that wasn't too far from home to send people to camps and retreats. They got together and they bought all this land up here and created Green Pastures.

"Now, everyone asks, why the name? It's taken from the Twenty-third Psalm. There an analogy is made between the Lord and a shepherd and his people and sheep. It is said that he makes us to lie down in green pastures. Now, for a sheep, this serves two purposes: one it is abundant, good food, and two, it is a soft and peaceful place to rest. In fact, sheep won't lie down if they aren't certain they can find food and if they are experiencing fear. So, green pastures represents that which brings you a sense of peace and well-being in your life. And here at Green Pastures, we hope to help you find that."

It was well said, and Jeremiah appreciated that. It filled him, though, with a sense of longing. He had never in his life had a green pasture in that way of thinking. His religion had always been a source of great comfort for him, but a sense of peace and well-being had never been his.

He looked around at his charges and wished that they might have the peace that he had never enjoyed. He believed they had a chance of achieving it, too, and he hoped that he might be a small part of that.

Cindy made it into the house and collapsed on her couch, shaking like a leaf. She had done it. She had confronted the lion in his lair. The question was, what was he going to do about it?

That thought drove her off the couch and she triple-checked her door and windows to make sure everything was locked up tight. She thought about calling Geanie to come stay with her and lamented the lack of a roommate.

"What have I done?" she asked herself.

There was much hilarity as the kids made their beds, changed into pajamas, and got ready to go to sleep. Ben was showing off his new flashlight, a silver metal one a foot long that looked almost too heavy for his arm when he tried to lift it. While the kids admired it he turned the light on, shining it on the ceiling.

"It looks cool, but it doesn't make any more light than mine," Tray said, flicking on a cheap, orange plastic one decorated with Halloween black cats.

Jeremiah smiled. Tray was right. Despite their physical differences and probably about thirty dollars in cost, they worked about the same. As the kids slid their flashlights under their pillows, he tried not to laugh. He hadn't even thought to bring his own flashlight, which he could disguise in his hand and was almost a hundred times more powerful than theirs. The camp, after all, had electricity, and for the short stints that they would be outside in the dark he could see well enough without one.

Jeremiah studied the schedule he had. They would be sharing meal times and some of the outdoor activities with the five other groups that were at the camp. They would, however, be having their own study, prayer, and worship times. Some of those the timing was necessitated by the Sabbath. His kids would miss out on a couple of fun-sounding activities on Saturday, but there was still more than enough to keep them entertained and stimulated. He had been working on some appropriate group reflections and lessons and he was beginning to think that the experience might even be good for him. He dealt very little with children and young adults and had missed the bar mitzvahs for all but two of the boys in the group.

Finally everyone had gone to the bathroom, some of them twice, and were settled down in their bunks. Jeremiah turned out the cabin light and then returned to his own bunk.

As soon as the lights went out the chattering turned to whispering as kids who went to different schools became acquainted or reacquainted and others shared in gossip or storytelling.

Jeremiah let the whispering go on for about an hour. At that point he spoke, startling them all. "Okay, now that we've all caught up, time to go to sleep. No more talking. We have a big day planned tomorrow and you're going to be hating life if you're tired."

There were a couple of groans but he was gratified that they did as told. He wasn't sure if it was because of the lecture he had given them earlier or because he was their rabbi and they were afraid to cross him just yet. Either way he prayed it would last. Once silence descended the breathing patterns around the cabin quickly changed as kids began to fall asleep. When the last one had, he allowed himself to relax.

It hadn't been a terrible day and he found himself actually starting to look forward to the next one. He allowed his mind to go blank as his muscles relaxed.

Jeremiah had just fallen asleep when he was jolted awake by whispers outside the window.

12

JEREMIAH SAT UP SWIFTLY, STRAINING TO LISTEN TO WHAT WAS BEING SAID.

"We have to do this fast and get out before we get caught."

"You think this is going to work?"

"He's in there asleep and this is our one shot at him. We have to take him out now."

"I don't like this."

"Too late to back out now."

He glanced around, looking for something he could use as a weapon. There was nothing in the cabin. He knew there was a fire extinguisher attached to the wall outside next to the door, but he needed something before he stepped foot outside.

He could feel the adrenaline beginning to take over as he slid off his bunk and slid Ben's flashlight out from under the boy's pillow without waking him. Jeremiah hefted it in his hand. It could definitely bash in an enemy's skull. He also grabbed Tray's small, orange plastic flashlight. Then he paused near the door, listening. Normally he wouldn't go out the front door, but the movement he could hear outside seemed to be focusing itself around the window. Whoever it was, they weren't pros.

He crouched low to the ground and eased the door open a crack. He counted four different voices total. How many others might be present but silent? The smell of rain hung in the air.

He burst out of the door, hooking to his right. The moon shone weakly through the rain clouds, and it vaguely illuminated two figures standing close together, peering at something in the taller one's hands. The shorter one turned with a strangled cry as Jeremiah began to swing the heavy flashlight.

Something in the way he stood, though, seemed wrong. At the last second Jeremiah twisted his arm so the flashlight didn't find its mark. He switched on the small one and shone it full in the face of a scared-looking kid with freckles and red hair. The light fell on his companion as well, revealing two rolls of toilet paper in his hands. They both screamed in fright. Feet came pounding across the porch from the other direction as inside the cabin his kids were waking up.

He flashed the light on the newcomers and discovered that they, too, were kids carrying toilet paper. One of them also had a tube of toothpaste with the cap already off.

Lights flicked on inside his cabin and at several others nearby.

"I think you'd better explain yourselves," Jeremiah growled.

"She put us up to it!" one of the kids wailed.

"Who?"

"Ginger Weston. Stuart and she broke up and she wanted to get back at him before he did anything."

"And what was your plan?"

"We were going to TP the cabin and write some stuff on the windows with the toothpaste," another boy admitted.

Jeremiah could see two other counselors jogging toward them. His kids had clustered in the doorway and were talking excitedly.

"What's going on?" the first counselor to arrive asked.

Wildman ran up right behind him. "Jimmy, Kyle, what are you doing here?"

Two of the boys squirmed under his stare.

"Brad, Wes, I think you need to explain," the other counselor added.

"Cabin raid," Jeremiah said, beginning to shake as the adrenaline left his body.

The other counselor groaned and shot a weary glance to the youth pastor. "Great, and it's only the first night."

"Okay, you boys come with me and we'll get this sorted out," Wildman said. "If we stand out here any longer the whole camp will be awake."

Wildman, the other counselor, and the four boys trooped off the porch. Wildman shot a glance over his shoulder at Jeremiah. "Nice catch, by the way."

"Thanks," Jeremiah said, tightening his grip on the heavier flashlight even more. If the pastor had even suspected that he had almost killed one of the kids, he would be horrified.

Jeremiah took a deep breath and turned around to see nine kids staring at him wide-eyed.

"Back inside," he ordered.

They scurried to do as they were told and were all sitting on their bunks when he walked in. He gave Ben and Tray back their flashlights and then addressed the kids.

"No retaliations."

Disappointed whines greeted him and he put up a hand to silence them. "At this point anything you do will only serve to make things worse and escalate the problem until somebody gets hurt."

"You're just saying that because you're a rabbi," Stuart accused.

"No, I'm saying that because I've seen things like this before. Sooner or later pranks get out of hand. Back to bed."

There was more groaning but they did as he asked.

After they had all settled Jeremiah returned to his own bunk and wondered just how long it was going to take for him to fall asleep.

The rain that he had smelled in the air began to fall and the sound soothed him. If they could just sleep undisturbed through the rest of the night everything might be okay.

The rain picked up in intensity and he allowed his muscles to relax. It was always a pleasant feeling to be dry and sheltered when it rained.

Cindy dozed fitfully on the couch, too afraid to go to bed. She should have called someone to come be with her. Hours passed and nothing happened. She could hear the sighing of the wind outside. She went over and over what had happened in her mind. If Max was the killer then she was dead. But if he wasn't the killer, what then?

It was after two when she heard something scratch at the glass at one of the kitchen windows. She bolted upright, heart in her throat.

"It's just the wind," she whispered to herself. "The wind pushing a twig from one of the plants. That's all."

Then it came again, louder, and it took all her strength to keep from screaming. She pulled her cell out of her pocket, ready to make a call.

The scratching stopped and she waited. Then there was a crash on her front porch and the scratching began again on the front door.

Terrified she hit Mark's speed dial number.

"What is it?" Mark asked moments later, sounding like he was talking in his sleep.

"Someone's outside my house!" Cindy squeaked.

"Cindy? Hang up and call 911. I'll be right there."

She did as she was told, hand shaking so badly she nearly dropped the phone twice.

When the operator answered, Cindy blurted out, "Someone's trying to break into my house."

The operator asked her a question, but all Cindy could hear was a sudden, heavy pounding on her door. She jumped, screaming, and dropped the phone. It hit her foot, bounced off, and slid underneath the sofa.

"Who is it?" she shrieked.

"Let me in!" a man bellowed.

She screamed again and ran toward the hallway, but stopped halfway down. There was something about the voice that hadn't sounded quite right. It sounded loud and angry but something else as well.

"Open up!"

Drunk. Whoever was out there was drunk. She hesitantly walked back into the living room. In her experience most psycho killers didn't announce themselves to the entire world by showing up drunk on your front porch.

"Who is it?" she asked, feeling like an idiot.

"Max. Open up, I need to talk to you."

What if it was a trap? What if someone else was sneaking around the back of her house and was breaking in? What if while she was busy talking to Max someone killed her?

"Max, you're drunk and I don't want to talk to you."

"I guarantee that you do," he said.

Even drunk he managed to sound arrogant and domineering.

"What do you want, Max?"

In the distance she could hear sirens. Emboldened she moved closer to the door.

"I want to confess my sins."

"I'm not a priest," she said.

"No, but you're going to want to hear it nonetheless."

He was getting tired, she could hear it in his voice. She bit her lip. The police were coming, including Mark.

"Tell me."

"Not until you let me in."

She turned on the porch light and looked out through the peephole. Max was standing there, swaying, holding on to the doorframe for support. She couldn't see anyone else around. Every fiber of her being told her to wait for the police.

Hurry, a voice seemed to whisper inside her mind, one she was slowly learning to trust.

She opened the door and stood aside. He staggered in and she slammed and locked it after him, praying that she was keeping danger out and not locking herself in with it.

"Happy St. Patrick's Day!" he roared.

It was after midnight so he was correct. And what St. Patrick's Day would be complete without someone getting completely drunk and making an idiot of himself?

"So, confess," she said, leaving her hand on the lock.

He held up the picture that she had given him of the rancher's wife. "I killed her."

"I knew it!"

"We were childhood sweethearts. We lost each other. When we found each other again she was married to him. I didn't care. I pursued her relentlessly. We . . . we had an affair. I begged her to leave him, but she wouldn't. She swore she loved him. I threatened to tell him. I was mad with jealousy. Then . . ." Max crumpled onto the floor and began to cry. "She killed herself. How could she do that?"

The sirens were turning onto her street as Cindy stared at Max.

"I paid so many people to cover it up, say it was an accident. I couldn't bear people knowing she had committed suicide.

He found out anyway, but I didn't tell him. He said I'd taken everything else from him and he would ruin her memory, her reputation. He forced me to buy that ranch in exchange for his silence."

"That's it, that's your confession?" Cindy asked as she heard feet pounding up the walk. She unlocked the door and opened it.

"How could she leave me!" he wailed.

Officers flooded into the room, guns drawn. "I'm okay," she shouted, hoping someone heard her. Mark was steps behind the others.

"What the—" he stopped short. "Cindy, what's going on here?" he demanded.

"I'm still sorting that out," she admitted. "Max. Why did you come here, just to tell me this?"

Max looked from the police to her in confusion. Then suddenly he let out a strangled cry and grabbed at his left arm and he slumped all the way to the floor.

"Heart attack!" Mark shouted.

Max looked up at her and the pain and fear burned through his alcohol-induced haze. His lips moved and she dropped down next to him. "I think you were right," he gasped. "Someone's killing . . . don't know . . . who . . . but—"

His eyes rolled back and his entire body went slack. Mark dropped to the floor and began performing CPR, but Cindy knew it was no use.

"He realized what was happening and whoever killed Dr. Tanner did the same thing to him," she said.

Hands reached down to pull her to her feet and then guide her over to the couch. Officers placed themselves between her and Max, obscuring her view of the body purposely.

"He wasn't behind the murders. And when he started to get suspicious, he was killed for it." She looked up at the nearest officer. "And he wouldn't have been suspicious if it wasn't for me."

She pressed her hand over her mouth.

I got him killed!

She didn't know how long she sat there before Mark came and sat beside her on the couch.

"I'm not sure what just happened, but I want you to know it wasn't your fault," he said.

"How do you know that if you don't know what happened?"

"Because I know you."

Tears streaked down her cheeks. She watched as Max's body was removed from her living room floor.

"He died in my living room," she whispered.

"Yes, he did."

"How am I supposed to keep living here after that?"

"You just do. You learn to cope. Or you can't and you move somewhere else."

"I can't afford somewhere else."

"Then you cope."

"How do I start?"

"You start by telling me what happened."

For Jeremiah the morning came too soon. Stuart had the bad taste to look like the only one who had gotten any rest and to say that he had slept great, which got him hit with flying pillows. The rain had let up just before dawn but the storm clouds hadn't moved on.

Jeremiah led his group over to the main meeting hall adjacent to the mess hall. The boys took seats on the floor on the third step up from the stage area. Other groups were trooping in, most looking as sleepy as his group.

The morning meeting had just started when one of the counselors came running in, face pale.

Jeremiah watched as Wildman moved to intercept him. They were speaking quietly but he could still read their lips.

Slow down, Wildman said.

Zac asked if he could take some pictures of the birds outside while everyone else finished getting dressed. I said yes. Fifteen minutes later he was gone.

He wandered off and got lost, you think?

He must have. He had a watch so he couldn't have lost track of time. It's my fault. I shouldn't have let him go.

It's okay. We'll find him.

Jeremiah shook his head. If the kid was lost and they organized a full-scale search for him they would likely ruin any chance of tracking him and get other people injured or lost in the attempt.

He stood up quietly and went to join the two men.

"What is it?" Dave asked him as he walked up.

"Lost kid?"

"Yes," Dave said, looking startled.

"No need to create a panic or lose anyone else in the search. I'm pretty good at tracking. Just show me where you last saw him and let me take care of it," Jeremiah said.

"I don't—" Dave hesitated.

Jeremiah locked eyes with him, willing the other man to go along with his plan. Slowly Dave nodded. "Okay," he said.

"Good. Watch my kids while I'm gone."

"Of course."

"Give me a minute."

Jeremiah went back to his group and whispered to Noah, telling him what was happening and that he was to make sure the kids listened to Pastor Dave until he got back.

"Do you need my help?" Noah asked.

Jeremiah shook his head. "I've got this one. Just keep it quiet."

The boy nodded and Jeremiah returned to the counselor. "Which cabin is yours?"

"Redwood. I'll show you."

"No, I don't want any more footprints there than are already present. How tall is Zac?"

"About five six."

"How much does he weigh?"

"He's a skinny kid. I wouldn't say much over one twenty."

"Did he take anything with him?"

"His camera and a backpack."

"Great. Now, take care of the kids that are here and try not to worry too much."

Jeremiah left the building. His map of the cabins and buildings was in his pocket, but he didn't need it. He had memorized the layout of the camp as far as he could from the crude drawing. He walked briskly toward the Redwood cabin, careful not to step on any tracks on the ground. As he got closer he started studying the tracks that were there, the ones made by the kids as they headed to the meeting that morning. He saw the erratic tracks of a grown man showing indecision and haste—the counselor. Finally when he reached the front of the cabin he found a single set of tracks heading off in a very different direction.

He followed them for a few meters, studying them. The kid who had made them was about one hundred and fifty pounds. *Or one twenty with a thirty-pound backpack*, he thought to himself.

Unlike the counselor's steps these were in a straight line, determined. *Not what I'd expect of a kid wandering around trying to take photographs.*

About a dozen meters from the cabin the tracks changed. The kid had begun to run. Jeremiah scanned the area with his eyes for telltale signs of any animals that might have scared the boy into running.

Nothing.

He scanned the ground to either side looking for tracks of animals or humans but there were only his and the boy's. Any other tracks had been washed out by the rain overnight.

What were you running from, Zac?

Jeremiah began to follow the tracks at a brisk jog, keeping his eyes moving, looking for something, anything, that could explain what Zac was running from.

After a mile the boy had stopped and set his backpack down on the ground beside him. Jeremiah had been right; the bag weighed roughly thirty pounds. *What could he have put in that backpack that he wanted to carry it around with him?*

The boy had rested about five minutes and then continued at a fast walk. He was heading straight for the bridge and the road out of the camp.

And finally Jeremiah realized what was going on. Zac wasn't running *from* something; he was running *to* something. The road. The way out.

Zac isn't lost. He's running away.

13

JEREMIAH CURSED UNDER HIS BREATH. *WHY ARE YOU RUNNING AWAY, ZAC?* There were dozens of possible reasons, some worse than others. He stood and surveyed the land. The boy was heading for the bridge and the road out of the camp. He needed to reach him fast and make it back to camp soon. He was going to need help dealing with the issue and he wanted to get back before the whole camp knew the boy was missing. If it was a problem that could be solved, it wouldn't be helped by everyone knowing what Zac had tried to do.

Jeremiah closed his eyes and visualized the road down to the river, including all its twists and turns. Zac was following the road. That meant he couldn't if he hoped to catch him before the river.

Jeremiah turned and plunged off the trail, headed straight through the trees and down the hill. As he ran, he kept his eyes moving, constantly sweeping across the ground checking for signs of loose earth, rocks, and roots. He made micro adjustments as necessary to keep from tripping or sliding.

He could hear the rush of the river well before he could see it. It finally came into view and he slowed, scanning both banks for a figure. Seeing nothing he started checking the ground for footprints.

Nothing new showed up in the mud. He turned his attention to the river and noticed that it was at least a foot higher than when they had crossed it the day before. He glanced up at the sky. The clouds were still present though the rain had ceased around dawn. He stared at them contemplatively. They were dark and thick and he didn't like the looks of them.

He looked back at the river. Another foot and the water would have risen to the level of the bridge.

The sound of running footsteps pulled his attention back to the road as he stepped behind a tree where he could see whoever was coming long before the person would be able to see him.

Around the bend a figure appeared, a boy of about sixteen wearing a backpack and running. His breathing was labored and Jeremiah could hear the sound of it as he neared and see the rapid rise and fall of his chest.

Just before the bridge the boy stopped and bent over with his hands on his knees as he struggled to catch his breath.

Jeremiah stepped out quietly, moving to stand between the boy and the bridge. "What are you running from, Zac?"

The boy jerked his head up and shied away from him, eyes wide like a frightened deer. His body was tense, poised for fight or flight though he was in no shape to do either.

"I'm Rabbi Silverman, but you can call me Jeremiah," he said, squatting down on his heels. By making his appearance physically smaller it would have a soothing reaction on the boy who was tapped into his more primal instincts. A smaller profile was generally less threatening. Also, by squatting down, he hoped to give the erroneous impression that it would take him longer to react or give chase. In fact he had coiled all his muscles in preparation for sudden defensive or offensive movement.

He picked up a rock from the ground and pretended to study it. Emboldened by his seeming lack of interest, Zac took a step forward. "What do you want?"

"At the moment? I just want to know what it is you want."

"I want to leave."

"Why?"

"I don't want to have to go back home."

"What's wrong with home?"

"I don't want to talk about it!"

"But I do. And I can't let you leave unless I know why."

"You'll let me leave if I tell you?"

"I didn't say that."

"But you just said—"

"Why do you want to leave, Zac?"

The boy paced up and down before him, looking first at the woods, then at the river and back again.

"The only way out of these woods is across this river," Jeremiah said at last. "And the river is swollen from all the rain so the only real way across it is over this bridge. And the only way across this bridge is through me."

"Why are you doing this to me?"

"I'm not doing this to you. I'm simply pointing out what's necessary for your escape plan to work."

"My parents are getting a divorce."

"Lots of people's parents are getting a divorce," Jeremiah pointed out.

"Yeah, but mine are fighting and screaming at each other constantly. They'd rather fight and make each other miserable than do anything else. I don't think either of them really loves me."

"I'm sure they do, even if they're not capable of showing it."

"You don't know!"

"You're right, I don't know exactly how it is for you. Tell me where it is you think you can go that will be better."

Zac wiped at his eyes. "My grandparents in San Diego said I could come live with them. My parents won't even hear me out on the topic!"

Jeremiah stared hard at Zac. The boy wasn't part of his congregation and he didn't know the parents. He had zero weight to pull with them. Still, they might be willing to listen to someone with an outside perspective.

"The thing is, Zac, if you run away they'll only drag you back. You think your life is hard now? Imagine what it will be like with them questioning your every move, having your friends and teachers report on what you do and say. And if they are that unreasonable at the moment, they might even accuse your grandparents of kidnapping."

The boy's eyes grew wide. "No!"

"Yes. I'll make you a deal, though. You come back with me, you promise no more running away, and I'll do everything I can to help you with your parents so they'll let you move in with your grandparents for a while."

"Really?" the boy asked. The light of hope flickered in his eyes.

"Really."

Zac wiped his eyes again. "Okay," he said at last.

Jeremiah stood slowly and walked over to him. He extended his hand and the boy shook.

"Deal?"

"Deal," Zac said, meeting his eyes.

"Good, now let's get out of here. I'm starving."

"Me too," Zac admitted.

It started pouring down rain as they were headed back. The road was growing slippery. The group had transitioned from the meeting hall to the dining hall by the time they returned. Dave saw the two of them enter and he grabbed the other counselor and made a beeline for them.

"Here's the deal," Jeremiah said. "As far as anyone needs to know, Zac here was helping me move some camp equipment in out of the rain."

"What happened?" the other counselor burst out.

Zac stared at his shoes and Jeremiah answered for him. "That's between Zac and me. Suffice it to say, it won't be happening again. We're all good here," he said, putting some forcefulness into the last sentence to make himself clear. He didn't want anyone trying to get Zac to open up and share any more than he already had.

"We're good, Rabbi," Dave said.

"Excellent. Zac, rejoin your cabinmates."

Zac and the other counselor were halfway to the table when Jeremiah called after him. "Thanks for the help!"

Zac waved and flashed him a grateful look.

"That was nice of you," Dave said.

Jeremiah shrugged. "Nothing served by embarrassing him at this point. Now, we've got a real problem on our hands."

Dave's eyebrows shot up. Clearly he was curious as to what constituted a real problem in Jeremiah's book.

"The river rose quite a lot in the middle of the night and now that it's raining again it's going to get a lot higher. I'm concerned that before long it's going to be over the bridge."

"That is a problem," Dave said. "Come with me."

Jeremiah fell into step with Dave as they left the dining hall and headed for the administration building. A couple of camp officials were inside. Dave headed to one of them.

"We've got a problem. The river is rising, fast. I think we need to consider evacuating the camp."

"We've had quite a bit of rain, but it's not enough to threaten the bridge," the man said.

"I was at the bridge twenty minutes ago. The water was less than a foot below the bridge *before* the rain started back up," Jeremiah said.

The man's eyes widened. "That's not possible. The river can take a lot more water than what we've seen."

"Then maybe you have congestion downstream, a log jam somewhere or debris clogging the river and causing it to dam up. I don't know what the problem is. I just know what I saw," Jeremiah said.

The man picked a walkie-talkie up off a table. "This is Admin to everyone out in the field. Can I get eyes on the river? I'm hearing that it's up over a foot and I need that confirmed."

"I'm near the bridge. I can be there in ten," a voice came back.

"Thanks. Let me know what you see."

To Jeremiah and Dave he said, "If the river is rising that fast then the bridge could be in trouble. This storm is set to continue until Sunday."

"There go all our outdoor activities," Dave said. He glanced up at Jeremiah. "I don't like it."

"I'm deferring to your judgment on this one."

"Let me use the phone," Dave said. "I need to make a phone call."

The man waved Dave toward a landline.

Moments later Dave was on the phone with the church. "Hi, Geanie, it's Dave. Listen, I need you to call Arnold and see how fast he can get the bus back up here to the camp. There's a storm and the river's looking to wash out the bridge.

"The bus is where? Great. Okay, call whoever you can and get me drivers for the two vans. Find out if anyone else is free who has a pickup or an SUV. No, I don't know off the top of my head who drives those. Give the drivers this number," he said, reading off the number taped on the top of the phone. "And call me when you know something. Thanks, Geanie."

"Cindy wasn't there?" Jeremiah asked.

Dave shrugged. "I don't know. Probably not if Geanie's answering the phone."

Fear tugged at Jeremiah but he refused to let it take hold. "So, no bus?"

"No. It's with the senior citizens' group at some special event two hours from the church in the opposite direction from where we are."

"Will the vans hold enough?"

"No, that's why I was asking her to track down members with large vehicles. It's okay. If we have to we can get people across the river in groups and then take our time getting down the rest of the mountain and getting home."

The walkie-talkie squawked and both turned expectantly.

"Admin, are you there?"

"This is Admin. What do you see?"

"River's rising and fast. We've got less than six inches before it hits the bridge."

The man holding the walkie-talkie clenched his fist. "Check downstream to see if anything's blocking the river."

"Will do."

The man dropped the walkie-talkie back down on the table. "If the bridge gets washed out whoever's on this side will be stuck here for a couple of days at least. Get the youth leaders and tell them to call their drivers. We're evacuating."

Jeremiah and Dave ran back to the dining hall and told every adult they encountered what the situation was, sending several of them back to the administration building to make their own phone calls.

Chuck grabbed a microphone and stood up on the nearest table. "Attention everyone."

The noise died instantly.

"I've got some bad news. Due to all the rain we're going to have to cut camp short."

Disappointed sighs went up around the room.

"It's cool, though, because we'll reschedule this with your churches for some other weekend in the next month or so and you can all come back. Now, what I need you to do is head back to your cabins and grab your gear. Meet back at the meeting hall in twenty minutes. Don't worry about busing your trays. Okay, move!"

Kids jumped up from their tables and went streaming outside. Jeremiah saw Noah leading his cabin out and he fought his way through the crowd to follow.

Once they made it into the cabin he said, "Don't worry about leaving things neat. Just grab your gear and let's move."

It took him less than a minute to stow all his stuff. Noah was done almost as quickly and the two of them went through the cabin helping some of the others pack as fast as they could.

They beat most of the other groups back to the meeting hall and while they waited Jeremiah ate one of his protein bars, grateful that he had packed them.

Cindy woke up with the alarm at seven after only three hours of sleep. She groaned as she hit the alarm clock and pulled herself up to a sitting position. She reached for the phone and called Geanie's cell and explained to her what had happened.

After a lecture about calling when she needed someone Geanie ordered her to take the day off. Reluctantly Cindy agreed.

"There go all my sick days," she sighed as she hung up the phone.

Her clothes from the night before lay crumpled in a heap where she had left them. The sight of the green shirt reminded her of her meeting with Max and also reminded her that it was still St. Patrick's Day.

She got up and began to get dressed for the day. She grabbed the shamrock-covered T-shirt she had bought on clearance the year before and paired it with some black slacks. Then she checked her email and surfed the web for a few minutes.

Finally she had run out of excuses to avoid the living room. She walked down the hall slowly and winced as the spot where Max had died came into view. She felt herself starting to sweat and she averted her eyes and headed into the kitchen. When her home had once been invaded and vandalized it had felt terrible, but nothing compared to this.

As she grabbed herself a glass of orange juice and drank it, she couldn't help but think about what Joseph had said, about the people who had been murdered on his property. Two people had been killed in his house and she wondered how he lived with it.

She should probably call her landlord, Harold, and tell him what had happened. Maybe at the least she could get him to pay for having the carpet steam-cleaned.

She contemplated her food choices in the refrigerator and none of them sounded good to her. She finally decided to eat out and with a feeling of relief she grabbed her keys and her purse and headed for the car.

She locked her house door behind her, then came to a stop. There, partially blocking her driveway, was a military green Hummer, an H1. She remembered then that Mark had said that someone would be by probably late in the day to take possession of the vehicle that had once belonged to Max.

She walked around it and checked the clearance with her mailbox and realized that she would have just enough room to squeak her car out past it. She got in and after a few angling maneuvers finally eased out of the driveway.

Once on the street she hit the gas, eager to put the memory of Max and his late night visit behind her. She drove quickly toward downtown and then glanced at the clock and realized that most places wouldn't be serving food until lunchtime.

She passed a few houses and businesses displaying festive holiday flags and she remembered that the pub served breakfast. She had never been there that early and she wondered if they served corned beef hash or corned beef omelets. It was St. Patrick's Day; they had to be serving corned beef all day long, she reasoned.

She had to park a block away. Several cars were parked out front, clearly having had the same idea that she did. When she walked up to the door, though, she was disappointed to see a hand-lettered sign proclaiming: *Closed for private event. Open to public at 10 a.m. Happy St. Patrick's Day.*

She checked her watch and debated whether her stomach could hold out for another hour. She turned and started walking toward her car. When she got there another car was parking next to her and a familiar figure got out.

"Cindy! Here for the corned beef?" Gary asked as he walked over to her.

"And the green 7-Up," she said with a smile. "It looks like the pub isn't open to the public for another hour, though."

"Yes, but I know the owner," he said, giving her a wink. "Come with me. I talked to the Realtor and unfortunately that couple is putting a bid in on a different house. Sorry, but we'll get another bite soon."

"Do you think we need to drop the price?" she asked.

He shook his head. "It's too early to think about that. Besides, it's already priced under market value. If that weren't the case I might be saying something different."

They paused in front of the restaurant and Cindy glanced at the sign as Gary reached for the door.

"You're sure it's okay?"

"Positive," he said as he put his hand on her back and steered her inside.

"Wow, there's a lot of people here," she said, taking in the twenty customers clustered around a few tables getting a head start on the day's festivities.

"It's a private party. Mine, actually, that I'm throwing for a new client."

"Not me?" she asked with a weak laugh.

"No, shame on me. Given how much you love corned beef I should have thrown it for you. I should have at least thought to invite you," he said, leading her to a table.

"It's fine," she said. "I was teasing."

"Yes, but a client is a client and here I am showing favoritism."

"Well, if you insist on feeling bad about it, I'll take a corned beef sandwich."

He laughed loudly, but she noticed that nothing about his face from his mouth to his eyes was actually smiling. A chill danced up her spine.

"So, who is this new client?" she asked.

"A businessman who likes to revitalize areas by bringing in new housing and businesses."

"Oh, that would be nice."

"Yeah."

Guilt flooded Cindy. She should tell him about Max. It hadn't hit the papers yet and she was pretty sure the police hadn't awakened him in the middle of the night just to tell him a client was dead.

"Here, I'll introduce you."

Cindy got back up from her table and Gary led her over to another table where a man in his forties stared up at her with cold, black eyes.

"This is my newest client," Gary said. "Frank Butler."

Max's rival.

"Frank, I'd like you to meet someone."

Why is he working with Max's rival?

Frank looked her up and down and then purred, "Hello, Cindy."

And she remembered what Gerald had told her about people she didn't know knowing her name. She turned and ran toward the front door.

She was almost there when something grabbed her hair and yanked so hard her feet slid out from underneath her and she crashed to the floor on her back, knocking the wind out of her.

She looked up into a pair of leering eyes.

"Oh, no," she whispered as realization hit her. "You're the one who's been killing people."

"Oh, yes," Gary sneered. "It's me."

14

MARK AND PAUL STOOD WITH THE CORONER AND SURVEYED MAX'S BODY. "You think it's the same poison that killed the doctor?" Paul asked.

The coroner nodded his head. "I don't have any test results yet, but I'd be willing to bet on it."

"We should check out the restaurants and the bar at his hotel. It's possible that's where Dr. Tanner was having breakfast when he was poisoned," Mark said.

"That's possible," the coroner said, "but if you're trying to decide where this guy got liquored up last night I'd like to make a different suggestion."

He walked over to a bin on a counter and fished a crumpled up piece of green paper out of it. "This was in his pocket."

Paul was the one wearing gloves and he gingerly took the paper and unfolded it. It was a flyer and Mark read it over Paul's shoulder.

Get your green on at O'Connell's Pub. Two for one green beers and three-dollar corned beef sandwiches.

And there, at the bottom of the flyer, were the restaurant's address and business hours.

"They're open for breakfast," he and Paul said at the same time.

"I feel the need for a corned beef sandwich," Mark said, heading to the door.

"Right there with you," Paul answered.

Terror gripped Cindy as she stared into Gary's leering face. "How could you?" she asked.

"Simple," he said. "You know how tough it is to be a Realtor right now? I needed this sale to go through or I was finished, everything I've worked to build, lost."

"But why did you kill Max?"

"Why? Because Max was weak! He came in here last night, got himself good and drunk, and told me that he was pulling out of the deal. You had filled his head with the idea that people were dying because of him. I couldn't let the deal fall through. Not after everything I've sacrificed.

"So, I killed him and found a new partner, one with a little more . . . imagination," Gary said. He hauled her to her feet and another man moved to pin her arms behind her back.

She turned and stared at the owner of the pub. "You're okay with your brother killing people?"

"Okay with it?" Gary said, laughing. "He helped! Whose idea do you think the poison was?"

She turned, scanning every face for an ally. Her gaze finally fell on Frank Butler. "And you, you're okay with your real estate agent killing people?"

Gary laughed even harder as Frank grinned at her. "Okay with it? He helped too!"

She turned and stared at Gary, the skin on the back of her neck prickling. "How is that possible if you only became partners last night?"

Gary smiled. "Well, I'll tell you. Those board members are surprisingly hard to sway. No, we realized that they needed a greater motivation to sell the property, something that would make them give it away if they had to, just to get rid of it."

"What are you talking about?" she asked.

"Let's see how clever you actually are. What would make them desperate to sell?"

"If, if there was something wrong with it."

"Bingo."

"But if you poison the water, then the land is useless."

He just continued to smile at her in that maddening way until suddenly she realized.

"If there was a tragedy . . ."

"Ding, ding, ding. Give the lady a prize."

"The campers!" she shouted, lunging toward him.

He laughed as the man behind her managed to keep her from taking a step. "Thanks to Mr. Butler, they're going to be dead campers within the next few hours."

The kids, Dave, Jeremiah!

She stomped down with all her might, nailing the instep of the guy holding her. He loosened his grip ever so slightly and she elbowed him with her good arm and spun out of his grasp.

Gary lunged for her, but she twisted to the side, slamming into the beam that held the dartboard. She reached up and snatched the darts from the board and ran for the door.

Someone tripped her and she fell hard, but remembered to hold her hand out away from her body. Her sore shoulder slammed down with a crack, and she bit her tongue, tasting blood, but she managed to hold the darts in a death grip. She scrambled to her feet, twisting as she did so, and slammed her back up against the wall of the restaurant. The door was ten feet away. Two guys stood between it and her, and others clustered around.

She switched all but one of the darts to her left hand and raised the single one in her right while trying to ignore the throbbing in her shoulder.

"Look, little missy wants to play," Gary sneered. He took a step forward and she focused on his face.

It's just like being at home. She threw the dart and nailed him in the eye. He fell to the floor screaming and she refused to look as she grabbed a fresh dart. She didn't want to see the result and she certainly didn't want to take her eyes off the other men.

"It's St. Patrick's Day, boys! Anyone else up for a game of darts?" she shouted.

She could see them exchanging uneasy glances. "In case you're wondering, that wasn't luck. I can pick you all off one at a time," she said.

"You don't have enough darts to get us all," a man a few feet from her said.

"No, but I can guarantee you a couple more of you will lose an eye."

She had seen that trick in an old western on TV once and she prayed it would work here. As it turned out, none of the guys facing her were eager to be the first either, especially not with Gary on the floor still screaming and thrashing about.

"I'll call your bluff," one man toward the back of the room said, pulling a gun out of a holster under his jacket and pointing it at her.

"We can't have gunfire in here!" the pub owner roared. "Put that thing away."

Sweat rolled down Cindy's forehead, stinging her eyes. They had a standoff. But there were more of them and there was no way they were just going to let her walk out of there.

With a shout a guy rushed her, forearm up to cover his eyes. She let fly and the dart sailed into his open mouth and he dropped like a stone, a horrible choking sound emanating from him. She grabbed another dart from her left hand.

Three darts left. She stepped to her left, easing slowly down the wall in the direction of the door. She raised the dart and aimed it at one of the two guys standing between it and her and he retreated, moving farther into the restaurant.

That left one man between her and the door and he didn't look like he was going to scare as easily.

"I have no idea who you are," she said, addressing him while still trying to keep her eye on the rest of the room. "You could leave Pine Springs and I wouldn't be able to tell anyone who you were."

"Yeah, but we know who he is," one of the other men said.

"Yes, but of the rest of you, I only know who Butler and O'Connell are. The rest of you I don't know. I would never have to see or think of any of you ever again. I'm just saying, a dozen men can walk free with no fear of reprisal from *me*."

Butler chuckled. "My men are loyal. If you're trying to get them to turn on me, it won't work."

"So, then maybe I should skewer you next," she said.

He smiled. "I don't think you have what it takes. I, after all, am not attacking you. You're only acting in self-defense. You forget, my dear, that oftentimes the best defense is a strong offense."

She refused to bandy words with him. She returned her attention instead to the guy by the door. "Let's you and I walk out of here together, as friends," she said.

He smiled at her. "I've been watching you. And I know how long it takes you to aim."

"Meaning?"

"Meaning, I'm too close," he said, rushing forward.

She slammed the dart into his carotid artery as he grabbed her. They fell together and this time she lost the darts when her hand hit the floor.

It's over, I'm dead.

Suddenly the front doors burst open and light poured in. "Police! Nobody move!" she heard Paul shout.

She pushed away from the man and Mark reached down to grab her as officers rushed into the room.

"Remind me never to play darts with you," he said.

She started laughing hysterically and it faded quickly to sobbing.

They moved all the campers down to the bus pick-up area and waited for the vehicles to begin arriving. Two Jeeps began ferrying some of the camp employees across the river in waves.

"We should move everyone down across the river. There's still quite a drive on this side of it for the buses," Jeremiah warned Dave.

Dave shook his head. "I agree, but there's just nowhere down there for them to turn around."

"How about on that side of the bridge? We could walk everyone across now, get down the mountain a little way."

Dave shook his head. "I'd agree with you, but we have the same problem as we do up here. Unfortunately I think we're just going to have to wait it out."

One staff member was still in the admin building, receiving calls and updates via the landline. Every few minutes he came out to give a report.

We're not going to all make it down the mountain, Jeremiah thought.

Leaders for each church were huddled together where they could receive the reports. Jeremiah preferred to stay with his kids. Since they had gotten a lift from First Shepherd he was content to let Dave be the one getting the reports. He was still close enough, though, that he could hear much of what was said.

The first bus arrived and was met with cheers by the kids who were starting to feel the anxiety coming off of the adults. It was from the Methodist church on the outskirts of Pine Springs. The driver pulled up and hopped off while the kids from the church piled on board. The counselors started slinging bags underneath the bus as fast as they could.

"I passed the bus for Baptist Brethren on the way here. It was broken down on the highway," the driver told the leaders. "I promised the driver I'd pick up his kids. We should have just enough room if some people sit triple to a seat."

"Listen up," one of the counselors who had found a bullhorn said. "Everyone from Baptist Brethren, you're getting a ride with us, so step forward."

There was a lot of jostling as the kids hurried to get onto the bus, tossing their bags to the counselors. Counselors from every group had stepped forward to load as quickly as possible. When everyone was on board the bus headed back down.

Two more buses from churches much closer to the camp than theirs arrived and were sent off as quickly as possible. Once they had left Jeremiah made his way over to Dave.

"Not everyone's going to get here in time," he said.

"I know," Dave answered, worry creasing his face.

The roar of engines preceded the arrival of both First Shepherd vans. The driver of the first one hopped out and made a beeline for Dave just as the staff member arrived with the update.

"Near as I can tell the next nearest bus is at least forty-five minutes away," the man said.

The van driver shook his head. "They won't make it then. The water's at the bridge. There's just enough room for the vans to turn around. I say we hustle everyone down there and try to ferry everyone across. It'll be a long walk down the mountain to reach a place where some of the buses can pick up, but we can help with that too. The important thing is to get everyone out."

Dave grabbed the bullhorn. "Okay, everyone from First Shepherd and the synagogue who can't hike fifteen minutes pile on these vans. We'll meet you on the other side of the bridge. Everyone else, follow Rabbi Silverman down to the bridge."

Kids scurried to do as instructed. Jeremiah noted that only the twins from his cabin moved toward the vans while everyone else fell in line behind him.

"All right," Jeremiah boomed, forcing his voice to project out over the crowd. "If you're from First Shepherd or the synagogue and you're hiking down to the bridge, you're with me. Let's move out!"

Jeremiah headed down the mountain with about twenty kids and two counselors following him. Behind him he could hear Dave continue to issue directions. "Those of you who are from other churches, we're going to need to get everyone to the other side of the bridge. Those who can't do the hike, wait here with me for the vans to return. Those of you who can hike, follow Rabbi Silverman and his group down."

Jeremiah set a quick pace, glancing back quickly to make sure that everyone was with him. Bags were weighing several down and he had to stop a couple of times to help kids shift them to better carrying positions. After a couple of minutes the vans passed them, taking the turns at speeds that even he thought were a bit reckless.

I should have insisted we move all the kids down. The buses could have still gone up to the top to turn around but then come back down and loaded on their way down the hill.

It was too late to change anything. His kids and the kids from First Shepherd stayed right with him. A group from one of the other churches raced by, clearly making it a game to see who could reach the bridge first.

The rain, which had been misting for a while, began to come down steadily again. When they were nearing the bridge, the vans passed them on their way back up.

When the bridge finally came into view Jeremiah's heart sank. Water was already rushing over the top of it, covering the boards. A couple of boys from another group were venturing out onto it.

"Don't!" he shouted.

They ignored him and stepped forward. The water, though shallow, was swift and the boards were slippery. It was only moments before both boys were swept off their feet. The one farthest onto the bridge went down face-first and didn't move.

Jeremiah dropped his backpack and sprinted forward. Zac appeared next to him.

He looked down at him questioningly.

"I'm your helper, remember?" the boy said.

Jeremiah nodded curtly.

Noah raced up beside them. "What do we do?"

"Zac, I want you to brace yourself with your back to the downriver side of the bridge and very carefully inch out. Noah, lock wrists with him and do the same. I'm going to stay on the ground as anchor. We'll form a chain. Zac, grab the nearest boy and see if he can grab his buddy. Then, work your way back. If you lose your footing, hold on because we're going to pull you back."

Zac nodded and he and Noah clasped hands. Noah did the same with Jeremiah and then, doing it just as Jeremiah had said, Zac inched his way out onto the boards. He slipped once, but grabbed the rail with his free hand and remained upright.

Then, very carefully, he grabbed the boy's wrist next to him. "Grab your friend!" he shouted.

When everyone had linked up Zac began to retrace his steps with Noah and Jeremiah pulling gently to help give him some momentum. It was only a matter of time before Zac lost his footing too and when he did Noah and Jeremiah moved fast, pulling hard and yanking all three boys off the bridge and onto the muddy shore.

Jeremiah knelt down and examined the unconscious boy. There was a nasty gash on his forehead. Jeremiah pounded his back and the boy began to cough out water before breathing in normally.

With Noah's help, they all moved out of the way of the vans, which were once again descending. Dave was in the front seat of the rear one and yelled out the window, "That's everyone from up there!"

Jeremiah held his breath as he watched the vans roll slowly across the bridge. On the far side kids tumbled out as soon as they stopped and were led further down the hill as the vans then did a series of forwards and reverses until they had turned around.

The water was nearly halfway up their tires as they crossed back over. They maneuvered around and then Zac helped

Jeremiah put the unconscious boy across the laps of three boys after they climbed into the front seat. Kids kept piling in both vans, crouching and standing when the seats were full until no more could fit. The vans rolled back across the bridge. The first one made it across and the second one was almost there when the tires began to spin and slip.

Around him kids began to pray and the van slowly, painfully rolled forward until its front tires gripped the ground on the far side. It lurched onto the road and the kids around Jeremiah gave a cheer.

They hadn't yet realized what he already knew. The rest of them were stranded. He looked around. There were twelve boys, two girls, and himself left. The water continued to rise over the bridge and on the far side he could see the first van driver arguing heatedly with the second.

Dave intervened and finally a consensus was reached. Slowly Dave grabbed the bullhorn from the person who had it. "We can't get the vans back across and it's too dangerous to try and walk or swim over. When the river goes down in a day or two we can get you out. There's plenty of food, water, activities. The rest of you are just going to continue to have camp without us."

Dave's voice cracked at the end and he lowered the bullhorn. Jeremiah nodded and looked down at his charges. "Well, you heard the man," he said, trying to force himself to sound cheerful. "Back to camp!"

"But we just hiked down," Bobby said.

"I know, Bobby. I know."

Mark walked over to Cindy where she sat huddled underneath an emergency blanket. "I just got off the phone with Geanie. Apparently they already sent out the vans to pick up everyone at camp. It's been raining there and the river was rising so they were evacuating everyone. She said they should be in cell phone reach in a little while. I guess they made arrangements to spend the night at a covered stadium and try to finish some of the camp activities there."

"Thank you," Cindy said.

"It's going to be okay. You did it. You caught the bad guys."

"And nothing's going to happen at the camp?"

"Nothing's going to happen at the camp," he said with a grin.

An ambulance was pulling away from the curb and she was staring at it with tears in her eyes.

"The three guys . . . you . . . uh . . . they're going to live," he said. "We arrested everyone else, including Butler. It's only a matter of time before these jackals start turning on each other."

She nodded and he sat down beside her. "Geanie's going to come take you home."

"How come people always think I need to be driven home?" she asked him, looking up at him with dazed eyes.

"Because sometimes you do," he said gently.

They made it back to the cabin and this time everyone stood in the middle of the floor, looking to Jeremiah for direction. It was a marked contrast to the last time. This time, though, he had five extra kids, two of them girls. He refrained from tossing his muddy bag back up onto his old bunk, instead dropping it on the floor nearby.

"Noah and I will take this bunk," he said. "Girls, you take this one," he said, pointing to the bunk to his left. "Everyone else will rotate between these three bunks and the floor. We'll raid the other cabins for extra pillows and blankets."

He was surprised that there was no grumbling, just a quiet muttering as people laid claim to their spot. It was cramped, but he wasn't about to split his charges over two different cabins when there was only one of him.

"Get washed up and let's go raid the kitchen and get something to eat," he said.

He sat down with a sigh and Noah approached him.

"Are you okay, sir?"

Jeremiah nodded. "We just have to keep things fun and light. We could be up here for a few days. Got any ideas?"

"One," Noah said with a grin. He whistled loud and everyone turned to look.

"Listen up, crew! I officially declare this cabin home base for the Swiss Family Silverman!"

The kids started smiling at that and there were a couple of weak cheers. But Noah wasn't done yet.

"Since we are castaways, the old rules don't apply to us. After all, we've already broken rule number two. There are girls in our cabin!"

The boys started cheering loudly and the girls clapped their hands.

"In light of the situation I declare rule number one, lights out at ten, null and void!"

There was more cheering and even Jeremiah started laughing.

"Castaways, we need a flag!"

"We can do that," one of the girls, Sarah he thought her name was, volunteered.

"We need a motto!"

"We've got that covered," Stuart said, pointing to him and Bobby.

"And we need somewhere to pillage!"

There was silence as the kids looked around at each other.

Jeremiah leaped to his feet. "To the kitchen!" he roared.
They all screamed in response and raced out the door.

It seemed forever before Cindy finally made it home. Geanie tried to stay with her, but Cindy forced her to go. If she was going to be able to continue to live alone she knew she had to make it through the night.

As soon as Geanie left the silence descended and her fear returned. She tried dialing Dave's cell and was relieved when he answered.

"Dave? It's Cindy. I can barely hear you."

". . . terri- reception . . . off mountain . . . but . . . couple days . . ."

"Where are you?"

". . . at . . . stadium . . . camping inside . . ."

"When will you be back?"

There was a burst of static and then she lost the call. She tried calling back, but it went straight to voicemail. She put her cell down on the counter. At least they were safe off the mountain.

A minute later her cell chimed to let her know she had a text. It was from Dave and it said, "Back tomorrow."

She took a deep breath. Everything was fine.

Food and the clean-up from it and breakfast ended up taking forever. When it was done a heavy curtain of rain isolated the camp. Jeremiah found the candles for lighting at sunset on the Sabbath in the office and took them to their cabin. *The kids are an evenly mixed group, for a wonder.* Six of the boys were his. Sarah was also from the synagogue. Brenda and the other six boys were from the church. They turned off the lights in the cabin, with the blessing of the castaways, and lit candles. Jeremiah took a minute to explain why they did what they did to observe the Sabbath.

The kids sat up and talked, but exhaustion was taking its toll and they were asleep well before the curfew they had been so excited to break. Jeremiah waited until they were all asleep and then blew out the candles. He wanted to leave them burning but fourteen kids in one room in a wood cabin asleep with burning candles seemed like a recipe for disaster.

Then he lay down, flipped onto his side so that he could watch the room, and fell asleep.

Jeremiah awoke to the sudden, overwhelming feeling that something was very, very wrong. He sat up slowly, eyes probing the darkness. He could hear the kids snoring softly and his eyes fell on each still, sleeping form. Fourteen. They were all there.

Unlike the night before there was no sound coming from outside, nothing that should have awakened him. Still, he knew that unlike the toilet paper raid this was real and very dangerous.

He rose and moved across the cabin silently, maneuvering around the kids sleeping on the floor, straining his senses for a sign of what it was that had awakened him. There was nothing. No movement, no sound.

No sound.

He slipped out of the cabin, grateful that he had slept in his clothes. He silently removed the fire extinguisher from its mounting. It made a good weapon both for the chemical spray inside and for the heft of it. He slowly moved around the cabin,

183

looking for something that could have frightened the animals and the insects into silence.

The farther he walked the more certain he was that something was wrong. He had almost completed his loop of the building when he saw a blinking red light. He approached and discovered a small black box attached to the power lines.

A bomb, he realized.

15

Jeremiah turned and leaped back up onto the porch, kicked in the door, and shouted, "Everyone out, move, move, move!"

Startled kids fell out of their bunks and landed on the kids who were on the floor. They all struggled to their feet and ran toward him. He stepped aside. "Head for the trees!"

The last kid out the door tripped, sprawling at Jeremiah's feet. He picked the boy up, threw him over his shoulder, jumped off the porch, and sprinted toward the trees with the rest of them.

Once they hit the tree line they turned and stared at him, eyes wide with bewilderment and fear.

"Hit the dirt and cover your heads!" he roared as he dropped the kid he was carrying onto the ground. Jeremiah threw himself down on his stomach and the kids did the same.

How long before it goes off? he wondered. *And who in this country would do such a thing?*

When the explosion came he was ready for it, but the kids were not. Their screams of terror hurt him. If he closed his eyes he was back in Israel witnessing a car bombing or synagogue desecration. Cold fury settled in the pit of his stomach. They should not have had to be witnesses to such violence.

Flaming pieces of the cabin rained down all over, but fell short of their vantage point.

"All my stuff was in there," he heard one child whisper.

Another one asked, "What made it blow up like that?"

"It was a bomb," Jeremiah said. He didn't see any need to lie to them. It wouldn't help them in the coming years and certainly not in the coming minutes.

"Did someone try to kill us?"

"Will they try again?"

"Why?"

"Where are they now?" Noah asked.

That was the question that was foremost in Jeremiah's mind. It was possible that the bomber had detonated it from miles away. It was also possible that he was in the area, watching the cabin burn and looking at them.

"We can't stay here," Jeremiah said. "Everyone follow me and be quiet. Noah, bring up the rear. If you see something, whistle."

Without standing up he turned around and began crawling on hands and knees farther into the forest. He turned his head and saw that the kids were falling into line behind him.

Jeremiah just had to figure out how to make their movements silent. The thought of pushing deeper into the forest with teenage campers with no outdoor skills made him shudder. There was nothing he could do about it, though, but keep moving and stay alert.

Fifteen minutes into crawling, some of the kids were starting to grumble. Surprisingly, the loudest complainers were not the two girls, Sarah and Brenda. Fourteen kids aged fourteen to eighteen were not Jeremiah's ideal comrades-in-arms and the complaining made him grit his teeth. Jeremiah turned his head and whispered to the boy behind him to be quiet and to pass it back. As soon as he did he knew it was a mistake as one kid after another practically yelled out "What?" to the one in front, followed by a louder "Shhhhhh!"

I could have done better with a herd of rampaging elephants.

Jeremiah could take no more and came to a sudden stop. He waved all the kids in a semicircle around him and placed Noah in the rear, facing the direction they had come. Before Jeremiah could say anything, Noah turned around.

"Sir, you said to whistle if I saw anything but what if I only heard something?"

"Wha . . ." Jeremiah started to say.

Just then Jeremiah heard some twigs snap a short distance to his left and held his fingers to his lips. He could hear the noises moving away slowly and he figured that it would be better to be walking than crawling. They needed distance and fast. "Everyone stand up quietly. Huddle up."

"What are we going to do?" asked Sarah who was holding Brenda's hand in a vise-like grip.

"We are going to move up the hill farther into the tree line. Each person step into the footprint of the person in front of you."

All the kids nodded their heads that they understood, but they could not hide the growing fear in their eyes. Only Noah, Sarah, and Brenda seemed to be relatively calm.

"Sarah, because you are shorter than the others you walk behind me and tell me when I take steps that are too large."

"Okay," Sarah whispered.

"Noah, walk drag," Jeremiah said to the boy.

"Drag what?"

"Sorry, drag means you follow at the rear. You stop every ten steps and scan the entire hillside from the front of the line all the way back down the hill. Pay special attention to the flanks, sorry, the sides left and right. If you see, hear, or even smell something whistle once. Got it?"

"Got it."

"The rest of you, do not look around. Do not talk, cough, or sneeze. Do not blow your nose or scratch your bug bites. Look only at the footprints in front of you and move quietly like a cat. Okay?"

All the kids looked at each other but they all nodded that they understood. He could tell that he had really scared them with that. "Let's go and remember, quiet like a cat." Jeremiah turned around slowly, slanting away from where he had heard the last twig snap. Jeremiah said a silent prayer for the kids and himself. *Adonai, calm their beating hearts and soothe their fears, and guide my feet to the safest path.*

Thirty minutes later they had walked more than half a mile from the camp and could only see a soft glow from the fire that had been the cabin. The walk had been surprisingly quiet and uneventful.

Thank you, thank you, Jeremiah prayed.

They were moving up toward an overhang near the top of the hill. Jeremiah stopped at the edge of a small clearing and waited for the kids to gather around him.

"I want you all to sit down and rest for a few minutes," Jeremiah said.

Stuart asked "What is happening?" in a shaky voice.

"Shhhh," said Sarah.

"That's okay. I don't know what is going on. Someone didn't want us staying in the cabin tonight. Maybe they needed it for firewood." Jeremiah knew the joke fell flat when not one kid smiled back at him. "Rest and catch your breath while I look around this clearing, and no talking."

Jeremiah waved Sarah and Noah over to him as he moved away from the main group. "Sarah, you watch out for the other kids and keep them quiet. Noah, go back down the trail about ten minutes, then sit and listen. I will whistle when I want you to return to the group."

Both kids nodded and moved off to their duties. Jeremiah waited for the kids to be out of sight and then he moved to his left skirting the clearing. He took deep breaths to steady himself as he assessed the situation.

I never thought that it would happen again. Outnumbered and unarmed in the wilderness. Jeremiah shook his head to chase the thought from his mind.

He made it all the way around the clearing having heard nothing but the creatures of the night. Whistling once, Jeremiah slowly walked up to the rest of the kids. He had been gone for half an hour. Sarah stood and walked over to him.

"I told them to close their eyes and relax their muscles one at a time. In two minutes they were all asleep," said Sarah.

"Very good thinking."

"Thank you, sir. What are we going to do now?" she asked.

Noah came into view walking very softly. When he reached the other two he held out his hands in a questioning gesture.

"It is going to start raining soon. We need to find shelter," Jeremiah whispered to the two kids. "I saw a small cave on the other side of the clearing that should be large enough for all of us. Did you hear or see anything down the trail?"

"All quiet," Noah reported.

"Good. Let's wake the others and get to the cave before we all get drenched."

With mild amusement, Jeremiah noticed that the kids lined up in the exact same order as before and also stepped in the tracks of the person in front. *Maybe there is hope for them after all*, Jeremiah thought.

A few minutes after they were all in the cave the rain began to fall. "Whew, that was close," said Noah. "What now, sir?"

"I think we should take inventory," Jeremiah said.

Cindy sat straight up in bed, heart racing. She glanced at the clock. It was midnight. She was sweating profusely and shaking. She struggled to figure out what had awakened her. Had it been a nightmare, a sound? She got up and checked her phone and cell phone. No calls. She made the rounds of her house checking the doors and windows. Everything was shut up tight.

She sat back down on her bed, hands still shaking. She had a sick, twisting feeling in her gut and she thought she was going to throw up. She hadn't felt like this since Lisa had been killed.

In a blind panic she picked up the phone and called her mom, waking her for a change.

"What on earth is wrong?" her mom asked.

"Hi, I just had—are you and Dad okay?"

"What? What kind of question is that for the middle of the night?"

"The only one that matters in the middle of the night. Are you both alive, well?"

"Yes."

"Daddy too?"

"Yes, he's right here asleep."

"Are you sure he's asleep?" Cindy asked, her throat constricting.

"Listen for yourself," her mom said.

A second later Cindy relaxed as she heard her dad's snoring. "Thank you, God," she whispered.

Another, terrible thought occurred to her. "Did anything happen to Kyle?"

"No, you worry too much."

"But he was doing that bungee jump . . ."

"You didn't watch it?" her mother demanded, her voice suddenly icy.

"No, I—"

"Cindy, you should support your brother."

Cindy wanted to scream. "Mom, it's not the time! Is he okay?"

"You want me to go wake him up and ask him?"

"He's there?"

"Yes, he came home to visit for the weekend. It wouldn't hurt you to do that occasionally."

"Yes, Mom, please go check on him."

A minute later she could tell her mom was holding up the phone again, her brother's snoring was as just as loud, but still distinguishable from their father's.

"Thanks, Mom," she whispered. "I'll call in a day or two."

She hung up before her mom could ask her any questions. She cradled the phone to her chest. If her family was safe, what else could be making her feel this sick?

Jeremiah.

She dialed his cell, knowing that there was lousy reception at the stadium, but hoping for a miracle. It went straight to his voicemail and she didn't bother leaving a message.

You knew he wouldn't pick up, she told herself, trying to stem the rising tide of panic that threatened to overwhelm her. *He's fine; there's nothing wrong.* Her stomach twisted harder and she let the phone fall from her hand as she hit the floor on her knees and began to pray.

"Inventory?" Sarah asked Jeremiah.

"Yes. We need to see what we have with us that can be used. Not all of us are in pajamas, so we may have useful items in our pockets."

Everyone not in pajamas began emptying their pockets, placing all the items on Jeremiah's handkerchief. It looked rather meager.

"Let's see. One flashlight, one pocketknife, one half empty pack of cigarettes and matches, one lipstick and one compact, and one of the ten-page camp information booklets."

"What are we going to do with makeup?" one of the boys sneered.

Sarah jumped up ready to pound on the boy, but was restrained by Brenda and Noah.

Before Jeremiah could answer, Noah said, "Well, the mirror in the compact can be used to signal planes or rescuers and the lipstick can easily write on paper. Did you bring a pencil?"

"Everybody calm down," said Jeremiah. "I'm not even going to ask who provided the cigarettes. We all need to get some rest. Boys, please all go to the left side and Sarah and Brenda and I will be on the right."

Noah, Brenda, and two others had been sleeping in their clothes, including jackets, as had Jeremiah. "Boys, give your jackets to those in pajamas," Jeremiah said as he handed his to Sarah.

Jeremiah signaled Noah and Sarah to the mouth of the cave. "We need to keep watch. Sarah, could you take the first shift for two hours and then wake Noah?"

"Yes, sir," Sarah replied.

"Noah, you wake me after your two hours, okay?"

"Yes, sir," said Noah.

"Listen you two, stop calling me sir. Call me Jeremiah or Rabbi, but not sir."

"Yes, si . . . er Rabbi," said Noah.

Jeremiah heard Sarah wake Noah around two in the morning. After Sarah was asleep, Jeremiah got up slowly. He stripped off his overshirt, leaving his black undershirt on, which blended into the night. He pocketed the knife and flashlight and moved to Noah's side. "I am going to scout around the area. Can you stay awake till I return? It may be more than two hours."

Noah nodded affirmative. Jeremiah patted his shoulder and before Noah could turn his head to acknowledge the gesture, Jeremiah slipped into the darkness. Moving at a speed that only years of training could provide, Jeremiah made it all the way back to the campgrounds. He eased his way into the administration building, checking his progress every few steps.

He wondered why the bomb makers hadn't bothered to take out all the buildings, or at least that one. He checked the phone but it was dead.

He searched around and retrieved three dark blue blankets, a well-stocked first aid kit, and two spools of fishing line plus a package of fishhooks. Using one of the blankets as a sack, he also grabbed several bottles of water, a small pan, and a dozen cans of soup. He raided the cabinet with camp logo sweats and T-shirts and grabbed what he could, using it to wrap the cans so they wouldn't clink together.

He searched quickly for anything else that might be of use and finally picked the lock on one cabinet. Inside he found paintball equipment and he grabbed a pistol and loaded it.

Jeremiah was back at the cave a short two hours after leaving. He was beside Noah before the boy even knew he was there. Startled, Noah asked, "Where did you get all the loot, Rabbi?"

"The campgrounds. Now help me cover up the kids."

"But the cabin was blown to smithereens."

"True, but not the administration building."

They didn't expect anyone to survive the bomb blast.

Sunrise in the mountains was always dramatic and this morning was no exception. The problem was that the cave faced east and the sun's rays entered the cave early. Everyone was awake before 6:30. Several of the kids looked worse for wear and to Jeremiah looked like they could easily go into shock. To prevent that, he got everyone with clothing on to look for some dried twigs and branches while he passed out the clothes he had gathered to those in pajamas. They looked like a group of carnival clowns in baggy sweats and oversized shirts, but at least they were dressed.

"Rabbi, how do we open the cans?" asked Brenda, holding up the soup.

"Here, use the P38," said Jeremiah, taking a small metal device from his wallet.

"What's a P38?" asked Sarah.

"It's really a can opener," said Jeremiah. "The U.S. Army issued them in cases of rations. It is called a P38 because some smart-mouthed GI said it took exactly 38 pushes to open a C-ration can."

"Does it take 38 pushes?" asked Noah.

"You will soon find out, but to answer the question, yes, 38 pushes is all you need."

Sarah, Brenda, and Noah all tried using the can opener but without any luck. Jeremiah took the device and quickly opened two cans of soup and poured them into the pan along with some water from one of the bottles. It took no time for the soup to cook over the small fire they had set in the back of the cave. Each of the kids took turns drinking their share straight from the pan. Bobby asked, "Is this what real camping is like?"

"Pretty close," said Noah.

"Okay, everyone, come here so we can talk," said Jeremiah. All the kids gathered close to him and as he looked at each and every face he could tell that this group would do whatever he asked without question or discussion. They were starting to move and act as one, behaving perfectly. It reminded him of a movie he had once seen. *Stepford kids,* he thought. *I can't believe these are the teenagers our congregations are always moaning about.*

"This cave is too exposed from below. We need to find another location for shelter that will give us some protection. Noah, Brenda, and I are going out to look for a better spot while Sarah and the rest of you stay here. Sarah is in charge, so listen to her, please."

"Sarah, keep everyone away from the entrance. You position yourself in the opening behind the bush and watch below. We will be back soon."

Jeremiah could see that everyone understood and that there would be no problems. What he was unsure about was having Noah and Brenda with him out in the open but he knew that three pairs of eyes were needed.

Ten minutes into the scouting expedition, Brenda whistled, signaling that she found something. When Noah and Jeremiah approached Brenda they could see that she had found another cave with a well-concealed entrance. This cave was even larger than the first one. In addition there was a small stream not thirty feet away.

In no time at all, everyone was relocated to the new hideout.

"Rabbi, are we going to catch fish in the stream?" asked one of the boys.

"No, no fish in that stream I'm sorry to say. We are going to use the fishing line and the hooks plus this morning's empty soup cans to set a warning signal, though. I think some of you would call it 'fishing for men.'"

The boy looked puzzled until Sarah said, "A burglar alarm."

Jeremiah took the fishhooks and tied them onto the fishing line every two feet. Sarah placed some stones into the soup cans after Brenda had punched holes in the sides close to the can top. She then tied short pieces of fishing line to each can and gave them to Jeremiah. Jeremiah and Noah then took the fishing lines with the hooks and cans attached and stretched them out around the hillside about fifty feet away from the cave. Using the knife, Jeremiah cut branches from several aspen trees. He then sharpened one end of each branch making a simple spear. These he took back with him to the cave. When he arrived there he found a large pile of mountain apples lying on one of the blankets. "Where did these come from?" he asked.

"I found them when we were looking for a new cave," said Brenda, flushing. "When you men went to set the burglar alarm some of us went out and picked the apples."

Okay, not automatons after all.

Jeremiah did not want to bring everyone down but this could not be allowed. "Thank you, Brenda. That showed initiative. However, until we know who else may be out here, we must avoid leaving the cave in daylight unless I am going also. Does everyone understand?"

Everyone nodded.

"Now we're going to stay put for a while."

"Rabbi, we are down to one bottle of water," said Sarah.

Jeremiah took the three empty water bottles and quickly and silently went to the stream and filled them. When he returned to the cave he opened the first aid kit and removed the water purification tablets and dropped one pill into each bottle.

"What was that you put in the water?" one of the boys asked.

"Iodine tablets."

"Isn't that like poison?" asked Brenda.

"Well, it can be, but these are specially made to make water safe to drink. It will taste a little funny but will not hurt you.

You just have to wait for the pill to dissolve, then gently shake the bottle and it is ready to go," explained Jeremiah.

"Is that another army thing?" Bobby asked.

"Yes, armies everywhere use them. Where is Tray?" Jeremiah asked.

"He's checking out the back of the cave," said Sarah.

"How long do we have to stay here?" asked one of the boys.

"Yeah, and where are we? I'm lost," said another.

Suddenly Jeremiah was being swamped with questions. *Don't let them panic now.*

"We are about a mile to a mile and a quarter from the campgrounds which are on the other side of that hill over there," he said as he pointed out of the cave's entrance.

Tray returned from his scouting the rear of the cave. He was carrying something that was wiggling. It was a mountain lion cub.

Jeremiah was up in a flash and through clenched teeth hissed, "Take it back now!"

Startled, Tray dropped the cub. The cub let out a loud cry when it landed on the rocky floor. Jeremiah grabbed the cub and vanished into the depths of the cave before anyone could blink an eye.

He could hear the kids muttering in surprise behind him.

"How did he move so fast?"

"Where did he go?"

"Is he like a ninja rabbi?"

When Jeremiah returned to the kids at the front of the cave he was doing all he could to control his anger.

"Rabbi, I . . . I . . ." stammered Tray.

Jeremiah held up his hand to cut off the boy. "It's okay, you didn't know that you never handle wild animals, especially in their lair. This place is not safe. We have to leave now."

"But it's daylight and you said—" one of the boys began in a very small voice.

"I know what I said, but we don't want to be here when the mother lion returns. She is not going to be happy and neither will I," Jeremiah barked, startling all the kids. "Pick up our stuff and let's move now!"

Jeremiah gave one spear to Noah and the third to Brenda. Taking his own spear and tucking the paintball gun into the back of his waistband, Jeremiah moved slowly to the front of the cave and began checking the surroundings for any signs of their attackers.

I should have checked the cave myself. He came to a sudden stop. *No, please not now.*

"What was that?" exclaimed Noah.

"What is that smell?" Sarah asked.

"She's back," Jeremiah said.

"Who's back?" Tray asked.

"Mother!"

16

JEREMIAH SLOWLY LOOKED AROUND THE CAVE ENTRANCE AND FINALLY SPOT-
ted the big cat lying directly above. At that instant the burglar
alarm was tripped. Looking quickly down the slope Jeremiah
could see two men coming up the hill. One of the men was
hopelessly entangled in the fishhook-laden line and had fallen
onto a large boulder, hitting his right shoulder. The fall had
caused the man to lose his weapon and he could not reach it
while still tangled in the trap. The second man was yelling at
him to be quiet.

Jeremiah saw his chance for action.

Gesturing to the kids to stay put and be quiet, Jeremiah
jumped out of the cave and while in the air he spun around
to face the lioness. The lion, having been distracted by the
two men down the hill, was startled when Jeremiah suddenly
appeared below her. She immediately coiled her muscles and
flew directly at him. Holding the spear above his head cross-
wise with his hands close together, Jeremiah caught the lion's
front paws on the spear, and in one smooth movement, he fell
backward, pulling the lion with him. Jeremiah hit the ground
on his back and placing his feet on the lion's belly, he flipped

the animal about fifteen feet down the hill and directly on top of the second gunman coming up the hill. The crash of the 300-pound cat into the man's chest killed both him and the lion instantly.

Jeremiah was up and moving down the hill, headed for the man tangled in the burglar alarm. In less than three seconds he was on the man who was attempting to pull a pistol from his belt.

No choice . . . no choice, Jeremiah thought as he struck the man with his clenched fist, arcing in an upward motion directly under the man's sternum, causing his heart to explode. The man crumpled to the ground dead.

Shaking with rage Jeremiah turned to look back at the cave and saw all the kids staring at him with expressions ranging from shock to horror. Jeremiah had wanted the men alive so he could find out what was going on. In seconds all that had changed.

Kids saw it all . . . Adonai, what have I done to these young minds?

He grabbed both men's pistols and signaled Noah to him. The boy came, face white, but he met his eyes.

"Have you ever been trained to fire a gun?" Jeremiah asked him quietly.

"I've played paintball with my uncles, but never a real gun," Noah said.

Jeremiah nodded and handed Noah the paintball gun. "It's loaded. Be careful with it. Put it in the back of your waistband and untuck your shirt to cover it. Don't let any of the other kids look at it, touch it, nothing. Understood?"

"Understood."

Jeremiah took a deep breath. "Noah, do you know what one of these paintball guns can do?"

"It can knock you down and give you really nasty bruises."

"And that's with padding. Use it up close on a person without padding and you can break an arm or a leg. Shoot them in the throat and you kill them. This is not a toy. Again. No one else touches it but you."

"I understand, Rabbi," Noah said, taking the gun from his hand and tucking it into the back of his pants.

"Good, help me by resetting the burglar alarm while I try to calm the others down."

"What about them?" Noah whispered, gesturing to the bodies.

"Leave them as they are."

"But—"

"But, nothing," Jeremiah hissed. "If anyone else comes up the hill they will think the lion killed both men. We have no shovels and a pile of rocks will be a dead giveaway. No, leave them exactly as they are."

Returning to the cave, Jeremiah noticed that the girls were calmer, although both had red eyes and a few tears still rolling down their cheeks. Moving everyone away from the entrance to the cave and making sure they were comfortable, Jeremiah sat down and tried to calm his own nerves. It was not over. He knew that. Professionals never worked this kind of job with anything less than two two-man teams. So, there were at least two more to deal with. *So, where are they and how long before they get here?*

Sarah came and sat down next to him.

"Are you okay?" he asked her, dreading the answer.

She nodded, but her eyes said otherwise. "Do you think the lion suffered?"

He stared at her in amazement. She had just witnessed him killing two men and she was concerned about the lion.

"No, her neck was broken: she never knew what hit her."

Sarah bit her lip. "What about the cub?"

Jeremiah heaved a sigh. "It won't survive long on its own," he admitted.

"Are you going to kill it?"

"It's either that or let it starve."

She shook her head. "There's a third option."

"We can't take him with us," Jeremiah said.

She glared at him. "I wasn't suggesting we do that."

"Okay, what's your suggestion?"

"When we get out of here, we can contact the zoo, and we can lead some of the keepers out here and they can rescue him. The zoo only has one lion and he's really old."

"You like the zoo?"

She nodded. "I want to be a veterinarian."

He gripped her hand. "Okay, Sarah. You help me, you keep these kids together, and I promise you that when we get out of here, we'll come back and rescue the cub."

She nodded and then threw her arms around him and hugged him. Startled he hugged her back quickly, then pulled away. Sarah turned and went back to the others.

Moving very far with fourteen shell-shocked kids was out of the question. *Not knowing where we are doesn't help. We need a map.*

Suddenly he remembered the camp information booklet and he pulled it out of his pocket. He flipped through it and found exactly what he needed. There, covering two adjacent pages, was a map of the entire preserve, and fairly detailed too.

Jeremiah sat studying the map for several minutes before he noticed that the rain had started again. He wondered how long it had been coming down. *You're losing your touch. You could always process dozens of information feeds from all your senses* at once. *You would have heard the first drop even before it hit the ground. This is not good. If we are all going to survive this, I have to get myself together.*

He knew what the problem was, though. *I don't want to go back to that life.* In light of all the things he had been thinking and feeling for the past several weeks, this was a revelation. And that revelation gave him strength.

Jeremiah silently rose and turned his face toward heaven. He stood there letting the rain wash over him for several minutes. Feeling refreshed he returned to the cave and studied the map again.

Sarah and Noah came over and sat in front of Jeremiah. "Where did you learn the move against the man caught in the burglar alarm?" asked Noah. "Did you learn that in the army?"

Not there. I can't tell them that, though.

"No, I was just very lucky. I saw him reaching for a pistol and knew I had to stop him."

"But you hit him . . ." said Sarah.

Jeremiah cut her off and quickly changed the subject. "According to the map in this booklet, there is an abandoned logging camp about two miles from here. There is a fire road near the camp that we could follow down off the mountain. We will have to wait till dark before we can use the road, but we can head to the logging camp now."

"Assuming the rain stops, right?" asked Brenda as she sat down next to Noah.

"Traveling in the rain might be the smart choice. The rain will wash away our footprints. With the remaining daylight it will be easier to see the mud we're walking through and try to keep from slipping. Using the road in the dark, on the other hand, would allow us to move as if we were in stealth mode."

"Stealth mode?" asked Sarah.

Okay, don't scare them. They have to keep the others calm.

"Yes, stealth mode." He could see in their expressions that they were paying close attention. "There are at least two more men on this mountain with us. It won't be long before they find the two down the hill, and when they do we don't want to be anywhere near here. They will believe we are moving farther into the preserve and we must help them with that."

"How long will it take us to get to the logging camp?" asked Noah.

"I was thinking about two hours."

"I can walk two miles in less than thirty minutes," Sarah said.

"Yeah, in the mall while window-shopping," quipped Noah, at which point both Sarah and Brenda punched him on the shoulders. "Ow."

"I'm sure you can, but there are fifteen of us and we are in the forest," Jeremiah said while trying not to smile. "We do need to move from here quickly and I was thinking of a way to do it. Get everybody up and ready to travel."

All the kids were ready to go in five minutes. Sarah, Brenda, and Noah each carried one of the makeshift spears while Jeremiah had cut up one of the blankets and made a simple backpack to carry everything else. Jeremiah and Noah had already retrieved the burglar alarm as the girls got everyone up and in line.

"Okay, gang, we need to create a distraction," said Jeremiah.

"You mean by like making loud noises?" asked Brenda.

"No, this would be a visual distraction. When we leave the cave we need to make as many footprints as we can. Then a short distance later we will get back in single file and make only one set of prints. Let's go."

Within ten minutes of leaving the cave they had fanned out and trampled the grass, shrubs, and flowers and then re-formed into a single line three times.

These kids learn fast, Jeremiah thought.

Forty-five minutes after they left the cave they were over halfway to the logging camp. Jeremiah halted the group and made sure that each kid drank some water. This was accompanied with sounds of gagging, choking, and spitting.

"This tastes awful," said Bobby just before he took another long swallow from the bottle.

"Yeah, but it's safe," said Noah.

"Okay, Noah, take the lead and move up this ridgeline walking only on the rocks."

"Where are you going?" asked Brenda, with panic in her voice. Sarah and Noah grabbed Brenda's hands to calm her down.

"False trail," he said. "I'm going to leave a false trail. I will catch up in a few minutes."

Brenda's nodding said she understood but her eyes showed that fear was still there. Jeremiah turned to the left and started trampling the dirt as he headed away from the group.

Noah started up the ridge with the others in tow and Sarah walking drag.

That girl is something. Quietly listens to everything, then takes charge when and where she's needed. Not afraid to be a girl but smart and analytical as well.

Jeremiah was not a smoker. His training had taught him how to smoke but not become addicted. Every five minutes he would light one of the inventoried cigarettes. He would let it burn down, then flick off the flame and drop the butt in the mud without covering it up.

His watch indicated that it was nearly noon and he had been walking for thirty minutes. As he finished his false trail, he removed the compact from the backpack. He tied the open compact to a tree branch so that the late afternoon sun would hit the mirror. If anyone was following, the flashing light off the mirror would convince them they were on the correct trail. Jeremiah figured this could give them another hour's cushion, more if they were lucky.

Sitting on the ground beneath the mirror Jeremiah removed his shoes and socks, using the laces to tie them around his waist. Then he carefully began climbing the tree. Fifteen feet above the ground, Jeremiah jumped from his tree to the nearest uphill tree. He caught a branch near the end and it bowed down but did not break. As the branch started moving up, Jeremiah scrabbled hand-over-hand up the limb toward the tree trunk. He repeated this pattern ten times until he was several hundred feet away from where his tracks ended. Climbing down the tree, Jeremiah started running up the hill toward the ridgeline.

He caught the kids less than a quarter mile from the logging camp. As he approached the kids Sarah whistled to signal Noah to stop.

"What happened to your shoes?" she asked.

"I can move faster and quieter without them," he replied.

"Yeah, stealth mode, right?" she said.

Observant too.

Jeremiah left Sarah and ran up hill to Noah. "Go back down the trail and send Sarah up here. You stay there and walk drag," Jeremiah said to Noah.

Before he had finished putting on his second shoe Sarah was standing beside him. She was slightly out of breath but looked to be in good enough shape to continue.

The logging camp is just around this hill. We must approach it carefully.

"I think we should climb a little higher so that we can see down into the camp," Jeremiah said to Sarah. "I am going to lead you up there and find a good spot to rest without being seen. I am then going to go down to the camp and check it out, okay?"

Sarah nodded understanding, then immediately started moving up the hill. The kids started after her, once again in the same order and single file. Jeremiah had to turn away to hide his grin from the kids. He just could not help it. Thankfully he did not burst into hysterical laughter, but he wanted to. He now realized that all the training he had received in his life had taught him nothing about children and group dynamics.

Jeremiah located a sheltered spot just below the top of the hill and under some trees. The kids except Sarah all sprawled out on the ground acting as if they had run a marathon. Sarah was sitting cross-legged with her back against a tree looking intently down on the camp.

"What now?" Noah asked as he approached Jeremiah and Sarah.

"You and I are going down to check out the logging camp."

Turning to Sarah he instructed, "Ask Brenda to help you keep the others together and quiet. We will be back soon."

"Don't be long. Some of the kids are getting hungry and a few others need a bathroom break . . . bad."

"They can go in the woods."

She pursed her lips. "Some people are cooler with that idea than others."

He had a feeling she was one of the ones who wasn't cool with the idea, but he didn't say anything, just nodded.

Jeremiah and Noah moved down the hill using trees for cover. Approximately fifty feet from the camp Jeremiah signaled a halt and crouched close to the ground. He placed his right hand, palm down, on the ground checking for vibrations. Nothing. Scanning the logging camp he could see three small buildings and one structure that looked like a carport, only much larger. In front of this structure was a large open area. He stared at it long and hard, and then he saw it. There, in the middle of the opening. Two parallel indentations. Helicopter skid marks.

"Great," Jeremiah hissed to himself.

17

Cindy had reached the church parking lot at noon and waited, wishing that Dave's text had said what time the bus would be arriving. She tried playing solitaire for a while using the passenger seat as a table, but twisting her shoulder hurt too much. She suspected that the fall had done more damage and cringed when she thought about what the physical therapist was going to say when she saw her again on Monday.

She prayed sporadically, still uncertain what it was that had awakened her in the middle of the night.

She considered going inside, but she wanted to see the bus as it pulled up. She half drowsed in her car. She hadn't slept much in the last few days and she was beginning to feel it.

The sound of an engine brought her fully alert and she sat up, peering eagerly through the window. A moment later one of the church's fifteen-passenger vans lumbered into sight. As it parked, the second one pulled into the parking lot behind it.

Her heart jumped into her throat. Both vans together couldn't carry as many as the bus could. She got out of her car and ran toward the first bus. Wildman descended from the front passenger seat.

"No bus?" she asked.

"We couldn't get it in time."

"Where's Jeremiah?"

"I was hoping you heard that part of the phone call. He's still up at the camp with fourteen kids. They're going to be stuck there for a couple of days until the rain stops and we can get back across the river. It's okay, though. They have plenty of food, water, games. Cindy? Cindy, what's wrong?"

She grabbed the front of his shirt in her fists and pushed her face next to his. "Where did you say Jeremiah is?"

"He's still at Green Pastures."

Her legs buckled under her and she collapsed onto the ground, screaming.

"What did you see?" asked Noah.

Above the logging camp Jeremiah inspected the helicopter skid marks. From where he was he couldn't tell how old they were. He'd have to get closer before he could determine if it was safe to take the kids down to the camp.

"Stay here and watch for my signal to come down."

Jeremiah moved the last fifty feet to the edge of the camp and came up behind the closest small building. There was nothing that he could see that was out of place when he looked through the window. He moved around the building and saw the front door covered by several cobwebs. *No one has entered here for some months,* he thought.

The other two buildings were the same way. Believing that no other people were there, Jeremiah moved to the center of the open area to view the skid marks. Kneeling down, Jeremiah pressed his fingers softly on the side of the mark in order to gauge how fresh they were. The mud in the marks was very soft, which meant the marks were at least three days old or more.

Jeremiah turned toward the tree line and waved for Noah to join him in the camp. When Noah arrived at his side, they checked to see if any of the buildings were locked. Surprisingly, none of them were. Noah started to enter one of the buildings but Jeremiah stopped him at the last second.

"Do not disturb the cobwebs. The less we change the area the harder it will be for someone to figure out we have been here. Go up and get the rest and bring them down the same path we took."

Noah nodded as he turned and retraced his steps back up the hill.

After Noah had left to get the others Jeremiah surveyed the logging camp. *Now what can we use in this place?*

Mark was sitting in an interrogation room across from Frank Butler and he was losing his temper. "Call off your dogs," he demanded.

Frank smiled insolently. "I do not know what you are talking about, Detective. I don't have any dogs. I'm more of a cat person."

Mark jumped to his feet, ready to punch the man, but Paul put a steadying hand on his arm and gave him a look that said, *Don't give him an excuse.*

"You know, the camp was evacuated yesterday," Paul said. "There's nothing for your goons to do up there except some tagging of buildings."

Mark's cell rang and he checked it. Cindy was calling. He left the room, wondering why she was calling. Once he closed the door behind him he answered.

"Jeremiah and fourteen kids are still up there!" she screamed in his ear.

"Cindy, what did you say?"

"Not everyone made it out before the river took out the bridge. They left fourteen kids behind and Jeremiah with them."

"No," Mark whispered. Fourteen kids and a rabbi were more than enough for a massacre that would scar the community forever.

"There's a fire trail, but there are logs down over the road and they can't get any emergency vehicles in there with the mudslides," Mark said.

"Someone needs to get in there. We need to send someone in a helicopter, an SUV, something. We can't just leave them there!"

"Calm down, Cindy, we won't."

Paul exited the interrogation room and gave him a questioning look. Mark told him what was happening.

Paul's eyes took on a steely glare. "I'm going up there."

"What, how? You don't even know for sure where they'll be."

"My sister has a Jeep. I've been to that area lots of times. If they're up there, I can find them."

Paul was already in motion toward the front door.

"What do you want me to do?" Mark called after him.

Paul turned and gave him a strange look. "You're a good cop, Mark. The best. Inside that room is a man who is your prisoner. And he's the only one who can call off a team of killers who are about to slaughter fourteen kids and a rabbi. If they haven't already. Do whatever you feel led to do."

Then Paul sprinted from the building.

"Cindy. Paul's on his way up there to get to Jeremiah and the kids. I'm going to see what I can do here to get the hit called off. You go home, sit tight. I'll be calling you shortly," Mark said before ending the call.

He turned to stare at the interrogation room. A monitor displayed what was happening inside the room, which was being recorded. He turned it off and glanced around. No one was looking his way.

"God forgive me," he whispered as he headed back into the room.

Jeremiah crawled out the door of the third building just as Noah arrived with the gang in tow. Seeing several kids dancing from foot to foot Jeremiah queried, "Who needs a bathroom break?"

Every hand shot into the air as if pulled by the same string.

"Okay. There are three stools in this building, which will be for the boys. Crawl through the door; avoid touching the cobwebs. Girls follow me to the next building. Sorry but there is only one stool in there."

When they drew closer to the second building Jeremiah whispered to the girls, "This one is cleaner. Don't forget to crawl through the door."

"Still in stealth mode?" asked Sarah.

"Yes. Anyone looking at the outside of these buildings must think that we have not been here. Stay inside until I return."

"No problem," said Brenda as she quickly crawled through the open door.

Jeremiah circled around the building and headed to the carport-like structure. There was not much to be found there. It looked like the logging company had done a good job cleaning out most of their equipment. As he approached the rear of the structure he heard an unmistakable sound.

Rattlesnake!

Great . . . dinner, thought Jeremiah. The sound was coming from a small stack of plywood near the back. Carefully he moved the wood with his sharpened branch. The snake slithered out the back toward the trees. Jeremiah easily speared the snake, pinning it to the ground. Using a nearby shovel, Jeremiah cleanly cut off the snake's head. After the body stopped writhing around, he picked it up and laid it out on a nearby workbench. *Timber rattler, short in length but large in diameter. Lots of meat.*

Using the pocketknife, Jeremiah quickly filleted the snake. Picking up the tail, he squeezed out the fatty tissue onto the meat. *I doubt there is any cooking oil or butter in those cabins.* Placing the meat onto a small piece of wood Jeremiah returned to the girls' building. Both girls were kneeling on the floor just inside the door.

"Okay, ladies, let's check this place out."

Unlike the equipment structure, the logging company left a mess in the small buildings. They quickly found the cooking shack. There were plenty of cupboards, a large sink with dish racks full of plates, silver, and glassware. The stove was a joke. There were two propane camp stoves, both of which had been charred from excessive use. There was a small refrigerator that Jeremiah was not going to open for any reason. *Who knows what is living in there?*

"Ladies, carefully look in those cupboards and tell me what you find. I will check these cabinets over here."

"Pots and pans in here," Brenda called out.

"Canned goods in this one," said Sarah.

Jeremiah found a dozen propane bottles but they seemed to all be empty. "Gas bottles over here, but they are all wrapped in plastic," said Sarah.

"Great, grab two for me, please."

Sarah handed Jeremiah two gas bottles. "Check the bottoms of the canned goods looking for any signs of rust," he said to no one in particular. Jeremiah quickly attached the gas bottles to the camp stoves. Using a stick match from the box on the shelf above the stoves, he lit them both. Both stoves lit, but the flames were not even. One side of all the burners had rusted through, leaving no flame on the opposite side.

"All the cans have rust except some canned peaches that are still wrapped in plastic," said Brenda.

"We need a large skillet. Did either of you see one?"

"There are five or six over here," said Sarah.

"Great. Take two over to the sink and rinse them out," Jeremiah instructed Sarah.

"Swell. Lost in the woods. Chased by assassins. Sleeping on the ground. No baths. And I draw dishwashing duty," moaned Sarah.

"In the interest of fair play, Brenda, you will wash the plates and silverware," said Jeremiah.

"Awwww," groaned Brenda while Sarah burst into hysterical laughter.

Handing his P38 to Sarah, he added, "You can open the peaches."

It was Brenda's turn to laugh.

Good, keep it light-hearted. They don't need to know how bad this is going to get.

"Did anyone find cooking oil in the cupboards?"

"No" came the reply.

Jeremiah took the frying pans from Sarah and placed them on the burners. Next he added some of the snake's fatty tissue and ground pepper to the pans. Taking a spatula from the shelf Jeremiah placed several pieces of meat into each pan and he was met with the sound of sizzling flesh.

"That smells good," said Noah as he crawled through the doorway.

"Dang! There goes my last fingernail. Here, you do this," complained Sarah as she thrust the peaches and P38 into Noah's chest.

Everybody started laughing at once.

"Sounds like a party in there," one of the boys outside yelled.

Four minutes each side . . . don't over or under cook this beastie . . .

"Food, food, food!" the kids outside started chanting.

"Noah. Go tell everyone to quiet down. We are not out of this yet . . . and remember, we are not alone up here," Jeremiah said to the boy.

"Sarah. Come over and watch the pans, please. Turn the meat over in two minutes. Four minutes per side. When done put them on the platter Brenda is washing now, and put more of this grease and meat into the pans. Can you do that?"

The expression on her face said it all. *Do I look like I am five?*

Jeremiah crawled out of the building. "Guys, let's go build a dining table." Jeremiah led the kids to the carport structure. After he had checked for additional creatures he helped the boys haul wood to the center of the area. Noah then took charge and directed the table and bench assembly, while Jeremiah returned to the cooking shack to check on the girls.

As Jeremiah crawled through the door he overheard the girls talking softly.

"You're right. I thought the Rabbi said there were no fish in the streams here."

"So where did he get this much meat? It had to be five or six big ones."

Before they could ask him, Jeremiah grabbed up the platter and headed for the door. "Bring the dinnerware and the spatula, please," he said over his shoulder. "Oh, and don't forget the peaches."

Everyone was seated around the table eyeing the "fish" on the platter. Several of the younger boys were visibly drooling.

"Before we begin, we must give thanks to HaShem for bringing us safely here and providing this meal." All the kids bowed their heads without a single sound.

"Adonai, we praise you for bringing us this far and we ask your guidance as we travel this wilderness and partake of this bounty."

"Amen," half the kids chorused at the end.

Mark sat quietly at the table in the interrogation room, tears streaking down his face. Blood covered his hands and clothes. He had turned the interrogation room into a torture chamber. Across the room Frank Butler was slumped on the floor, unconscious.

Mark had broken every vow he had ever made to himself about not hurting others. He'd also just ended his career. And he'd probably go to jail when people realized what he'd done.

And it was all for nothing.

He had finally gotten the weasel to agree to call off his assassins. He thought he had won, saved all those lives. It would be worth it.

But he had forgotten the most important thing. No working phone lines, and no cell reception. Just like they couldn't call up the mountain to warn anyone of the massacre, Frank Butler couldn't call to stop it.

The door was locked, the camera was off, and the room was soundproof. He pulled out his gun and stared at it. After what he had done not only was his life shattered, but any hope of convicting Frank Butler was gone with it. Any bit of evidence they had or could get would be thrown out because of the stain of his actions. He had let a killer go free.

It would have been worth it if he could have saved anybody. Because, in the end, he'd rather save a single life than catch a killer after the fact. Most murders were single acts, often born of intense passion and not likely to be repeated.

He stared at Frank. Not so with him. The man had been so arrogant, so remorseless. It couldn't have been the first time he had killed. And if he walked free, it wouldn't be the last.

"Maybe I can still save some lives," he whispered. "At least I can stop him from killing again."

He hefted the gun in his hand. It was too late to make it look like an accident. He could claim there had been a struggle, but his fellow officers would know better, and ultimately, they would do the right thing and put him away.

Paul, did you know what I was capable of, how far I'd go? Mark wondered.

He dragged himself to his feet and moved to stand over the man on the floor.

My victim, Mark realized as he aimed the gun at his head.

18

Jeremiah watched as Noah carefully scooped pieces of meat to each person. All eyes then turned to the rabbi for permission to start.

"Begin."

Flashing forks caused the meat to disappear faster than anyone could have predicted. Fortunately there was enough for all to eat their fill. When it came time for dessert everyone commented on how great the peaches tasted. He smiled, knowing from experience that a simple can of peaches could taste like heaven to a man lost in the wilderness. As much as he wanted to indulge in them, he avoided it, choosing instead to only eat a small meal of the snake. He needed to stay awake, probably for a long time still. That meant he could only consume a small amount of food and only protein.

Not surprisingly, most of the kids started looking very drowsy after they ate. "Noah, girls, pick up all the things on the table and take them to the cook shack, please."

Once the meal had been cleared Jeremiah had the remaining kids lie down on the table and benches. Minutes later they were all fast asleep.

Entering the shack, Jeremiah could see the girls busily cleaning up the pans and dishes while Noah was carefully putting everything back where it had come from.

"Rabbi, where did you find that fantastic fish? Didn't you say there were none in the stream?" Sarah finally asked.

"Yeah, and how many were there? That was a lot of meat," chimed in Brenda.

Noah just smiled. Jeremiah realized he knew what they had really eaten. Signaling to Noah, Jeremiah walked over to the girls. "Stay calm, promise?" he asked both of them.

After both had nodded yes, Jeremiah told them the truth. "It was only one, and it was a timber rattler."

Before the girls could scream, Noah and Jeremiah had covered the girls' mouths. When they had calmed down, the men removed their hands. Both girls turned sputtering and spitting into the sink.

"But, but . . . but . . . it tasted like fish . . . where . . . how . . ." Brenda stammered.

"I can't believe you made me eat rattlesnake. . . . Ewwww . . ." blurted out Sarah.

"I didn't make you eat anything. You were hungry and assumed it was fish. You are accustomed to eating fish. The meat smelled like, looked like, and tasted like fish, didn't it?" Jeremiah asked.

"Yeah, but . . ." started Brenda.

"Rattlesnake is actually quite nutritious, and as you now know, tastes pretty good too."

Noah, changing the subject, asked, "What now, Rabbi?"

"It is close to four o'clock. It is still too bright out to risk moving right now. We will stay here till midnight before starting down the fire road. Right now we all need some rest."

"I set up another table for us to sleep on because the other kids have totally covered our dinner table," Noah told the girls. Turning to Jeremiah, he asked, "Guard duty?"

Before Jeremiah could respond, Sarah jumped in with "I'll take the first shift. I am totally weirded out by what I just ate."

"Me too. I'll go second," Brenda added.

"You girls stand guard together. Noah will go second and I will be last. Sarah, teach Brenda how guard duty works, Okay?"

"Rabbi, that means you will have a longer shift than the three of us," said Noah.

"True, but I am no longer growing and don't need much sleep anyway." *Thirty-two hours awake so far, well short of the ninety-two in that place . . . don't think it!* He took a breath. "If any of the kids wakes up and needs a bathroom, escort them to the shack and back. We don't need anyone aimlessly wandering around the area."

Everyone acknowledged the instructions and started for the door. "Are we going to make it?" asked Sarah as she crouched down to crawl through the doorway.

"Yes!" was all Jeremiah said before waving her out the door.

Right. When did you turn into Mister Happy? All things being equal, the odds say none of us will make it.

Cindy paced her bedroom, having moved there to pace after having accidentally stepped on the spot where Max had died when pacing the living room. "Come on, Mark, call me back. Tell me what's going on," she said out loud.

She tried his cell again, but he didn't pick up. The longer she went without hearing the worse she felt. It was going to be dark soon and all she could think of was Jeremiah and the kids on the mountain, fighting for their lives.

If they haven't already lost them, she thought. She slapped herself lightly on the cheek. *Don't think that way!*

She couldn't take it anymore. She had to do something.

Mark heard a soft knock on the locked door to the interrogation room. Then a scratching sound. Someone was picking the lock. It was now or never. His finger tightened on the trigger.

The door swung open. Mark turned to look. Kneeling at the door was his wife.

"Traci?" he asked, his mind racing.

She stared from him to Frank's unconscious form and then back at him. "Mark?"

"It's not . . ." he stopped. It was exactly what it looked like and she would know even if he tried to deny it.

She stood and swung the door closed behind her. "Put the gun down, honey."

"What are you doing here?" he asked.

"Paul called me. He told me what was happening. He said that he thought you were going to need me. He wanted me to tell you he was sorry."

"I'm sorry for everything," he said.

"I'm not. You haven't done anything yet that I'm ashamed of, and I'll stand by you no matter what comes."

"They're going to come in here at any moment," Mark said.

She shook her head. "There's a very hysterical lady outside demanding that they send every available officer to Green Pastures in armored trucks."

"Cindy," Mark groaned.

"I kind of figured it had to be. No one's going to be looking for us for a while."

She put her hand on his arm and he dropped it, taking his finger off the trigger and sliding the safety on like he always did whenever he was around her. She wrapped her arms around his neck and he clung to her like he was drowning.

"Help me, Traci."

"I'm here."

The group walked back to the dining area. Noah climbed up onto the second table he had constructed and settled himself for a nap. Without saying anything Jeremiah pointed out the best guard locations to the two girls. As Brenda moved to her position, Jeremiah whispered to Sarah, "I'm going to scout the area for activity. I will return here from the direction of the cooking shack."

She nodded.

Jeremiah began his scouting trek by returning to the trail they had made coming down into the logging camp. He then turned and moved down the ridge for about fifteen minutes. He then turned half right heading in the general direction of the fire road. Carefully making his way through heavy brush and undergrowth, Jeremiah took extra care not to leave any tracks or damage any bushes. Thirty minutes later he arrived at the fire road. He figured his location to be about two miles away from the logging camp. Turning uphill toward the camp, Jeremiah carefully inspected the road.

This is not a good road. This would be very difficult at any time, but in the dark it is going to be very dangerous.

The road had not been used for a long time. It was full of ruts and holes, all of which contained muddy water. There were no shoulders to speak of and there were rocks and boulders everywhere. About a half mile from the logging camp, he could see there were a couple of large trees lying across the road.

What's that sound?

Instantly, Jeremiah was off the road, lying behind a large boulder, holding the open pocketknife at the ready. He lay there not moving or breathing for nearly a minute until he heard the sound again. *A vehicle . . . maybe a Jeep . . . someone's coming. But who?* he whispered to himself as he drew a shallow breath.

Can I make it to the fallen tree? No! Great! he hissed to himself. *I'm on the wrong side of the road to take out the driver . . . can't move now . . . too late for that . . . think.*

The Jeep appeared about fifty feet away. It was struggling to make headway on the messed-up road. *Get ready, breathe*, he said to himself as every nerve and muscle tensed for what was to come.

Forty feet to go.

Good, a convertible with its top removed. Breathe.

Thirty feet.

Dive through the passenger opening, knife extended. Breathe.

Twenty feet.

Whoever this guy is, he knows how to wrestle that Jeep. Breathe.

Ten feet.

One last breath. Tense up the proper muscles. Get ready . . . ready . . . steady . . . NOW!

Jeremiah sprang through the passenger opening with his outstretched arm tipped with the skinned knife blade. One foot from the man's throat, he realized who it was.

NO! Paul . . . it's Paul . . . Hold . . . Hold . . . NO!

Jeremiah jerked his hand to the right, just missing Paul's throat, and slammed into him with full force. Both men went flying out the driver side entrance and landed about five feet down the slope from the road.

"Umphhh!" issued from Paul's throat as all the wind was knocked from him. He was unconscious.

Close . . . so very close. Jeremiah stood and, taking Paul's feet, turned him around so that his head was elevated. Using his hand, he scooped some water from a puddle and sprinkled Paul's face.

The Jeep had continued for a few feet, then flipped over onto the driver's side. The engine was racing. Jeremiah ran up and turned off the ignition.

Maybe we can right this . . . Sure . . . with ten men and a boy, maybe . . . or . . . two men and fourteen kids, yeah. Jeremiah climbed back to where Paul was lying.

Paul was starting to revive.

"Come on . . . wake up!" Jeremiah splashed more muddy rainwater on Paul's face.

"Whaaa. . . ." Paul said, reaching for his sidearm. "What happened and who are y . . . Jeremiah! Thank heaven, I have been looking for you. Where are the kids? What happened at the summer camp? Did you see what happened? Was it an accident? What hit me? Why am I covered in mud?"

"Take it easy. Breathe a little. The kids are all fine and unless I miss my guess are fast asleep."

Jeremiah wasn't sure that Paul got that, but his anxious expression was starting to relax. Paul gingerly raised himself onto his elbows. Taking a few quick breaths, he tensed and then stood up in one smooth motion.

He didn't learn that at the police academy.

"Asleep?" Paul asked.

From his expression, Jeremiah could tell Paul was feeling better. So much so that he was speaking in his "cop voice."

Before starting up the fire road, the two men inspected the Jeep. "We should be able to get this righted with all of us working together. We can then get out of here," Paul said.

I don't think so . . . Oh, we can right the Jeep all right, but it won't carry us all, will make too much noise in the night air, and don't forget those cursed headlights . . . No, we are walking out of here.

The two men retrieved some water bottles and another flashlight from the Jeep.

Jeremiah took about ten minutes to explain the chain of events up to but not including how close Paul came to permanent sleep. He also left out the part about the two dead men and the mother lion.

"Unbelievable! One teenager alone doesn't act like that. Get a group of them together, like your fourteen, and they become a totally unmanageable mob. No! You must be sugarcoating," Paul said with an incredulous and unbelieving expression on his muddy face.

Cops! Always so suspicious.

"Rabbis don't believe in sugarcoating." Jeremiah took his handkerchief from his pocket and handed it to Paul. "Here, clean your face. We are fairly close to the logging camp where you can witness my words firsthand. Oh, and be prepared to apologize. How did you come to know we needed help?"

It was Paul's turn to explain.

"Cindy, a roomful of bad guys, and a handful of darts. That had to be something to see."

"She made quite an impression on them, some of them quite literally," Paul said.

As they moved Jeremiah kept his eyes roving, searching for signs of the enemy.

"Why aren't you two together?" Paul asked.

"Excuse me?" Jeremiah said, stumbling over a rock in the road.

"You like her. What's the problem?"

Jeremiah stared hard at Paul. He had no desire to talk about anything with Paul, least of all Cindy and his problem. "Just liking someone isn't always enough," he said at last when Paul continued to stare at him.

"Is it because she's Protestant?"

It would be easy to lie and tell Paul that was exactly the problem. It wasn't, though. He wished they shared the same religion, but his past was the real problem. The truth was he couldn't see himself with anyone, especially anyone as curious as Cindy. He could never tell her who he really was, what he really was, but sooner or later she would start asking questions he wouldn't be able to answer.

Out loud he said, "I'm a rabbi. It's expected that I'll marry a nice Jewish girl."

"I think you would have already married a nice Jewish girl if that was all that was going on."

"I'd rather not discuss my love life while we're fighting for our lives."

"You have anything better to discuss?" Paul asked pointedly.

"How we're all going to get out of this alive."

He moved ahead faster, unwilling to continue the conversation. He stopped at the edge of the logging camp. Moving to his left, he came into line with the cooking shack.

"Why did we just do that?" Paul asked.

"Guard duty."

"Guard what?"

Checking the time, Jeremiah whispered, "We have been posting guards, lookouts if you prefer, each time we stop and stay in any location longer than ten minutes. Right now Sarah and Brenda have the duty. They are scheduled to wake Noah in fifteen minutes. It is arranged that I approach the camp from this direction only."

"What happens if someone approaches from another direction? Do the guards open fire?" Paul asked sarcastically.

Taking several deep breaths Jeremiah replied, "No! The guard will sound the alarm, a single whistle, and then everyone will freeze."

Jeremiah was beginning to think it would have been better if Paul had stayed home. The rabbi and his castaways were doing just fine, thank you. Jeremiah issued one short whistle and started walking toward the cooking shack. Paul trailed behind, chuckling. When the men walked past the shack, Jeremiah could see Sarah crouched down behind several old tires in the front of the open structure. She was looking intently up at the ridgeline to her left.

"Unbelievable," Paul muttered.

Sarah waved her right hand, low to the ground. Jeremiah knew immediately that she had seen something. Turning toward Paul, Jeremiah placed a finger on his lips and pointed to the woodpile to their left. Both men moved quickly and took cover. Jeremiah, crouching low, moved to Sarah's side.

"I heard some noise from down the hill. As I was turning to look a flash of light caught my eyes," Sarah reported.

"Where was the flash?"

"There, under that very tall tree on the left side of the hill we came down earlier. Brenda has seen it too," said Sarah, indicating Brenda's position.

"Where are all the kids and Noah?" asked Jeremiah.

"The boys' bathroom shack."

Paul approached the two. "What is going on here?"

"We are not alone on this mountain," Jeremiah whispered. "Under that tall tree on the hill is at least one of the people tracking us."

"Brenda, are they still there?" Jeremiah whispered, turning to the girl.

"Yes."

"Okay, keep your eyes on them."

"Got it," she responded.

Jeremiah turned his head back to Sarah and whispered, "Go get Noah, and both of you come back here."

Sarah nodded and left. She was moving very quietly and quickly. She skirted around behind the buildings. By going that way she couldn't be seen by the men on the hill.

"Wow! Who taught her that?" asked Paul.

"She taught herself."

Two minutes later, Sarah and Noah were crouched down in front of Jeremiah. Their faces indicated concern but an almost total lack of fear.

"We can't really leave this place right now. There is still too much daylight. We are just going to have to stay here under cover. As long as they think we are here, they won't come looking. They will wait for nightfall. We've got about an hour. Go back and get all the kids and bring them here. Don't use the door. It can be seen from the hill. Break out one of the rear windows and have the boys exit there."

Noah and Sarah nodded, then left.

"What did you do to those kids? They are not normal," said Paul.

"Nothing. All the kids in this mob, as you called them, are great. They do as I ask immediately and without question."

Jeremiah moved closer to Paul. "There is a two-man hunter-killer team on the ridge. They will stop at nothing to eliminate the survivors of the bombing at the summer camp. The only reason they aren't rushing us now is they saw the two of us come into the logging camp. They are now discussing how to deal with three men instead of two."

"Three?" queried Paul.

"Three. Noah is six foot two and 210 pounds and from three-quarters of a mile away . . . well, you understand."

"How do you know they are killers?" Paul asked.

Jeremiah took a deep breath. "We know this because professionals rigged the bomb on our cabin to blow us all up. We know this because professionals like these always work as a pair of two-man teams. We know this because we killed the two-man team that found us this morning. Well, technically, the mother lion killed one of them. We know this because of the clothing they wore and the equipment they carried."

"Killed?" said Paul as he jumped to his feet. "Mother lion? What the devil is going on up here?"

"Get down!"

Crack!

Thump!

Thud!

Paul's body hit the ground hard. Just like that, he was gone.

19

"EVERYBODY GET DOWN AND FREEZE!" YELLED JEREMIAH.

Who would bring a Barrett on a job like this?

"Keep your heads down. Do not look up until I tell you to. Brenda, do you still see them?"

"Yes. What happened?" she replied.

With an angry edge to his voice, Jeremiah responded, "Just keep watching the hill. Do not lose sight of them for any reason. Got that?"

"Got it," Brenda said in the tiniest voice Jeremiah had ever heard.

"Noah?"

"Rabbi?"

"Go get one of the blankets and bring it to me."

A minute later Noah approached Jeremiah at a crawl. He offered the blanket, averting his eyes from the policeman's body.

In the hardest-sounding voice Jeremiah could manage he said, "Look at him. This is what war and killing really look like and not like that antiseptic event of this morning. Look at him. You must look. It will help you decide if the army is still what you want. Look!"

Noah looked and then he crawled away a few feet and threw up for several minutes.

"Where is his head? What could do something like that?" Noah groaned.

"A Barrett," Jeremiah said. "A Barrett sniper rifle can do this. Hit a person anywhere, even the arm, with a fifty caliber bullet and they are dead. Messy dead."

Softening his voice, Jeremiah continued, "We're dealing with a trained sniper. I'm sorry to be so hard on you."

Noah nodded, but didn't say anything.

Jeremiah draped the blanket over Paul's body before any of the other kids could see it.

The skies opened up and it began to rain again. The sun was also getting lower in the sky. Jeremiah checked his watch. *Forty minutes until darkness.*

"Girls, are they still there?"

Simultaneously, the girls answered, "Yes."

"Who has the best view of our bad guys?"

"I think Brenda does," said Sarah.

Moving carefully over to Brenda, Jeremiah said, "Okay, ladies, I have the duty. Relax and rest your eyes for a while."

Jeremiah could hear the breath slowly being released from both of the very tense girls.

Ten minutes later Jeremiah thought he heard something. *What now?* This sound was not the snipers moving in. Nor was it a vehicle coming up the road. *What is it?*

Helicopter.

"Everybody up. We are leaving now! Same as earlier, single file. No talking. Sarah, lead out that way. Noah, drag. Now move!"

The castaways were completely clear of the logging camp and a quarter mile down the logging road in less than five minutes. *I would take this group over most trained soldiers any day.*

232

Running to the front, Jeremiah whispered to Sarah, "Stop at the fallen tree."

At the tree, Jeremiah waved the group to form around him.

"The tree is too long for us to go around, so we will have to go over. Noah, you go first so you can help the others down on the other side. Whistle when you are ready."

Jeremiah cupped his hands for Noah to step in, and up he went.

Noah whistled.

"Brenda, you're next. Put your foot here in my hands. Sarah, push her bottom if she starts to tilt in your direction."

In less than a minute everyone was over and he was finally standing alone.

Now it's my turn. Oh, boy, this could hurt.

Opening the pocketknife, Jeremiah moved back from the log about fifteen feet. *Ready, go.* Running full tilt toward the log, Jeremiah waited to the last possible moment, then launched himself at the tree. *Short!* Jeremiah knew he had not jumped high enough. He hit the tree first with his chest, then his face. He tried to ignore the explosion of pain.

Swinging his right arm downward as hard as possible, Jeremiah jammed the knife into the tree. *Hold, please, oh, please hold.* The knife held firm. Swinging his left hand around and over his right hand, Jeremiah pulled himself up the side of the tree. It was not easy considering how wet the log was. Once on top, he tried to free the knife. In answer to his plea, the knife did hold, but that was it. The knife was so firmly embedded that it was not coming out for many years.

Twisting around, Jeremiah could see the kids had moved a short distance down the road, with Sarah in the lead. Brenda and Noah were still below him. Releasing his grip, Jeremiah slid off the tree into the steadying hands of the two kids.

Jeremiah used a simple hand signal to Sarah, and the line began moving. Five more minutes and they arrived at the overturned Jeep. Jeremiah signaled Sarah to keep going, which she did. Jeremiah stopped to search the Jeep for anything that could be of use. There was not much to be had. He found one box of granola bars, two more bottles of water, and a hunting knife. When he stood up, he was face-to-face with Brenda.

The look of horror on her face said it all. Turning away quickly, Jeremiah pulled some rags from the back of the Jeep and pressed them onto his face, wincing against the pain. Turning back to Brenda, Jeremiah whispered, "Sorry about that."

"It's okay. The sight of your entire face covered in blood startled me. Can I help you clean up a bit?"

"Thank you, that would be nice." Jeremiah turned so his face could be seen in what little light was still in the sky.

"Do you still have the first aid kit?" Brenda asked.

Jeremiah reached over his shoulder into the backpack and handed her the kit.

"This is gonna, like, sting," she said just before putting iodine on to his wounds.

"Bring it on," said Jeremiah, smiling his biggest smile.

Brenda giggled while she continued working. "Some of these cuts need stitching."

After looking in his eyes, Brenda said, "Oh, no, you don't. I'm not sewing up anything, especially your face. I can't even get the cuts to stop bleeding."

"That's fine. Just put some Band-Aids on the worst of them. We need to get out of here," Jeremiah said.

They caught up to the rest in no time. It was really getting dark; five more minutes and it would be pitch black. This was going to get tricky. When Jeremiah caught up with Sarah, he indicated that she should slow the pace. Some of the younger and smaller boys were starting to have trouble keeping up. Three of them had already fallen in the ruts, holes, and muddy water on the road. No one had complained or made any sounds, but once it was totally dark the situation would surely change.

Jeremiah heard one of the boys toward the back of the line cry out as he fell down the hill off the road. The boy was sliding down the muddy bank very fast. He came to a stop and Jeremiah could hear crying.

Sarah stopped the line without being told to do so. She had everyone squat down and rest quietly. Jeremiah made it back up the line to where the boy had fallen.

"Who is it?" he asked.

Brenda replied, "Bobby."

"Everyone stay where you are. Noah, with me."

Noah and Jeremiah carefully made their way down the muddy slope. They found the crying boy about twenty feet down. His leg was badly broken.

"Bobby?" whispered Jeremiah.

"Yeah," came the tearful reply.

Jeremiah indicated for Noah to move around to the boy's head. The light was completely gone from the sky. Seeing the boy's leg to determine the nature of the break was going to be difficult. Gently placing his hands on Bobby's ankle, he started sliding his hands up the boy's leg.

"Ow! Ow! Ow!"

"Easy, I know this hurts," whispered Jeremiah.

Jeremiah took off the backpack. He removed one of the flashlights. Cupping his hand over the business end of the flashlight, Jeremiah switched it on. Sliding his hand slowly to the side, Jeremiah allowed the smallest beam of light to escape his hand.

Compound fracture. *Great.* Jeremiah could tell that the bone had broken skin. Using the hunting knife from the Jeep, he cut open the pant leg. Opening the first aid kit, Jeremiah removed several tongue depressors and handed them to Noah.

"In his mouth to bite on. I have to set the leg and it will hurt," Jeremiah whispered to Noah.

Jeremiah removed the collapsible hard plastic splints and two bandages, plus the antiseptic cream from the kit. He put a large amount of the cream on an antiseptic gauze pad. He also cut strips of the white tape.

"Bobby?"

"Yes."

"Bite down on the sticks Noah will put in your mouth. I am going to set your leg and it is going to hurt. Do you understand?" Jeremiah whispered.

"Yes."

"Good. Now take some deep breaths and when you are ready look up at Noah and he will insert the sticks in your mouth," Jeremiah said, nodding at Noah.

"Here we go."

Sticks in.

Jeremiah, swiftly and with steady pressure, pulled Bobby's leg while straightening it at the same time. The bone realigned itself perfectly. Noah had placed his arm on Bobby's chest holding him down while being ready to control the boy's arms. Not really necessary, because Bobby had passed out.

"Rabbi, he's not breathing!" yelled Noah.

"Shhhh. He has just passed out from the pain. He is going to be fine. You can remove the sticks," Jeremiah whispered.

Jeremiah placed the cream-covered pad on the wound opening, applying mild pressure to push some of the cream into the hole. Next came the adhesive tape strips to hold the pad.

Extending the splints, Jeremiah placed them on the boy's leg. The bandages were then wound firmly down the entire length of the splints.

"Pull Bobby toward you away from this tree. We will then pick him up and return to the road," Jeremiah whispered to Noah.

Noah moved the boy away from the tree. Jeremiah moved around and, placing Bobby's legs together, gently lifted him off the ground. Noah turned around and started backing up the slope. Five steps, then *boom*. Noah splashed down on his bottom and slid three feet back down. Noah struggled up and started moving again. *Boom!* Down he went again.

"Stay down for a minute. We need to think this out," Jeremiah said to Noah.

"How did you know that the gun was a Barrett?" asked Noah.

"Training. Lots and lots of training. Don't worry about it. The army has excellent training routines. They will teach you how to recognize weapons by their unique signatures. They will also teach you how to tell where the shot came from and how far away it was. They will teach you to recognize the sound of a bullet passing close by you and determine if it was fired in anger or was unintentional. Like I said, we can have a really long discussion after we get home."

"If we get home," moaned Noah.

"The army will teach you how to overcome those kinds of doubts too. If you are willing, they will teach you new ways to eat, sleep, bathe, dress, everything. They will teach you how to stay awake for seventy-two hours and still function at 100 percent. Now, let's figure out how to get up this bank and back to the road."

"Rabbi?" said Noah after a long pause.

"Yes."

"Can I try carrying Bobby on my back?" asked Noah.

"Good idea. I will help you lift Bobby onto your shoulders, then move directly behind you. I will use this spear to anchor each step you take. Lead out with your right foot," Jeremiah whispered.

Noah shifted the paintball gun that had been in the back of his waistband to the front of his waistband. Jeremiah took the opportunity to check both of the guns he was carrying and to reposition them so he'd be ready when it was his turn to carry Bobby.

Once Bobby was loaded on Noah's back and the two men were ready, Noah moved his right foot forward. While it was raised, Jeremiah pushed the spear into the muddy slope below the foot. Noah then placed his foot down partially on the spear. Left foot up, second spear into the mud, foot lowered. The routine was repeated until the men were on the road.

Jeremiah had fallen so many times he was now covered completely in mud. So much mud that if he lay down and closed his eyes he would be invisible. They put Bobby down on the road's shoulder. Jeremiah checked his vital signs. Searching through the first aid kit, Jeremiah located a small bottle of painkillers. Placing the bottle into his pants pocket, he placed the kit back in his backpack.

"Stay here. I'm going to check if we are being followed."

Two thumbs up came from Noah.

Jeremiah made his way back to the fallen tree. Holding his breath and calming his heart, he strained his ears. He was listening for a sound. Any sound. No people following close enough to hear. *The helicopter is on the ground, though. I can still hear the turbine.*

"Let's set up our burglar alarm," he said as he returned to stand next to Noah.

"Stay here," Jeremiah whispered to Brenda. "Oh, and watch Bobby. If he stirs, signal."

Once they finished with the alarm, they sat down next to Brenda.

"Should we make a stretcher for Bobby?" asked Noah.

"Not a good idea, at least not right now. The road is just too torn up. We would spend more time dropping him than making progress. Down the mountain, the road may improve and then we can reconsider. For now, we will take turns carrying him. You brought him up the bank, so I will take him next. We will switch every fifteen or twenty minutes."

"I will take a turn too," chimed in Brenda.

"Me too."

"And me."

"I'll take a turn."

"Thanks, everyone," said Jeremiah.

"No problem. After all we must work together. We are a team. Yeah, that's it, a team that has, like, done pretty darn good. I believe we need a new name. How about the 'Rabbi's Rangers'?" asked Brenda, who was getting high fives from those closest to her.

"I know, we need T-shirts," Sarah said, which was followed by a chorus of agreement.

"Let's calm down," said Jeremiah.

The kids started chanting "Rabbi's Rangers, Rabbi's Rangers."

"Thank you, all," said Jeremiah. He raised his right arm with clenched fist and immediately there was silence. "Rangers, move out."

Noah and Brenda helped load Bobby onto Jeremiah's shoulders. "Bobby, you awake?"

"Hmm?"

"Don't throw up on me."

"'Kay."

Noah signaled for Sarah to move forward, which she had already started to do. Sarah had instructed the kids closest to her to grab the belt or waistband of the person in front of them.

Each kid did so and then whispered to the person following to do the same.

It was now totally dark. *Blacker than black. This is going to be really bad. I hope no one else gets hurt.*

Jeremiah couldn't believe what was happening. The line was moving quicker than he had thought possible. He then realized why. *We are moving like a snake, weaving all over the road. Clever girl, that Sarah.* She was choosing the path of least resistance by moving around the boulders and ruts while avoiding the deepest of the potholes.

Anytime someone fell in the mud, the tug on the belt rippled up and down the line at which point everyone halted. Seconds later another tug signaled to start moving again. Jeremiah was relieved that no one had asked how far they had to go. They would have given up if they knew that the fire road wound up, down, and around the entire north side of the forest preserve. Nine miles. They had to go nine miles. At the pace they were currently moving, Jeremiah calculated that they would arrive close to the washed-out bridge at about three in the morning.

Sarah, on her own initiative, called a halt after an hour of walking. She whispered, "Five-minute break," which was passed back up the line. Jeremiah had been carrying Bobby the entire time. Brenda and Noah quickly lowered Bobby to the ground. Jeremiah turned to check on the boy only to find he was awake. His face looked calm but Jeremiah knew the boy was in pain. Reaching into his pocket for the painkillers, he removed two pills. Noah had retrieved one of the water bottles from the backpack. Jeremiah offered the pills and water to Bobby.

"I don't need those," Bobby said weakly.

"Take them. We still have a long way to go and besides, it is always smart to take the pills before the pain gets to be too much."

"My mom's a nurse and she says that all the time," said Bobby, taking the pills and water from Jeremiah.

During the rest break, Jeremiah walked up the line of kids. Virtually everyone was covered in mud. All the faces showed concern. However, none of them showed any panic.

"You guys are doing great. We will be out of here soon. Keep helping each other like you have been doing," whispered Jeremiah.

Some of the kids flashed thumbs up and others responded with "Rabbi's Rangers."

"Sarah, you are doing a terrific job. We are moving faster than I expected," Jeremiah whispered.

"Thanks. I learned to use my complete eyesight capabilities in Drivers Ed."

"Drivers Ed?" asked Jeremiah.

"You know, don't stare in one direction, which strains and tires your eyes. Keep your eyes moving. Don't ignore your peripheral vision, and so forth."

"Well, it appears to be working. Are you ready for someone else to take a turn leading?"

"No, I like it up here, and besides I have only fallen in the mud twice. Did you see the others?" asked Sarah.

"Yes."

"If their eyes were closed, they would be invisible. Plus they have put on twenty pounds of mud weight. What a mess."

"I know what you mean."

Before heading back to the end of the line, Jeremiah showed Sarah a couple new belt tug signals.

"Stop every thirty minutes from now on. We need to switch the person who is carrying Bobby," said Jeremiah before leaving Sarah to her task.

As he moved along the line, Jeremiah made sure that all the kids knew about the new signals and to pass them along accurately. Bobby was loaded onto Brenda's shoulders. Without any signal, the line was up and starting to move.

"Noah, stay extra close to Brenda in case she starts to fall," Jeremiah whispered. "I'm going to backtrack and check for a tail."

Thumbs up from Noah and the line was moving. Jeremiah moved back up the road a few hundred feet so that he could not hear the kids. He squatted in the center of the road sweeping his eyes and ears trying to pick up any hint of activity. Nothing. Jeremiah returned to the kids.

Twenty minutes later, the line halted. Bobby was moved to the next person.

"Are you ready?" Jeremiah asked Tim.

"Yes, sir . . . er . . . Rabbi," came the reply.

Thirty minutes moving, five minutes halted. No tails detected. Bobby switched to a different person.

This is going better than I could have ever imagined. The pattern had been repeated six times so far. Approximately one mile to go. Unbelievable. One hill left before the downward slope to the bridge.

Bobby was now loaded on Noah. This would be his third time.

Suddenly Jeremiah saw a flash of light. They were being followed. He was certain their tracks had been obliterated by the heavy rain that, unfortunately, was starting to let up.

These people are pros. They figured out that we had to take the road, that we had no choice.

Jeremiah gave three quick tugs on Brenda's belt. Within seconds, the line was moving much faster. The light was falling behind and then disappeared. Jeremiah could hear more and more kids hitting the mud. No sounds or outcries, though.

Jeremiah could just make out the crest of the hill in front of them. Five minutes later the rain stopped. There was a warm glow in the sky ahead.

It's too early for the dawn. City lights. Must be the city lights. It can't be; the city is too far away.

Thump. Thump. Thump.

The helicopter was coming.

It was the middle of the night and Cindy still couldn't fall asleep. The police had refused to send more people up the mountain after Paul to rescue Jeremiah and the kids. She had never figured out where Mark was, but she had talked end-lessly to the two officers who escorted her home to no avail.

She was praying, trying to think of every possible scenario, trying to believe the best.

She was failing miserably. The main road wouldn't be pass-able for another day at least and she knew that there were downed trees on the fire road that were blocking emergency vehicles. If Jeremiah and the kids were in trouble there was no guarantee that they were still anywhere in the vicinity of the camp and Paul was trying to make it in based on only his knowledge of the campsite itself.

They're going to need more help, she thought as she paced.

You can do this, a voice seemed to whisper in her ear. *You have the tools, you have the knowledge, and you have the map.*

She stopped still in her tracks, her mind racing. Then she grabbed her keys and headed out the door where her eyes fell on the green Hummer parked at the curb in front of her house. Slowly she approached it. It was an H1, the closest civilian equivalent to the military vehicle.

She held her breath as she put her fingers on the door han-dle and turned. It moved and the door swung open. There, in the ignition where he had left them were Diamond's keys. She opened the glove compartment and found a satellite phone. Her heart began to pound and her palms were sweating.

Mark had said he would be sending officers to collect the car, but it must have slipped his mind.

What are you thinking, Cindy? she asked herself. Every fiber of her being screamed for her to stop, but in her mind she could see Jeremiah clearly and Brenda and the other kids and their terrified faces. She started the car, closed her eyes, said a brief prayer, and stepped on the gas.

Five minutes later she was parking at the church. She took the keys with her, half afraid that someone else might make off with the Hummer while she was inside. She unlocked the main gate and ran inside where she unlocked the office. Within five minutes she was on her way back out to the vehicle with a big box containing a first aid kit, flashlight, a couple of blankets, bottled water, and protein bars. Carefully folded in her pocket was the map of the entire property that they kept on file.

She stowed the gear in the back and then hit the road. As she took the onramp onto the freeway it took all of her will-power to drive the speed limit with so many lives on the line, but she knew she couldn't afford being pulled over, especially in a car that she had technically stolen. Whatever minutes she might save by speeding could be more than lost by such an encounter.

After a brief debate she finally put on her Bluetooth, yanked out her cell phone, and tried calling Mark one more time.

"Cindy, this isn't a good time. What is it?" he asked, his voice tense.

"I've been thinking about it, and I'm not sure Paul is going to be able to find them. I have the map of the entire property with me and I'm going in to try and find them."

"It's too dangerous," he said.

"Please, don't try to lecture me and don't try to stop me. I have to do this. I feel it."

"How do you think you'll make it in even on the fire road?" Mark asked.

She bit her lip. Moment of truth. "I, um, sort of borrowed the Hummer."

"What!" Mark roared.

"It can get me in. I've also got Diamond's satellite phone so once I get in I can actually call out and tell you where to send the cavalry."

"Cindy, this is ridiculous. You turn around and take that Hummer back right now. This is a job for professionals. Don't make me call the car in and have road blocks set up to catch you."

"I was afraid you'd say that. That was why I almost didn't call you. Look, you do what you feel you have to, but I'm not stopping. Jeremiah, Paul, and those kids are out there and they need help. I've got equipment and the map and I'm already on my way. Lives hang in the balance and minutes could make all the difference. I swear to you, in this thing I will drive over any road block I see. The only way you're going to be able to stop me is if you have an officer shoot me."

She bit her lip, her head swimming with disbelief at what she'd just heard herself say.

"What has gotten into you?" he asked quietly.

"We can talk about that once everyone is safe," she said.

"Call me at the first sign of trouble," he said after a long pause.

"I will."

20

SUDDENLY THE FOREST BEHIND THEM WAS BATHED IN BRIGHT LIGHT AS THE helicopter closed in on them. Again, Jeremiah gave three tugs on Brenda's belt. As before, the pace quickened. The helicopter was two miles behind and closing. They were searching the road and the forest to either side.

They crested the hill. Two quick belt tugs, a pause, then two more tugs. The entire line dropped down to the mud in the middle of the road. Each person grabbed scoops of mud and covered their face and hands. They lay motionless, face up. As the helicopter and its light approached everyone closed their eyes. The light washed over the entire line. Not once did it hesitate; it just kept moving. In seconds the light had moved off them and down the hill.

Wait, wait.

Jeremiah got up, wiping his face, and started moving to the front of the line.

"Up, we have to move," he said to the kids as he passed by.

Reaching Sarah, Jeremiah said, pointing north, "Move off the road that way. We are close to the campgrounds and the bad guys will be waiting for us. Let's go. Same pace. Stop in fifteen minutes. Okay?"

A simple nod and Sarah was up and moving. Fifteen minutes later the group was halted under some trees half a mile north of the road. Brenda was lowering Bobby gently to the ground with Noah's help. Jeremiah moved up the line collecting the three jackets that had been given to the youngest kids. Returning to Noah, they made a stretcher using the spears and the jackets. They rolled Bobby onto the stretcher, then lifted it up to test it out.

Jeremiah gave Bobby two more pills, which he took gratefully. Jeremiah moved over to Sarah.

"I think the river is about half a mile in this direction. When you get close, move along it to your right." After a short pause, he asked, "Are you okay?"

"I'm doing fine. I have never walked this far in my life. I actually feel good although the pace was starting to make me short of breath."

"Good. You can slow the pace down. Don't become winded."

She nodded.

"Let's move out," Jeremiah said to a smiling Sarah.

The Rangers' progress had actually improved. The ground was not nearly as muddy or slippery. Jeremiah lagged behind for several minutes. He was looking for the flashlight. Nothing. After a few minutes he caught up with the kids. He was slightly, and only slightly, relieved that he had seen no sign of the flashlight. Unexpectedly, the line stopped and Jeremiah moved up beside Sarah.

"What's wrong? Did you see or hear something?"

"No, Rabbi. There ahead," she said, pointing at the river, "is a footbridge across the river."

"No bridge was shown on the map."

"It is only three months old. The scouting council built it as our community service project."

"Scouting council?" asked Jeremiah.

"Yeah, the Girl and Boy Scout troops in town. Noah's dad was the engineer and Tray's and Bobby's dads provided the materials. Almost all of us in this group donated a minimum of twelve hours labor. Pretty neat, huh?"

Minutes later the Rangers were squatting near the bridge-head. Jeremiah, Brenda, and Noah went out onto the bridge with several feet between them. Each person wound an arm around the right side wire.

"Three," said Noah, who was in the middle of the bridge. The three jumped up and down twice.

Good, seems solid enough.

"Three," said Noah again. The three tried to get the bridge to sway back and forth, but it was still solid. Returning to the riverbank, Jeremiah approached the group.

"The bridge seems to be safe. Sarah will go first." Turning to Sarah, Jeremiah continued, "When you get across go straight onward into the trees. Stop about twenty feet in."

"Rabbi, the trail turns left and goes down the other side of the river," Sarah said. "Shouldn't we follow that?"

"No. As you know, we are close to the camp. We have no idea what awaits us there. It will be better for us to hide and rest, at least until the sun comes up."

Jeremiah turned and addressed the entire group. "We are going to cross the river here. Do not look around. Just look straight ahead. Sarah will lead out. Next person will follow fifteen feet later."

"Why?"

Because I don't want them to be able to kill two of us with the same shot. Out loud he said, "So we don't overload the bridge and start it swinging back and forth."

Jeremiah stood by the bridge and as each kid started over, he reminded them to go straight into the woods. Brenda and Noah, carrying Bobby on the stretcher, were last. Jeremiah checked the area quickly, then crossed over. Once they had assembled around him, Jeremiah passed out some first aid towelettes.

"Clean around your eyes, nose, and mouth."

Jeremiah then passed around the box of granola bars and bottled water.

"We are going to hole up here till sunrise, so everyone get some rest. Oh, and no snoring," said Jeremiah, as the group giggled.

Jeremiah moved over to Bobby.

"How you doing, champ?" he asked.

Jeremiah looked down at the broken leg. He could tell it was beginning to swell. Opening the first aid kit, Jeremiah removed the two instant ice packs. Squeezing them to break the inner pouch, he shook them to mix the chemicals. He placed the ice packs gently on the wound area. Next he opened the emergency thermal blanket, spreading it out. He placed the blanket on Bobby and tucked it in on both sides.

"Rabbi, is it smart to use that? It is like, shiny," asked Brenda.

He whispered to her so Bobby couldn't hear. "I wish it wasn't so shiny too but we need to make sure that he stays warm. The last thing we need is for him to go into shock. He has been doing good so far, but staying in one place without movement will cause his temperature to begin to fall, and then he will be in big trouble."

Brenda nodded understanding.

"Rabbi?" asked Sarah, who had crept up behind Jeremiah.

"Yes?"

"We need to post guards. I will go first. Noah, can you go second if needed?"

"Good idea, but I will take this shift. You have been on point for over five hours and Brenda and Noah were the last to carry Bobby. You three have been utterly fantastic, awesome . . ." Jeremiah trailed off. He just did not have words for what these kids had done and for the first time in many years, he was getting emotional.

Jeremiah left the group in the capable hands of Sarah, Brenda, and Noah. He positioned himself just upstream of the bridge and inside the tree line.

What a night, and unfortunately it is not over. At the least, we are on the correct side of the river. He slowed his breathing and heart rate. He sat listening. All he heard was the river and the sounds of the forest. He couldn't even hear the kids breathing.

There was something he needed to do and now that it was no longer the Sabbath and the kids were safe for a while he could do it. He debated. It would mean leaving them alone for at least two hours, maybe more.

He returned to the camp and told Noah what he needed to do. With the boy's assurances that they could handle whatever arose, Jeremiah turned and melted into the wilderness.

It took him over an hour to make it back to the logging camp. When he did he wrapped Paul's body in the blanket he had laid over it earlier and carried it into the forest.

He had no idea how long it would be before they could send someone to retrieve the body, but he didn't want to leave it out to be violated by the animals and the elements. He went back into the camp and got a shovel.

Jeremiah began to dig. The earth was soft and the grave didn't have to be deep. Three feet deep would be enough to protect the body from animals. It was shallow enough, though, that after a few days the smell of decomposing flesh would help him find it again.

After half an hour he had it deep enough. He carefully shifted Paul's body into it. He sat back and recited from the

Psalms as was customary. He chose the one he found to be most poignant to the moment.

"The LORD is my shepherd; I shall not want. He maketh me to lie down in green pastures: he leadeth me beside the still waters. He restoreth my soul: he leadeth me in the paths of righteousness for his name's sake. Yea, though I walk through the valley of the shadow of death, I will fear no evil: for thou art with me; thy rod and thy staff they comfort me. Thou preparest a table before me in the presence of mine enemies: thou anointest my head with oil; my cup runneth over. Surely goodness and mercy shall follow me all the days of my life: and I will dwell in the house of the LORD for ever."

Finished, he picked up two fistfuls of dirt and let them fall down on top of the body before he stood and shoveled the dirt over Paul.

"Dayan Ha'emet," he said, ripping his shirt on the right side of his chest. He was not family and yet there was no one else to mourn Paul who, if nothing else, he had been a brother-in-arms with.

"Praised be the name of G-d. He created the world according to his will. Life has a plan and a purpose. We hope for the coming of G-d's kingdom on earth, when things as they are, will be changed to things as they ought to be."

He had done what he could for the dead. It was time to attend to the living. It was time to stop being the hunted.

Cindy hit the fire road and felt her heart jump into her throat. From this point forward she was entering the danger zone and she could be attacked at any moment. She tried to keep back the fear that threatened to cloud her thinking as she drove cautiously up the road, keeping an eye out for kids, killers, and obstacles on the road.

Trees pressed in around the car, obscuring her vision of what lay to the sides of the trail. Branches scratched at the windows, making her cringe at the sound. The road curved a lot forcing her to grudgingly reduce her speed even further so that she could stop in time if a person or obstacle did present itself.

With every minute that ticked by on the dashboard clock her anxiety increased. *What if I'm too late? What if this minute Jeremiah's breathing his last? What if I could save the kids if only I hadn't slowed down?*

She prayed, desperately trying to drown out the fear and the questions that seemed to be trying to drive her mad.

Suddenly, she found a Jeep, upside-down on the road.

Paul!

Paul had said he was going up in a Jeep. *He must have been attacked*, she realized. Fresh waves of fear washed over her, but she forced herself to slow down and look to see if there was anyone inside the Jeep. There wasn't and she breathed a sigh of relief. She debated briefly whether to stop and look for him, but decided her best bet was to keep moving and make it to the camp.

Farther on several large trees blocked the path ahead, crossing the road. She turned the Hummer and headed into the forest, easing between the trees until she could get around the fallen ones.

A faint fork in the road appeared and she took the left branch, knowing it led to the camp site. The road continued to wind for another five miles, but finally brought her to the edge of the campground. She drove through slowly, looking for signs of occupation. At last she saw something that made her blood turn cold.

One of the cabins had been destroyed and there was a huge crater in the ground where it had once stood. Nearby trees showed scorch marks and she saw bits of wood scattered a long way in every direction. The roof of the closest cabin was half caved-in as well.

Cindy got out of the Hummer and walked gingerly to the edge of the crater. She peered inside. It was several feet deep, and in it she saw skeletons.

She fell to the ground and began to retch at the sight. When it didn't seem like she could possibly be sick anymore she dragged herself back to the Hummer, beginning to sob with sorrow and terror.

A few minutes later she reached Mark using the satellite phone, and attempted to describe to him what she had found.

"The skeletons were in the crater, under where the cabin was?" he asked.

"Yes."

"But the wood from the cabin itself was scattered for yards around?"

"Yes."

"Cindy, take a deep breath. It sounds like whoever those skeletons belong to, they were buried under the cabin long before it exploded."

"What are you saying?" she asked.

"It's not Jeremiah and the kids. Their . . . bodies . . . would have been blown clear with the pieces of the cabin from whatever explosion happened."

"Oh, thank, God!" she wailed, then began to sob even harder.

"Listen to me. Get out of there. You aren't safe. Come back out. We're putting a team together and we'll be going in with helicopters and SUVs shortly."

"I can't wait," she said. "It might be too late."

"Then at least please get out of that camp. You're completely exposed up there."

"I will. I'll call when I know anything more," she said before disconnecting.

Mark was right. She was a sitting duck, vulnerable. She had to keep moving. She picked the quickest route out of the center of the camp to get back under cover of the trees.

Once there she studied the map. There was an old logging camp a couple miles away. It would provide some form of shelter, but she doubted that anyone in Jeremiah's group knew of its existence.

"Think, Cindy! If you had fourteen kids to worry about and killers stalking you on this mountain, where would you go?"

The answer was so obvious that she felt like an idiot for even asking the question. "I'd get the heck off this mountain."

And as far as any of the campers knew, there was only one real way to do that, back down the way they had come up. They might try to forge the river even though it had washed out the bridge.

She set off down the hill. The rain was starting in again and she worried about the kids out in it even as the Hummer sloshed and slid through patches of mud.

Half an hour later Jeremiah found the trail of the man with the flashlight who had been following them down the fire road hours before. The rain had eased up, preserving the footprints, and the hunter had made no effort to hide them.

Jeremiah followed, swift and silent as a ghost. He found the place the man had turned off the road to eat and rest for a few minutes. He pressed on. As the trail became fresher, the blood began to sing in his veins.

The man was a professional, but he was being sloppy. He had no idea who or what he was up against or he would not have let down his guard as he did.

You should have gone home before you killed Paul, he thought as he pursued.

Somewhere off in the distance he could hear a low rumble. For a moment he thought it was the helicopter but realized almost instantly that it wasn't. *Something on the ground, something big.*

He slowed, almost upon his quarry. He can't find our trail; he's going slow and looking and in the meantime leaving a trail a blind man could follow. But where's his buddy in the helicopter?

A lightening in the trees a hundred yards ahead of him indicated the presence of some sort of clearing. Jeremiah slowed even more and circled to the left, moving away from the trail. It was possible that the killers weren't being sloppy but that they had laid a trap for him. At any rate they were much closer to the river and the kids than he would have liked.

As the clearing came into view Jeremiah could see the helicopter. It was down and the engine was off. Both men were near it, partially obscured from view. The sound of the other engine was growing louder. He could tell the moment that both of them heard it too. They listened for a moment and then moved to get in the helicopter.

Jeremiah leaped into the clearing, pulling one of the guns from his waistband, and shot the one on the passenger side of the helicopter. The man crumpled without a sound. It took only a moment for his partner to respond, shooting at Jeremiah from underneath the belly of the chopper.

Jeremiah resisted returning fire until he could get a clear shot. He began circling around, trying to keep trees between himself and the shooter. The engine sound had become almost deafening.

Friend or foe? he wondered.

Friend seemed unlikely, and the chopper pilot seemed to be thinking the same thing. He climbed into the cockpit, preparing to take off. Jeremiah sprinted forward, needing to get in a good shot before he could lift off.

A crashing sound in the trees drew his attention as a dark green Hummer punched through the underbrush and charged across the pasture. Jeremiah shouted in surprise and jumped back.

The vehicle slammed into the helicopter, sending them both skidding. Jeremiah sprinted forward, ducking behind the helicopter and running up alongside.

The man inside was dazed. Turning, he raised his gun. Jeremiah was faster and was able to shoot him in the arm, causing him to drop the weapon.

"How many more?" he roared.

The man stared at him long and hard. "Who are you?" he asked finally. "We weren't expecting . . . you."

"I'm the man who will end your life right here, right now unless you tell me what I want to know."

"I'm the last."

"Who hired you?"

"I can answer that," a female voice he recognized quavered.

He glanced over and saw Cindy climbing out of the Hummer. He yanked the man out of the helicopter and threw him face down onto the ground. He hit the man in the head with the butt of the gun to knock him out.

"What are you doing here?" he barked at Cindy.

"Rescuing you," she said, appearing beside him with a coil of rope.

He ticked his gaze over to the Hummer. "You think that thing will still run?"

She nodded. "It's a tank. It better."

Jeremiah stripped the injured man down to his underwear, making sure he had nothing he could use as a weapon. Then he trussed him and threw him into the back of the vehicle. He grabbed one of the protein bars from the box back there and wolfed it down, chasing it with a bottle of water.

He turned to Cindy then and hugged her fiercely. "Thank you for the rescue," he whispered.

She shook her head. "It's not over. Where are the kids?"

"Let's go get them."

Under Jeremiah's direction Cindy drove the Hummer to the bank of the river near the footbridge. Satisfied that his prisoner wasn't going anywhere he left him in the back of the car and led Cindy across the bridge. She had a satellite phone with her. What he would have given for one of those during the whole ordeal! They were almost to the camp when he heard a boy scream. A moment later he heard a shot.

He sprinted forward. *No, no, no!*

With Cindy on his heels he ran into camp and looked wildly around. He spotted Noah, standing off to the side, eyes wild, paintball gun drawn and aimed at the ground, hand shaking.

"What is it?" he asked as he crossed to him.

The boy looked up at him with dazed, fearful eyes. "You were right about one thing, Rabbi. These guns can kill."

Jeremiah looked at where the gun was aimed and nearly collapsed in relief. Noah had shot the head off a rattlesnake.

Jeremiah clapped the boy on the shoulder and then relieved him of the weapon. He cleared his throat. "Who's up for breakfast?" he shouted.

A minute later Cindy was thrusting the satellite phone at him. "Here," she said, "explain to Mark exactly where it is we are so they can send the cavalry to come pick us up."

Jeremiah took the phone. "Mark."

"Rabbi."

"Good to hear your voice."

"Yours too. Now tell us where the devil you are."

"Gladly," Jeremiah said, tears of exhaustion and relief filling his eyes.

Thursday night Cindy made it home and glanced at the clock, calculating the time difference between her and Rhode Island. She walked into her bedroom and sat down on her bed. She grabbed the phone and dialed the number she'd been meaning to call for the last four days.

She smiled when her brother picked up.

"Hey, Kyle, it's Cindy."

"Hi," he said, sounding genuinely surprised.

"How are things with you?"

"Great. The new show is doing really well. How about you? Somebody told me that you stopped another killer."

"Mom?"

"No, one of the guys I work with saw it online somewhere."

"Oh."

I guess some things never change.

"You should totally send me a newspaper clipping. Mom too."

"I'll think about it."

"So, what can I do for you?"

"Kyle, I just wanted to say 'thank you.'"

"For what?"

She pulled the darts out of his picture and stared at it for a moment. "For . . . everything. You saved my life."

"How?"

"You just did."

"Mom said you were getting weird. Are you okay?"

There was a knock on her front door and she got up and hurried down the hall to open it and see Jeremiah standing there.

"Never better," she told Kyle, unable to keep the smile from spreading across her face. "I'll talk to you later."

She hung up and welcomed Jeremiah in. He glanced around at the half packed boxes. "Moving?"

"Yes. I inherited a house a few months back and I've decided to move into it. Geanie's going to be my roommate."

"Congratulations."

"Thank you."

"Everyone's getting new homes," he said. "Zac, one of the kids, is getting to go live with his grandparents. He's very excited about that. And the zoo has a new lion cub courtesy of Sarah, another one of the kids from camp."

"Something in the air, I guess." She indicated the pizza and bottle of soda he was carrying. "What's the occasion?"

"Dinner."

"Why?" she asked as he put the food down on her counter.

He turned and looked at her and a shiver crept up her spine. "Because I think we have to stop waiting to have a reason to spend time together. I'm not going to wait until the next body shows up in Pine Springs before talking to you again."

He took her hand in his and her skin tingled and her breath caught in her throat.

"We're friends, right?"

"Yes," she said.

"Then I want us to start acting like it. No more ignoring each other, no more drifting apart. I want to spend time with you when the world isn't falling to pieces, not just when it is."

"I want that, too," she whispered.

"Good," he said, smiling into her eyes.

Mark answered his phone in surprise when he realized it was the coroner calling. "You know I'm suspended, right?"

The other man paused. "Things have been said."

"Do I want to know?"

"Probably not."

"I'm suspended for at least another three-and-a-half weeks and I'm under investigation. You shouldn't be calling me. Jackson is handling my active cases."

"I know, but I'm not calling about those."

"What is it?" Mark asked.

He glanced across the room to where Traci was curled up on the couch reading a mystery. He owed her everything. She had saved him. She was the reason he was going to survive whatever came.

"You know, word on the street is that you're going to be back on active duty next month."

"That would be nice," Mark said. "Seriously, though, why did you call?"

"We've finished identifying about half of the bodies that were buried underneath that cabin up at Green Pastures," he said.

"And?" Mark asked.

"They are several members of the cult that followed that Matthew guy about twenty years ago. Men, women, children. It looks like a mass suicide."

"Great," Mark muttered.

"One of the kids that we have a positive identification on was a ten-year-old boy. We ran the DNA several times and matched it to a kidnapping from back then. Police suspected that the cult was behind that and several other kidnappings, but could never prove it. It's official; the missing boy was one of the bodies."

"Who is the boy?"

"Paul Dryer, Junior, son of Ruth and Paul Senior."

"That's impossible," Mark whispered. "You knew Paul. He was killed last week."

"That's why I wanted to call you, so you heard it from me first. I'm sorry about your partner. But whoever he was, he wasn't Paul Dryer."

Discussion Questions

1. Everyone deals with death in different ways, finds different ways of healing. How do you lean on God when you experience times of mourning and do you allow those around you to help you during these times?

2. Cindy does something incredibly dangerous when she goes to rescue Jeremiah and the kids. Have you ever risked your life to save someone else? How did it make you feel?

3. The Bible says that no greater love hath a man than to lay down his life for a friend. How far have you gone to help a friend? Is there anyone you would lay down your life for?

4. At the end of this book Cindy comes to have some sense of perspective about the death of her sister, which helps her to deal with her own life and circumstances. Is there anything you need to gain perspective on in your life?

5. At the end of this book Cindy calls her brother, Kyle, to thank him for helping her even though he didn't know it. Is there anyone you should thank who might not realize how they have helped you?

6. Is there someone you've been meaning to spend more time with but you just haven't gotten around to it, a family member, friend, or even God? What can you do this week to strengthen that relationship?

7. Zac, one of the campers, tries to run away from home. Every year many kids attempt to run away from home. Do you know any kids who might need someone to talk to?

8. Volunteer opportunities abound at churches. Is there anything you can do to help out? Have you ever volun-

teered to work at a camp or help out with teens in some other capacity?

9. Mark goes too far and does something terrible in order to try and save people. Have you ever done the wrong thing for the right reason? How did you make amends?

10. Several of the characters in this story feel or are trapped. Have you ever felt that you were backed into a corner with no way out? What did you do? How did God help you in this situation?

Want to learn more about author Debbie Viguié
and check out other great fiction
from Abingdon Press?

Sign up for our fiction newsletter at
www.AbingdonPress.com/fiction
to read interviews with your favorite authors, find tips
for starting a reading group, and stay posted on what
new titles are on the horizon. It's a place to connect
with other fiction readers or post a
comment about this book.

Be sure to visit Debbie Viguié online.

www.debbieviguie.com

What they're saying about...

Gone to Green, by Judy Christie

"...Refreshingly realistic religious fiction, this novel is unafraid to address the injustices of sexism, racism, and corruption as well as the spiritual devastation that often accompanies the loss of loved ones. Yet these darker narrative tones beautifully highlight the novel's message of friendship, community, and God's reassuring and transformative love." —*Publishers Weekly* **starred review**

The Call of Zulina, by Kay Marshall Strom

"This compelling drama will challenge readers to remember slavery's brutal history, and its heroic characters will inspire them. Highly recommended."
—*Library Journal* **starred review**

Surrender the Wind, by Rita Gerlach

"I am purely a romance reader, and yet you hooked me in with a war scene, of all things! I would have never believed it. You set the mood beautifully and have a clean, strong, lyrical way with words. You have done your research well enough to transport me back to the war-torn period of colonial times."
—Julie Lessman, author of *The Daughters of Boston* series

One Imperfect Christmas, by Myra Johnson

"Debut novelist Myra Johnson ushers us into the Christmas season with a fresh and exciting story that will give you a chuckle and a special warmth."
—DiAnn Mills, author of *Awaken My Heart* and *Breach of Trust*

The Prayers of Agnes Sparrow, by Joyce Magnin

"Beware of *The Prayers of Agnes Sparrow*. Just when you have become fully enchanted by its marvelous quirky zaniness, you will suddenly be taken to your knees by its poignant truth-telling about what it means to be divinely human. I'm convinced that 'on our knees' is exactly where Joyce Magnin planned for us to land all along." —Nancy Rue, co-author of *Healing Waters* (*Sullivan Crisp* Series)
2009 Novel of the Year

The Fence My Father Built, by Linda S. Clare

"...Linda Clare reminds us with her writing that is wise, funny, and heartbreaking, that what matters most in life are the people we love and the One who gave them to us."—Gina Ochsner, Dark Horse Literary, winner of the Oregon Book Award and the Flannery O'Connor Award for Short Fiction

eye of the god, by Ariel Allison

"Filled with action on three continents, *eye of the god* is a riveting fast-paced thriller, but it is Abby—who, in spite of another letdown by a man, remains filled with hope—who makes Ariel Allison's tale a super read."—Harriet Klausner